Rendersella is a heartfelt and hope-filled modern fairytale that sweeps readers into a world where art, identity, and grace intertwine. With fresh, engaging prose and characters who leap off the page, Amy Anguish delivers a story brimming with heart. I could not get enough of Ella's journey to embrace her God-given worth and find love along the way. Inspiring and charming, this book is perfect for fans of sweet romance with a redemptive core.

— TABITHA M. CORVIN, AUTHOR OF
MALICE IN WONDERLAND

I0587853

Real-Life Fairy Tales
Book One

Rendersella

Amy R. Anguish

Scrivenings
PRESS
Quench your thirst for story.
www.ScriveningsPress.com

Copyright © 2025 by Amy Anguish

Published by Scrivenings Press LLC
15 Lucky Lane
Morrilton, Arkansas 72110
https://ScriveningsPress.com

Printed in the United States of America

All rights reserved. No part of this publication may be reproduced, stored in a retrieval system, or transmitted in any form or by any means—for example, electronic, photocopy, or recording— without the prior written permission of the publisher. The only exception is brief quotations in printed reviews.

Paperback ISBN 978-1-64917-486-4

eBook ISBN 978-1-64917-487-1

Editor: Denica McCall

Cover design by Linda Fulkerson—www.bookmarketinggraphics.com

Scripture quotations are from the ESV Bible® (The Holy Bible, English Standard Version®), copyright © 2001 by Crossway Bibles, a publishing ministry of Good News Publishers. Used by permission. All rights reserved.

All characters are fictional, and any resemblance to real people, either factual or historical, is purely coincidental.

NO AI TRAINING: Without in any way limiting the author's [and publisher's] exclusive rights under copyright, any use of this publication to "train" generative artificial intelligence (AI) technologies to generate text is expressly prohibited. The author reserves all rights to license uses of this work for generative AI training and development of machine learning language models.

For my dear friend, Katie Gilchrist. She's a great cheerleader, always up to be a second set of eyes, and the one who introduced me to West Virginia. Here's to 25 plus more years of friendship.

PROLOGUE

Fourteen years ago

"Once upon a time"—Daddy used his best fairy-tale voice as he read the story, snuggled on her bed — "there was a girl named Rendersella."

"Daddy!" Ella wiggled her shoulder against his side. "That's not what it says."

"It's not?"

"No, silly." Ella pointed to the page. "It's Cinderella."

"Oh, so it is." Daddy lifted a brow. "But I like Rendersella better."

"Why?" Ella looked up at her Daddy's face. He had been so serious lately. She liked him much better this way, like he used to be.

"Because it uses our name. Renders. And your name, Ella." He poked her in the belly. "And besides, it's funnier that way."

"I don't know if I want to be like Cinderella, though." Ella leaned against Daddy's strong arm.

"Oh? Why's that?"

"She has to do all the work for her mean old stepmother and stepsisters." Ella shrugged. "Who would want to do that?"

"Good point. But she also gets the prince in the end, so then she never has to work again, right?"

Ella pinched her lips together as she considered his words. "I guess. But do you have to marry a prince to have a happy ever after, Daddy?"

"Nope. But I hope whoever does marry you—many, many years from now—treats you like a princess." He drew her closer to his side. "Because that's what you are."

They sat quietly for a moment, and Ella soaked in the extra attention. It had been a good day. Mommy had even been able to go for a short walk with them earlier. That hardly ever happened anymore.

"Daddy, can we read the story now?" Ella could only sit quietly for so long.

"Of course, Princess." He smoothed out the page and began again. "Once upon a time ..."

This time, he said the name right, and Ella settled in for her favorite story. Cinderella was full of dreams, and Ella had lots of dreams of her own. She wanted to grow up to be an artist like Mommy. The days when Mommy got out the paints and gave Ella her own brush to use were her favorite.

They would go outside and find a pretty spot, and Mommy would say, "Ella, let's see if we can capture a little bit of God's beauty on this paper today."

Mommy was a wonderful painter. She could mix colors and make shapes that were almost exactly like God's. Ella was still learning.

Leaning over Ella's easel next to her own, Mommy would press a kiss to Ella's head, her headscarf tickling Ella's cheek. "You have to start somewhere. I wasn't always this good, either."

Other days, they would use pieces of charcoal. Or colored pencils. It didn't matter. Ella loved them all.

"As Rendersella rushed from the ballroom, she gasped. She had slopped her dripper!" Daddy's silly voice brought her back to the present.

"Daddy!" Ella tried to frown, but her giggles took over. Especially when Daddy added some tickles.

"What? Did I do something wrong?" Daddy set the book aside and blew a raspberry on Ella's cheek. "Huh? You sure are picky tonight."

Ella shrieked with laughter. Daddy always found the most ticklish spots.

"What's going on in here?" Mommy stood in the doorway, a cardigan pulled close around her thin body.

"Ella is being super picky about the way I'm reading the story tonight." Daddy glanced over at Mommy. "So I'm retaliating."

"Hmm. I thought you were trying to get her to calm down so she could sleep soon." A small smile winked at the edges of Mommy's mouth.

"I'm just wearing her out." Daddy winked. "Want to help?"

Mommy came closer and started tickling Daddy.

"Hey! No fair." Daddy didn't fight back, though. He told Ella the week before that they had to be extra careful with Mommy because her medicine to kill the bad germs was making her body weak. Ella joined in and helped Mommy instead.

A few minutes later, they were all in a heap, a few giggles still escaping.

"Well, Ella, are you worn out?" Daddy puffed beside her.

"I don't think so, Daddy. I still need to hear the end of the story."

He poked her in the side. "Somehow, I figured you'd say that."

Mommy pressed a kiss to her forehead. "A seven-year-old can't go to sleep not knowing how the story ends."

"Right." Ella nodded.

"You've heard this story so often you can quote it with me." Daddy bopped her nose.

"Daddy, please?" Ella blinked up at him, knowing she almost always got her way when she gave him this look.

He huffed again. "Fine."

They all snuggled in, Mommy on one side of Ella and Daddy on the other. He read the words right this time and much too quickly reached the "happily ever after." Ella sighed. The end was her favorite part.

She couldn't wait to grow up and have her own happy ending.

1

Present day

Ella Renders stepped into the lobby of the Starbright Hotel. The light here was bright compared to outside, where the sun had barely crested the horizon. She strode straight to Kari White, who held out a key card before Ella could even ask.

"I could only get you as high as the third floor today. Room 312." Kari glanced up from her computer. "Hopefully that's still okay."

"That should be perfect, actually." Ella saluted her with the card. "You're the best."

She crossed the marble floor and stepped onto the elevator, her messenger bag bumping her hip with each step. The hotel was only five stories but still tall enough for what she needed. When it was originally built, the contractors carved out the mountain only enough to expose the flat land needed for the structure. They left the rest intact, which made for a nice view from the upper stories on the rear side. And this time of day, several deer liked to roam the edge of the man-made bluff for breakfast.

Ella slid the key into the door and slipped inside before she drew too much attention to herself. Now, to see if the deer would cooperate today or not. Slowly, she raised the curtains and studied the still-dim view before her.

"Come on. Come on."

There.

Movement to her right. Squinting, she made out three—no, four—deer stepping carefully through the trees a few feet away. A breath slipped from her lips, and she quickly pulled out her sketch pad and several pencils.

Maybe if she had a fancy camera, she could simply capture the animals to study later, when things weren't so rushed. But her phone was a bottom-of-the-line, hand-me-down piece of junk. Anything she tried to shoot through this window would come out blurry and useless. Sketching was the next best thing. Good thing Kari didn't mind her borrowing a room several days a week.

Every now and then, all the upper-story rooms were booked and she didn't get this chance. But when she did, she grabbed it.

Ella climbed up on the little table next to the window and crisscrossed her legs. *Okay, deer. How will you pose for me today?*

The graceful creatures didn't realize they were the object of an artist trying to capture their images. Their focus remained on the tender grass at the base of the trees and a few choice leaves. The sun rose higher, casting everything in a golden glow and sending coral streaks across the sky.

"This is beautiful, God," Ella whispered in reverence. "Thank You for sharing Your creativity. You knew I needed this sliver of peace, didn't You?"

As if in reply, a buck wandered into view directly across from Ella. She sucked in a breath and quickly worked on his outline. Majestic. She traced his antlers with her gaze and tried to mimic its crooked angles and points on her paper.

Flipping to a new page, she started another set, this time with several deer together. But a sound somewhere outside startled the animals. They all raised their heads, stiffening, before turning and leaping back into the shelter of the woods.

Her fingers loosened around her pencil. "Time's up."

Ella sighed, then rose and stretched. She'd been able to work for half an hour this morning. Not terrible, all things considered. But had she created anything worthy? Sure, it was always good to practice her sketching and work on new things. But eventually, she needed her artwork to bring in actual income. Because if she had to live with her stepmother, Angela, much longer ... well, she wasn't sure what she would do, but nothing that would end well.

She stashed her paper and pencils back in her bag. Time to face reality. Who knew the next time she'd be able to steal another moment like this?

"God, grant me peace and strength today. And please help me not to say anything I'll live to regret."

Another glimpse of the room proved she'd put everything back to rights. Okay. On to the next task on her list.

Pulling the door closed, she spun and her messenger bag slammed into something, throwing her off-center.

Make that *someone*.

"I am so sorry." She brushed her hair out of her eyes. The impact had flipped it every which way. "Are you okay?"

Her gaze moved up to the face of the person with whom she'd collided. Hazel eyes. Light-brown hair, the perfect length for running fingers through. Five o'clock shadow ... which was ridiculous, because it wasn't even eight in the morning. And what was she doing? Taking inventory? Though he did look familiar.

7

"I'm fine." His voice was mellow and sounded slightly amused. "Are you okay? I think you're more impacted than I am."

"How silly is that? I mean, you're the one who got whacked by my bag." If only she could bury her own head in that bag now. Why couldn't she shut up? So much for God keeping her from saying anything she'd regret.

"True enough." He grinned, and a dimple appeared in one cheek. As if all the assets she'd noticed before weren't enough. "But I've been hit with worse. No worries."

"Okay, then." She backed up several steps. "Um, have a good day." She offered a little wave, spun on the heel of her Converse, and hoofed it out of there. Could that have been any more embarrassing?

* * *

"What are you staring at?" Jake stepped into the hallway, where Chaz remained fixed in place after being run over by the vivacious blonde.

"I'm not sure." Chaz scratched his head.

"I don't think I know what that means." Jake nudged his friend. "But you're going to be late if we don't get a move on."

"Right. Sorry. I was walking down the hall when a woman with blonde hair slammed into me. She wasn't very big, but she must've been carrying an anvil in that bag. It packed a wallop."

"A blonde, huh?" Jake rolled his eyes. "Oh boy."

"No, seriously. I've never seen a girl like her before. She was all flustered—"

"You've seen plenty of girls flustered before." Jake shoved him as they exited the elevator. "Usually over you."

"Not like that. Not flustered because she was meeting me. I

think she was embarrassed. And I don't think she recognized me."

"Not recognize the great and mighty Chaz Prince?" Jake stepped back, pressing a hand to his heart. "What is the world coming to?"

"Stop already." Chaz made a beeline for the coffee machines on the other side of the lobby. "It was sort of nice, actually. Except she rushed away before I could find out anything about her."

"Your day really has started badly, hasn't it?" Jake stirred a big dollop of creamer into his own coffee. "You got hit by a bag, weren't recognized, and then you were abandoned." He *tsked*. "Maybe you should go back to bed instead of sticking to your original plans."

"Remind me again why we're friends?" Chaz perched on a stool with a Danish.

"Because I let you use my hotel for a major friend discount when you and your dad are at odds." Jake sat across from him.

"And because we turn the other way when you come in here for breakfast even if you haven't spent the night." Kari nudged him as she walked past.

"Surely there's more to it than that." Chaz tapped his chin.

"Because we understand each other?" Jake shook his head. "No, that can't be it. *Hmm.* Let me think some more."

"Don't think too hard. You might hurt something."

"Ain't that the truth?" Kari joined them, her own cup of coffee in hand. "What are you trying to figure out?"

"A girl ran into me upstairs, but I didn't recognize her." Chaz ducked his head. "Which makes sense, considering this is a hotel and guests come from all over. She's probably from out of town."

Kari slowly lowered her cup. "Were you on the third floor last night?"

"His favorite." Jake propped his feet up on the one unused stool. "Though I can't figure out why. The suites are on the fifth floor."

"I'm not using one of your suites without paying, and you won't let me pay you anything when you have open rooms." Chaz shook his head. "Besides, I like seeing the deer in the mornings."

"They're such a nuisance. Isn't it almost hunting season?" Jake tapped the table.

"Don't you dare." Kari punched her brother.

"Good grief! What's with you?" Jake rubbed his shoulder.

"There's no reason to kill those deer. They aren't causing any trouble with the hotel. They're probably one of the unsung perks, honestly."

"There you go." Chaz finished off his last few drops of coffee. "Okay. Time to face the beast."

Jake lifted an eyebrow. "Probably not a good idea to refer to your dad as an animal. Especially when you're about to ask him for a promotion."

Kari shoved her brother. "Good grief, Jake. Can't you be the least bit serious?"

"Only when I have to be."

Chaz shook his head. "I'll see you both later. Hopefully without me having to move in permanently."

"You've got this, Chaz." Kari stood too. "Guess I better get back to the desk in case anyone comes in wanting a room."

Chaz waved to his friends and headed out into the chilly morning. Autumn had arrived overnight, it seemed. He should've grabbed a sweater before coming here last night. But he'd needed time away from his dad to figure out what to say today. Because it was past time to face the issue. Time to assert some independence and prove he had what it took.

As much as Jake joked, Chaz's dad could be a bit gruff,

especially when it came to business matters. He hadn't built the most popular art gallery in the area by being lazy, that was for sure. But hadn't he also raised Chaz to know everything there was about the Prince Gallery? Surely it wouldn't be that big of a step to let him take on more.

Chaz cranked the engine and put his Jeep in gear.

Only one way to find out.

2

"Is it safe?" Ella peeked out from behind the desk as Kari took her place again.

"Are you kidding me right now?" Kari nudged her with a foot. "It was you?"

"Yes. But in my defense, I had no idea he was walking by when I rushed through the door." Ella rose up enough to peek over the counter. "Is he gone?"

"He's gone." Kari shook her head. "Though why you'd avoid Chaz is beyond me."

"Chaz?"

"Chaz Prince. Jake's best friend." Kari typed something on the computer.

"Prince? As in, the Prince Art Gallery?"

Kari finally glanced her way. "Yes. Why?"

Ella let her head fall back and bang against the wall. "So much for that dream."

"Wait. You want to get your artwork in the Prince Gallery?" Kari turned around.

"What artist around here doesn't wish for that?" Ella shook her head. "But it doesn't matter. I'm not good enough."

"Not good enough? Are you kidding me right now?"

"Kari, I've never even finished school. Maybe if I took those last few classes ... or at least had more instruction." Ella spread her fingers, noticing a few of them were smudged with pencil lead. "I mean, watercolors elude me."

"And who says you have to use watercolors? Don't you prefer pencils and oils anyway?"

"I do, but I think it's because I've never learned watercolors. Can you imagine the sunrise I could paint with them?"

"Everything I've seen of your work has been awesome. I don't know why you can't recognize it too."

"Who are you talking to?" Jake's head appeared over the counter. "Oh, hey, Ella. What are you doing down there?"

"She was hiding from Chaz." Kari blabbed the secret before Ella could stop her.

"Chaz? Why?"

"She's the one who bumped into him upstairs." Kari pointed to the ceiling.

"Really?" Jake frowned. "What were you doing upstairs, Ella?"

Kari scrambled to straighten some papers. Up to this point, she'd kept Ella's secret. Would Jake disapprove of Ella using the rooms for her art?

"I sent her up for something. She was rushing to bring it to me. No big deal." Kari slapped the stack of credit card receipts down on the counter and smiled at her brother.

Jake narrowed his eyes, glancing between the two of them. He shook his head and muttered, "Whatever. I'm running to the hardware store. That toilet in 422 is running again."

"Sure." Kari waved him off.

Ella rose to her feet. "Is he going to be mad if he finds out about our arrangement?"

"Probably not." Kari shrugged. "I mean, he doesn't like the

deer, but they're not actually hurting anything. Honestly, knowing you draw them several days a week might make them look better in his eyes."

"Will he tell Chaz it was me who ran into him this morning?" Ella pressed a hand to her forehead. "I hate to think I ruined all my chances because of a simple mishap."

"Nah. Probably won't even think about it." Kari glanced at her watch. "But if you don't scoot, Jake won't be the only one you'll be in trouble with."

"Oh, man!" Ella squeezed her friend in a quick hug. "Thanks, Kari." She darted outside toward her old truck.

She turned the key in the ignition, and nothing happened. "Come on, Humphrey. Don't die on me now." Why her father had given the truck such an old-fashioned name, she had no idea, but she couldn't bear to quit using it.

After a few sputtering coughs, the engine roared to life. Ella breathed easier and drove out of the parking lot. Goodbye, Starbright Hotel—hello reality.

Too bad Ella had ended up living the rotten part of the Cinderella story. Angela was the closest thing to an evil stepmother who existed in the real world. She even came with an evil stepsister. Though thus far, Bellamy was more annoying than evil.

If Ella didn't arrive at the flea market before it opened, and Angela found out, her evil would be unleashed. The flea market booth was Angela's way of purging all of Ella's mom's old things. One day at a time, Ella was losing every last piece of the mother who'd passed thirteen years ago.

A few cars already sat in the flea market lot. It was open only three days a week, but this town seemed to pull in shoppers from all over West Virginia and beyond, so they stayed busy.

"Morning, Ella." Sam waved from booth ten. He

straightened a few cowboy hats then moved on to his baseball cap collection.

"Ella, you don't happen to have any butter dishes, do you?" Marjorie from booth fourteen leaned over an old rolltop desk.

"Nope. Fresh out. But if you need a gravy boat, I saw a few of those." Ella withheld the fact that they'd once belonged to her grandmother from England. No need to rub more salt in those wounds.

"Thanks, dearie. But I need a butter dish."

Finally, Ella made it back to booth twenty.

Bellamy lay sprawled across Daddy's old wingback chair, filing her nails. "'Bout time you got here."

"The market doesn't open for five more minutes." Ella slid her bag behind the register stand.

"You know Mama wants you here at least ten minutes early." Bellamy cocked an eyebrow.

"I had some trouble getting my truck to start." Not a lie, though not the complete truth, either.

"Interesting. Especially since you were gone long before I left this morning." Bellamy leaned forward and perched her chin on her fist. "Wonder where you were."

No way was Ella about to go down that road. Bellamy was one of the last people on earth Ella wanted to share her artwork with. Bad enough she already had to share the house.

"I didn't realize you were working here today. No classes?" Ella straightened a stack of her mom's dinner plates so she wouldn't have to meet her stepsister's eyes.

"None I felt like attending." Bellamy tucked her file into a sparkly bag and leaned back, crossing her legs. "Figured I might as well contribute to the family business." Her laugh grated on Ella's nerves worse than her truck's brakes on a mountain road.

So many things were wrong with that statement. Bellamy had what Ella desired most—the ability to work toward a degree. Instead, Bellamy flaked out and skipped classes as if they weren't worth more than gold. And in some cases, they were. Because the "family business," as Bellamy called it, was no longer in existence.

Daddy's coal company had long ago been sold for a profit. The money received from that sale, however, was no longer around. Angela and Bellamy had no money-management skills or any compunction about running around and buying whatever they wanted when they wanted it. If Ella hadn't stashed her bit away in an account Angela couldn't access, she would be completely destitute. As it was, she needed a job with an actual income ... and soon.

* * *

Chaz straightened his spine before heading into the gallery. Time to beard the lion. Or was he a dragon? Either way, there he went again, comparing his dad to a beast. Jake was right— not the best approach.

After strolling through three of the rooms, he found Dad tucked away in the back, sorting through canvases in a storage closet. Strange. Dad didn't usually do menial work.

"Dad?"

The older man straightened, still moving his gaze back and forth between two paintings. "What do you think? This one with more golden hues or the other with more blues? I need something for that empty spot in the front room."

Chaz couldn't resist raising an eyebrow. Dad was asking his opinion. Better get this right. Maybe it was the opening he'd been praying for.

The one on the right showed a forest path bathed in

afternoon sunlight. Nothing moved among the trees, but it was warm and welcoming.

The left one included more of a swamp area, with cypress roots and Spanish moss. While it didn't emit coldness, it also wasn't as welcoming. Not somewhere you'd want to go stroll.

"Let's do the gold." Chaz nodded to emphasize his decision.

His dad studied them both for another minute, then set the blue one back in the closet. "I think you're right. It's what I reached for initially, but sometimes I second-guess myself. They're both good."

"They are. But this one is a place I'd actually like to visit."

Dad's lips twitched behind his goatee. "That thought hadn't even run through my mind, but I see what you're saying."

Chaz followed his father back through the rooms of artwork. Many of the paintings hanging around them were of the same style, though others were more modern and simplistic. Did he really have anything to offer that Dad wasn't already doing here? What was he thinking, wanting a bigger role?

As Dad hung the painting in the bare spot, Chaz offered up yet another prayer. *God, I really thought this was what I wanted. Why are these doubts springing up now? Is this from You?*

Dad finally turned and focused on him. "What's on your agenda for today?"

"Actually ..." Chaz rubbed the back of his neck. "I was hoping I could talk to you for a few minutes."

Dad blinked but then held a hand out toward the offices. "Let's go."

In his dad's office, Chaz sank onto a couch, but his dad walked around to the other side of the desk, seating himself behind the gold nameplate—Kingston Prince. Power play, or habit? Either way, it didn't make this any easier.

"What's on your mind?" Dad started to flip through his planner but then stilled and set it to the side, folding his hands on top of his blotter.

"I wanted to talk to you about stepping up and taking a bigger role here." Chaz slipped his fingers under his legs so he wouldn't fidget.

"A larger role." Dad leaned back in his chair. "What would that entail?"

This was good, right? Dad was willing to listen.

"I haven't hammered out all the details, but I'd love to help you in procuring new artwork—"

Dad held up a hand, stopping him in his tracks. So much for that good vibe a second before.

"New artwork? Why do we need new artwork? Our gallery is full. You saw the storage room a few minutes ago. All of our current artists seem very happy with their contracts. And our number of visitors has remained steady, if not risen, in the last few years. Why mess with a good thing?"

Why indeed.

Chaz tried to wrangle his thoughts into something he could communicate clearly, but they scrambled worse than the eggs his mom made for breakfast every morning. No discerning one from the other. He pressed a fist to his forehead.

"I need to *do* something. I need a purpose," Chaz groaned. "This is our family business. I love it and want to see it do even better. Not for me, but for all the people in West Virginia and beyond who consider this one of the best galleries in the state. Right now, you have me doing basic admin work."

"And do you think our gallery would still be okay and growing if we didn't have someone to do the admin work?" Dad crossed his arms over his sweater vest. "I suppose you think you're too good to work your way up the chain like everyone else?"

"That's not what I'm saying at all." This was always how it went. Talking to his father was like picking a fight with his toddler cousin. He was never going to win.

"Well, tell you what. When you can come in here with a coherent plan instead of grandiose ideas, we can start this conversation over. Until then, I'm pretty sure you have work to do in your office."

Chaz pinched his lips together. Protesting would get him nowhere, no matter how much he wanted to argue. He was twenty-six. His father shouldn't be able to cow him so easily. And yet here he was, headed back to his tiny little office with a tiny window and no nameplate. To file some paperwork and make sure a placard was printed for the painting his father just hung.

Yes. It was necessary work.

But couldn't he do more? He needed a better plan.

E lla straightened a stack of dishes that leaned precariously on one of the shelves lining the small booth. Bellamy had disappeared an hour ago, but Ella couldn't complain. Her stepsister was more hindrance than help. Not that it would keep Angela from paying her more.

Ella whipped a handkerchief out of her bag and tied it around her hair to keep it out of her face and prevent the dust from taking residence. Time to unload another box of her mother's fine china.

Despite the morning chill, not much of the cool air penetrated the large warehouse that contained the flea market. Ella rubbed a hand across her forehead and glanced around the booth. Several things had sold that morning, though probably not enough to satisfy Angela. Why she thought this was the best way to secure income for their family, Ella had yet to figure out. It would never bring in as much as her father's job had.

"Miss, do you have any casserole dishes for sale?" An older lady stood perusing the shelves from a distance.

"Only these over here." Ella motioned to her right.

"Oh. Well, that's not exactly what I'm searching for, but thank you." The woman shuffled past.

Emotions warred within Ella. Hard to decide whether to be elated or frustrated. She finished unpacking the plates edged with tiny pink roses and broke down the box. The market was fairly quiet right now. Maybe she could finish the drawing she started last week.

Ella slipped out her sketch pad and flipped to the right page. West Virginia was full of beautiful scenery—hills and valleys, trees aplenty, waterfalls and rivers, and wildlife. But Ella loved to incorporate a bit of its history and culture into her artwork too.

This page showed a valley not too far from their house. Near the bottom, a train track followed the curve of the hills, its black engine puffing alongside a stream with myriad cars full of coal behind it. The nature was for her mom. The coal was for her dad. Any way she could find to hold onto little pieces of them, she grabbed quickly.

Despite being interrupted by several more customers, she was able to get her train polished how she wanted it. It didn't show movement—one of those skills she wished she could take a class to learn. But still. It was nice.

She wiped her fingers on an old cloth and tilted her head. What else did it need? Maybe a couple birds?

"Excuse me."

She jerked, glad she had set aside the piece of charcoal she'd been using. "I'm so sorry." She jumped up from her stool in the corner. "I didn't even see you come in."

"No worries. You looked focused." Chaz Prince stood in her booth. What was the likelihood of her having an awkward run-in with him twice in one day? Did he recognize her from that morning?

"Oh, um. Sure." She stashed her pad behind a shelf against the front wall and wiped her fingers on her jeans, hoping against hope to remove all the evidence of holding charcoal earlier. The way she'd bumbled into him, she didn't want to risk him associating that girl with anyone who might also draw. No need to lessen her chances of being a Prince Gallery artist. "What can I help you with?"

"You look familiar." He squinted for a second as he met her gaze. "Do I know you?"

She blinked. "I don't think so. Have you been here before?"

"A few times." He crossed his arms and pursed his lips. "But I don't remember seeing you before."

"I'm usually here when the market is open." She turned her face away, hoping he didn't remember where he had seen her.

"So weird."

"Maybe I have a doppelganger." She gave a half-hearted laugh. Though in reality, it wasn't funny. Over the years, she'd heard way too many times how much alike she and Bellamy looked—"as if God had made them look like sisters even though they weren't related." She had to force herself not to gag at such words from well-meaning church members.

"Possible." He still stood there, not saying what he needed.

"So, you had a question?" Ella prompted.

"Right." He turned and faced the nearest shelf. "These dishes. Do you know how many you have of each?"

Her mother's china. He wanted her mother's china? Why? Usually women came looking for the nice dinnerware—not men. Especially not young men.

Maybe she could use this for good, though. She could offer him a deal—a percentage off if he'd consider hanging one of her drawings in his gallery. Stupid idea. Ridiculous. As if that would be an even exchange!

"Miss?"

She hadn't answered him. He probably thought she was an idiot, and she wasn't far from disagreeing.

"Right. Sorry. Last I counted, we still have a full twelve place settings of the dinner plates, salad-dessert plates, and ten soup bowls. Oh, and eight tea cups and saucers." She reached past him and looped her finger through the handle of the gravy boat. "Plus two serving bowls and a gravy boat."

"Wow. I didn't count that many."

"Some of them are still in boxes. We only have room for so much to be out at a time." She traced the pattern on the gravy boat. All her heart was wrapped up in the tiny rosebud-print dishes. They were supposed to have been passed down to her, after all.

They're only things, she reminded herself. *Just stuff that can break. Someday, I'll go to Heaven and be with my parents again. That's my happy ending to look forward to. Just have to get through the Cinderella part before that can happen.*

"And these prices are accurate?" Chaz pointed to the sticker on the bottom of the plate in his hand.

"They are." Though much too low considering the sentimental value she placed on them.

He nodded and set the plate back on the shelf. "I may be back. My mom has a set very similar to this one, but she's broken a few pieces through the years. Maybe I can replace them for her birthday next month."

"That's a sweet idea." And made more sense than him wanting them for his own house. Wasn't he a bachelor? She blinked the thought away. It didn't matter.

He lifted the gravy boat out of her hands. She didn't even realize she was still holding it.

"Tell you what. How about I buy this piece today to make

sure it really does match." He ran a finger over the tiny roses on the side. "That way I won't waste my money or your time."

"Sure." She nodded. "I'll wrap it up for you."

The newspaper crinkled as she molded it around the side of the dish and then stuffed it into the opening. Another memory leaving. No. The memories would stay. It was just a dish. She didn't need the dishes to remember her mother.

She blinked back the tears building behind her eyes and handed him the bag with the dish in it. He held out a debit card, and she quickly ran it through the reader attached to the tablet Angela kept for this booth.

As she returned his card, she noticed the black under her fingernails. The moment he pinched the card in his fingers, she jerked her hand back. Maybe he hadn't seen the charcoal.

"You okay?"

She nodded and forced a smile. "Fine. Have a great day. Maybe I'll see you again soon."

He hesitated another moment. Had he finally recognized her? He shook his head. "Maybe so."

And he was gone.

She wilted against the wall, sliding all the way down to the floor and covering her eyes with her hands. Deep breath in. Deep breath out. *Okay, God. What now? Are you opening a door for me to the gallery, or is this just a coincidence?*

* * *

Was that the same girl from this morning? Chaz questioned his sanity. With the handkerchief over her head, it was hard to tell, but where else had he seen someone with the same blonde hair? Surely, if she was, though, she'd have admitted running into him—literally—that same day. And she hadn't said a word. Hadn't even seemed to recognize him.

And what had been on her hands? He wouldn't have noticed the black smudges if she hadn't jerked away so quickly, drawing his attention to them. Had the newsprint she used to wrap the gravy boat transferred to her skin that much? If so, he'd need to unwrap it as soon as he got home and maybe even wash the dish before it became permanent. He'd never seen newsprint get under fingernails before, though.

With the way she'd jerked away and took forever to answer, things seemed off, as if she were hiding something. But at least he was on the right track for his mother's birthday. Assuming this was the correct pattern.

"Oh, I'm so sorry!" For the second time that day, a blonde bumped into him.

Stepping back, he untangled her from his torso. "It's okay. I'm sure I wasn't watching where I was going." He touched her arm. "You okay?"

"Yes. Just feeling foolish for running into you." She brushed a strand of hair from her blue eyes and blinked up at him. "Oh."

Uh oh. Here it came.

"You're Chaz Prince." One of her perfectly manicured hands fluttered at her chest.

"Guilty as charged." He studied the girl in front of him, but he couldn't remember meeting her before. It definitely wasn't the same girl from that morning, though she had several similarities. Besides, the girl earlier hadn't known who he was, and this one obviously did. Bumping into him twice in one day would be too serendipitous.

"Well, I'm terribly sorry, Chaz. So clumsy of me. And now I'm keeping you from wherever you were headed." She batted her eyelashes. "Can you forgive me?"

"Of course. Like I said, the fault is probably as much mine

as yours. Don't worry about it." He gave an awkward wave then sidestepped around her when she still didn't move.

The girl did look familiar, but nothing rang a bell. Just like the girl from the booth. Maybe they were related or something. He shook his head. No need to overthink it. One chance meeting in a hallway shouldn't make him so obsessed, even if the girl seemed to have literally walked out of his dreams.

He headed out into the late-Friday sunshine. Autumn was one of his favorite times of year. The colors, the cooler weather, the beginning of hunting season. Jake was itching to go, but their option right now was turkey, and wild birds tended to be much tougher than farm-raised. Deer season would start in a few weeks, though.

Speaking of Jake, his friend's ringtone filled the air as Chaz slid into his Jeep.

"Can't get enough of me, huh?" Chaz put the phone on speaker so he could drive.

"Ha. You wish." Jake's voice sounded muffled for a minute then came back strong. "Look man, I know you don't love turkey hunting—"

"Hate it. Almost as bad as duck hunting."

"Which isn't even really a thing here."

"Right. But we went to Arkansas a few years back and about froze our—"

"Anyway," Jake broke in, "my friend Mike has some wooded land, and they've been overrun with turkeys lately. He knows I love to hunt and called me to see if I was willing to try my hand at bagging one or two."

"You're only allowed to get one per day in the fall season." Chaz shook his head.

"Technically, yes. But this is also private property, so I figured the rules aren't quite as ... black and white."

Chaz chuckled. "Like you're a good enough shot to get even one."

"I believe that's a challenge, sir." Jake let out an evil-sounding laugh. "What's your schedule look like tomorrow?"

"Pretty open right now. You're serious about this?"

"It'll do you good to get away. Out in nature. One with God's creation." Jake's voice switched over to a pleading tone. "You know you want to."

"You're a mess. What if I told you I need to work on a plan to present to my dad instead?" Chaz turned into the driveway and parked behind his father's car.

"He went for your idea, then?" Jake's voice rose. "That's amazing!"

"Not exactly."

Silence.

"He said I needed to come in with 'an actual coherent plan and not some grandiose idea.'" Chaz sighed. "He doesn't understand why I want to bring in new artwork, new artists. He's set in his ways. He says why change something if it works?"

"So, while we're hunting turkeys, we'll brainstorm. I'm great at coming up with ideas."

Chaz grinned. "You're not going to let me get out of this, are you?"

"Why would you want to?" The grin in Jake's voice was evident by his lighthearted tone.

"All right. When and where are we meeting in the morning? And please tell me it won't be nearly as early as when we went duck hunting in Arkansas."

Jake hemmed and hawed, and Chaz braced himself for the inevitable. Hunting might be an enjoyable pastime, but it definitely wasn't restful. At least not with Jake White.

In the meantime, Chaz needed to see if this dish matched

his mom's. He crossed his fingers that it would. The girl who sold it to him was intriguing, a mystery itching to be solved.

She'd been so focused on whatever was on that paper when he first arrived, but he hadn't been able to get a good view of it. Here's hoping his hunch on these dishes matching was correct so he'd have an excuse to return.

4

Ella perched on a large boulder and quickly sketched the flock—or was a group of turkeys called something else?—in the field in front of her. Angela had given her the day off for some reason, and Ella wouldn't complain about having a whole Saturday to draw.

She'd left Humphrey at a park nearby and then wandered until she came upon the lovely sight. Turkeys were a rare treat. She didn't run across them often.

A tom ruffled his body then fluffed all his feathers out in a full display. Who was he trying to impress? Didn't matter. She'd gladly take advantage even if it wasn't meant for her.

"Thank you, God, for this day of quiet. For this beautiful location. And for the creativity You poured into this world. All these animals are different, and I love seeing each and every one of them."

Her whispered prayer was quiet enough it didn't disturb the birds munching on berries, buds, and bugs nearby.

She switched to a dark-gray pencil and worked on drawing individual feathers. The birds were so fluffy and plump. If she thought they wouldn't run away, she might try to get closer.

All around her, God had painted the trees in their autumnal

glory. Russets and goldenrods and crimsons and rusts were dotted through with the deep greens of pine trees. God's artwork always made her want to improve in her own craft. To capture at least a little bit of the glory surrounding her. She let out a deep breath.

Lowly, so she wouldn't startle the turkeys, she hummed "Oh to Be Like Thee." She might not have her earthly parents anymore, but she still had a Heavenly one. And He was the best.

Finishing up the sketch she was working on, she flipped to a new page and focused on a smaller bird. Maybe a hen? It was hard to tell from this distance.

The breeze rustled the trees. The turkeys gobbled and yelped at each other. Occasionally, other bird sounds filtered through from the surrounding woods. The peace trickled through Ella's soul, washing away all the frustration and sadness that surrounded her at home.

Home. The word almost didn't fit her house anymore. Most of her parents' items had been sent to the flea market booth or given to charity. Angela's style was much more flamboyant than theirs, so Ella kept mostly to her room. But even her room wasn't the same. Several of her items had gone missing over the last few years too.

"But one of these days, I'll be able to leave. Get out on my own, find some dishes similar to Mama's, maybe even have a little room to set up as a studio." She closed her eyes and leaned back to let the sun kiss her face. "One of these days."

How she'd do it, she had no idea, but she was determined. She would not live under Angela's thumb forever. Why stay with someone who had never liked her in all the twelve years they'd lived together?

And leaving Bellamy behind wouldn't be hard, either.

A turkey gave an extra-loud squawk and performed a flying

leap across the field. Well, that was interesting. She hadn't ever seen one fly before. Not that it had achieved any great height or distance, but still. It was more than she could do. The one time she'd tried to fly off the swing set as a child, she'd had the wind knocked out of her. She was afraid she'd died. And then, as she grew older, Angela had clipped her wings in other ways.

A few snapping limbs from the woods to her right clued her in as to why the birds might have scattered. Someone was coming. She quickly shoved her papers into her bag and stuffed her pencils into the front pocket. Had she inadvertently ended up on private land?

She scrambled to climb down from the boulder right as Chaz Prince stepped from behind a tree. *You have got to be kidding me! Where does he keep coming from? And why does he always show up where I am?*

She froze, only partway down, hoping he'd be distracted by the turkeys and not notice her hiding half behind the rock. No such luck. He zeroed in on her immediately.

She quickly held a finger to her lips and pointed across the field. He blinked, glanced that way, and straightened. That worked? He was distracted that easily? No. He looked back at her and held up a finger. Was he coming her way?

"Chaz?" A bellow broke through the silence, startling all the birds into the trees, distracting Chaz, and giving Ella a chance to finish climbing down.

She quickly walked in the direction where she had parked. Maybe he wouldn't follow her.

"Wait!" Chaz called.

No way. There was no way she could face him again after humiliating herself twice yesterday. Especially considering he hadn't seemed to recognize her in the afternoon. But he surely would if they kept meeting. And what excuse could she give for being here? Was it his land? Humiliation all over again.

"Chaz?"

Was that Jake's voice? Even more reason to leave. Jake knew who she was. And she wasn't ready for Chaz Prince to know about her yet. Not until she could get her artistic act together and be sure she wouldn't make a fool of herself like she had yesterday.

"Wait." Chaz sounded closer.

A stitch in her side slowed her down. Now what? Ella leaned against a thick tree to recover for a second. She willed her breath to calm, forcing her inhales and exhales through her nose instead of her mouth. Why did he keep following her?

"Where did she go?" Chaz stopped close enough she could see him in her periphery.

She eased further around the trunk.

"Chaz. There you are, man. What are you doing?" Jake rushed to his friend.

"I saw that girl again."

"You're going to have to be more specific." Jake leaned on his knees to catch his breath.

"The one who bumped into me at the hotel yesterday morning. The one I thought was a tourist. Do you think she lives around here? Why would she be on Mike's land?"

So it was someone's personal land. Good to know. She wouldn't trespass here any longer once she was able to get past the guys.

"Maybe she didn't realize it was private property. His land abuts a park not too far away." Jake straightened and pointed in the direction of her truck.

No. Not helpful at all, Jake!

"How far?"

"I don't know. Less than a mile, probably. I've never approached it from this direction before." Jake glanced around.

34

"Hey. Did you see any turkeys? Mike said they like to hang out around here."

"They were back there, but they ran off when you shouted." Chaz hooked his thumb over his shoulder but kept looking in the direction Ella needed to be headed right now.

"Really? Aw, man. I was sure we could bag one today."

"We still might. But I sort of want to see if I can catch that girl first." Chaz took a step in her direction.

Ella stiffened.

"C'mon. You've run into her two days in a row. If you're meant to meet her, maybe you'll see her again. We're supposed to be having guy time."

Chaz hesitated. "When did you start believing in fairy tales?"

"Happy endings aren't my idea. Kari keeps making me watch those cheesy romance movies. Maybe they're rubbing off on me."

"Pretty sure any woman you talk to would beg to differ." Chaz shook his head. "It feels important—seeing her randomly two days in a row."

"You sure *you* haven't been watching cheesy romance movies?" Jake draped his arm around Chaz's neck. "Come on. Maybe we can still catch up with the turkeys."

Chaz glanced behind once more then followed his friend back the way they'd come. Ella slumped and let out a deep breath. She and Chaz saw things much differently. He thought their meetings were important. She considered them something she wasn't ready for.

Every encounter so far had been far from professional. Hadn't even shown her in a good light. Instead, she'd been frazzled, frantic, and fazed. Not a good way to impress someone. Was it too late to change that? Had her unprofessional reactions completely ruined any chance of being featured in his gallery in the future simply because of these accidental meetings?

* * *

"She was over here when I first saw her." Chaz stopped by the boulder at the edge of the clearing.

"You're still hung up on that girl?" Jake frowned. "I thought we were here to find some hens. Not chicks."

"That was bad even for you." Chaz nudged his friend out of the way and climbed up on the rock, which offered a great view of the field. A spot of white lodged in a bush on the other side of the boulder caught his eye.

He knelt down and pulled it free from the branches. Paper. He focused closer. Not just paper. A drawing of a turkey.

A good drawing, at that.

She was an artist.

Now he was more intrigued than ever. A bubble of mirth welled in his chest. What were the odds?

"You done up there? Which way did the fowl go?" Jake rested his gun against his shoulder and shielded his eyes from the sun.

"That way." Chaz pointed across the field. "Good luck. Your holler sounded more like a moose than a turkey call."

"Ha, ha. Maybe if I *use* my turkey call, they'll come back." Jake pulled his call box from a side pocket on his backpack. "I chalked it up this morning, so it should sound nice and smooth."

"You and your calls. Are you sure it actually sounds like an animal?"

"Watch and learn." He rubbed the top piece against the bottom box, and a loud squeak sounded, similar to the noise a turkey would make. If it worked, Jake would never let Chaz live it down. They walked in the direction of the turkeys and found a spot near the edge of the trees with dense foliage to conceal them. Jake used the box again.

"Are you going to be terribly upset if you don't snag a turkey today?" Chaz crouched against a tree trunk.

"Nah. It's still a good day. Out in the woods with my good bud Chaz. Chasing wood nymphs and solving the world's problems."

"What problems have you solved today?" Chaz lifted a brow.

"I believe you said we need to come up with a plan to present to your dad soon." Jake pointed at Chaz.

"I believe I said *I* need to come up with a plan." Chaz pointed back. "Totally different."

"What are friends for if not to bounce ideas off of?"

"If I bounce too many ideas off you, the turkeys will never come back. We're supposed to be quiet so they'll think it's safe. Not that you're ever good at being quiet."

"Good thing too. Because if I were, I'd have never located you in that fancy gallery of yours. It gave you a reason to come out of your office." Jake winked. "I'd have purchased my art and you would've missed your chance at having the best friend a guy could ask for."

Chaz smirked. "You might disagree with that assessment if you knew my dad might've given you a discount on those pieces you bought for the hotel had you been quieter."

"What?" Jake smacked himself in the forehead. "I guess having you as a friend makes up for the discount. Mostly."

"Good thing too. Because seeing as you're still yammering, you're probably not snagging a bird today."

Jake's expression said he didn't completely buy Chaz's reason to quit talking, but he complied anyway. Chaz spread the drawing out on his legs and studied it. It was a quick sketch, but still detailed. Each feather showed veins and shading. The chest looked soft enough to touch. How had she captured such detail while crouched on a rock in the middle of nowhere?

"Whatcha lookin' at?" Jake broke the silence.

"That girl dropped a drawing when she left." Chaz held it up for Jake to see.

Jake whistled. "I had no idea."

"Had no idea of what?" Chaz leaned forward.

Jake's eyes widened. "That ... the turkeys around here got so big."

Jake's response wasn't believable in the least, but before Chaz could reply, something moved nearby. Both guys froze and waited to see what they were up against. One by one, the turkeys strutted their way back out into the open, gobbling and fluttering their wings. The run was large, with at least eight birds Chaz could count from his position.

Jake shifted slowly, lowering his weapon and waggling his eyebrows at the same time. "Let's do this," he whispered.

Chaz lifted one side of his mouth. Life was never boring with Jake around.

"Aim for the head," Chaz softly reminded him.

Jake scoffed. "I know what I'm doing." He lifted the gun to his shoulder and released the safety. Focusing, he let out a breath and pulled the trigger. The shot was true, and a bird near the front of the cluster fell, one leg still twitching.

"Nice." Jake lowered his weapon.

"Happy now?" Chaz grinned.

"Of course. But don't you want one too?"

"Nah. I'm good. I already got my prize." Chaz held up the drawing. "Maybe it will inspire a plan."

"A sketch of a turkey? I'm sure your dad will love it. Jump right in and give you whatever power you want in the company." Jake shook his head before rising to examine his kill.

"I didn't say I was going to use this as the plan. I said maybe it would inspire me." Chaz followed him over and snapped a picture for Jake to post on social media.

"Well, I can't wait to hear what your great plan is. Because if it's inspired by a turkey, it has to be a good one." Jake bagged his bird and loaded everything else into his bag. "I guess we have to leave now, since you don't want to shoot one. Unless you want me to shoot it and you take credit?"

"Pretty sure that's lying."

"I mean, it's only fair, since you're not going to use your one-bird-per-day limit. It's more like ... sharing."

"Let's just go." Chaz pointed in the direction of his Jeep. "And you better not get blood on my upholstery."

"Wouldn't dream of it." Jake loped beside him. "The bird, on the other hand ... Well, I can't speak for him."

Chaz shook his head. Several times today he'd wanted to throttle his best friend—like when he scared off the turkeys and the girl. But it had been a good day, anyway. Jake was right. Being out in the woods with a friend sometimes made the whole world look better.

And if he could find the master of this artwork, his world would look even better still. Especially if her drawing could inspire him to come up with a plan to convince his dad to offer him a bigger role in the gallery. Something told him she was exactly what he needed.

If only he could catch her.

5

"There's my girl." Fae slid over on the pew to make room for Ella. "I was beginning to worry about you."

Ella tucked a loose strand of hair back into her braid. "Angela insisted I finish *all* the dishes before leaving this morning."

Fae squeezed Ella's fingers with her own slightly arthritic ones. "Well, I'm glad it didn't take you too long."

It didn't, because Ella had hidden half the dishes under the sink to wash later. Not a perfect solution, but it got her out the door on time. Not that she'd ever admit as much to her sweet neighbor Fae.

"How was your week? Any blessings?"

Ella thought back over the last few days. "I had yesterday off. That was nice."

Except for running into the man she was trying to avoid. Or losing her favorite sketch of the turkeys. No telling where it had ended up.

Fae jerked her head Ella's way, her brows angling downward. "She let you have a day off?"

"Weird, right?" Ella smoothed her bulletin on her lap. "But I found a lovely spot with a flock of turkeys to sketch."

"Blessing, indeed." Fae nodded.

Ella pushed the not-so-great moments from her mind and focused on the blessings: Friends like Kari and Fae. The deer and turkeys. The lovely colors of the trees.

She took a deep breath of the wood-and hymnal-scented air.

Time to worship God.

As services were about to start, Angela and Bellamy sauntered up the aisle, waving at a few people and acting like they weren't awful. No. Ella needed to be more charitable. God loved Angela and Bellamy, so she should as well. Love your enemies and all that. She mentally shook her head. She knew what she should think but couldn't seem to make her heart behave.

As if Fae could read Ella's thoughts, she nodded at Angela and Bellamy, but then leaned close and whispered, "It's good they're here."

It was. And Ella knew it. But she struggled with their hypocrisy. And struggled even more to not be judgmental.

The song leader stepped up to the microphone. "Good morning!"

The services started, and Ella reined her thoughts into submission ... mostly.

The hymns of praise and prayer were easy to sing, lifting Ella's heart to help her face another week. If she didn't have faith, she wouldn't have made it this far. Thank God her parents had instilled in her a love for Him early on. Fae had helped nurture it more after they were gone.

A few titters around her interrupted the quiet as the minister took the pulpit. Strange. Brother Butterfield looked the same as he always did—his graying hair combed neatly, glasses perched high on his nose. Someone in front of her looked toward the back then ducked her head close to her sister to whisper. So, they weren't murmuring about the minister.

Ella started to follow the attention of the other girls then caught herself once her gaze reached Fae. Fae frowned and opened her Bible, running a hand over the ruffled pages. Ella tried to control her curiosity about the whispers like Fae was, but it niggled at her. The giggles and hushed conversations were quiet, but still audible. Who was causing such a ruckus? And why?

"Brothers and sisters, did you know we worship an artist?" Brother Butterfield smiled. "The best one, in my opinion."

Ella couldn't help but grin. He was speaking to her heart today.

"The Bible tells us from the very first verse, 'God created.'" The preacher nodded. "Creativity is all around us, from the colors in the trees right now to the various animals we find to even how unique and different we all are from each other."

Amen! Ella's heart sang.

"But did you know He created us for a reason?" Brother Butterfield glanced out over his glasses. "And not just because He was bored or wanted to see if He could make eight billion plus different people. Let's all turn to Ephesians."

Ella flipped to the book near the back of her Bible.

"Right here in chapter two, verse ten, it says, 'For we are his workmanship.' Some translations say, 'masterpiece.'" Brother Butterfield tapped his Bible. "'For we are his workmanship, created in Christ Jesus for good works, which God prepared beforehand, that we should walk in them.'"

Ella's margin was filled with a colorful picture of someone painting a human. Illustrating verses helped her remember them, and her Bible had color on almost every page now. She underlined the word "workmanship" and wrote "masterpiece" over to the side. It didn't make her feel like a masterpiece, per se, but she needed to remind herself God saw her that way.

"Not only did God say what He created was 'good' and 'very good' in Genesis, but here He calls us His masterpiece. It takes artists years and years before they consider any of their art good enough to call a masterpiece. And oftentimes, they still see the imperfections and flaws. So other people label their creations as a masterpiece for them. But God looks at you ... and me ... and says we're masterpieces despite our flaws and imperfections."

The thought settled deep into Ella's soul. Her favorite artist considered her to be perfect despite her imperfections.

"Now, if you look further into the verse, you'll see why He made us. To do good works."

As Brother Butterfield moved on to talk about various ways they could do good works, Ella's mind wandered to her own life. What did she do that was good? What did she do worth anything at all?

Her stepmother and stepsister cared if she was around only because they knew she'd do chores they didn't want to do. She worked the flea market booth because the tiny bit of income it allotted would hopefully allow her to take another art class in the near future—not because she wanted to sell her parents' possessions. She drew because her fingers couldn't stay still when God's beauty was all around her. But did that do any good?

No one ever saw her artwork except Kari and Fae. And they were biased.

Fae nudged her as they stood for a song. She mouthed, "You okay?"

Ella nodded and joined in singing, but the peace from earlier had fled. There had to be more to life than all this. But what could she do in her situation? She could barely afford the gas and insurance for her dad's old truck. What could she offer when she had barely anything?

The closing prayer flew by, then everyone started chatting and gathering their things to leave. Ella closed her own Bible, tucking her bulletin between the pages. Fae stopped her with a hand on her arm.

"You'll come have lunch with me today?"

Ella glanced a few rows up, where Angela spoke with some other ladies. "I'll try."

"Come. I made your favorite."

Ella's mouth watered. Fae's slow-cooker chicken and dressing was the best. Decision made. Not that she wanted to turn her down. "I'll be there."

Bellamy's laughter was louder than all the other noises in the church building. Ella glanced over her shoulder and noticed her stepsister not too far away. A few other girls their age hovered around her but kept glancing toward the back of the auditorium. Ella followed their gazes and froze. Chaz Prince.

"Anyway, he seemed completely okay that I bumped into him when he left the market the other day." Bellamy's words broke through Ella's sudden paralysis. "I expect him to come back soon if only to see me again."

Ideas clicked into place. If Chaz had run into Bellamy as he left on Friday, she would've told Angela. And Bellamy was obviously interested. Why not? Chaz had been named West Virginia's most eligible bachelor the last two years. Was that why Angela had given her the day off yesterday? To remove the chance of Chaz seeing Ella instead of Bellamy?

A small snort escaped Ella before she could stop it. Fae raised an eyebrow.

"Sorry. I'll tell you later, but needless to say, irony has

reigned in my life the last few days." Ella shook her head. "I'll meet you at your place in a little while. Gotta put a few dollars of gas in the old truck so it will start tomorrow morning."

Fae reached out and squeezed Ella's hand, leaving behind a folded-up bill.

Ella squeaked a protest, but Fae had already moved out of the row and was headed up the aisle. That woman. She peeked at the money and sighed. Fae would remind her it was a blessing, not charity. And it would be a huge blessing to be able to fill her tank instead of putting in a little at a time as she could afford it.

She followed her neighbor toward the door only to stop when Chaz stepped into her path.

"It's you."

She blinked. "I've never claimed to be anyone but me."

"Right." He lifted one side of his mouth, showcasing a dimple. "But I keep seeing you, and I never get to ask you your name."

She swallowed. If he knew her name, would it hurt her chances of displaying her artwork in his gallery? Who was she kidding? She wasn't that good.

"You do have a name, right?" He tilted his head.

"Yes, of course." She flipped her braid over her shoulder. "It's Ella."

"Ella." He reached out and took her fingers in his, giving them a light squeeze. "A pleasure to finally meet you."

Wow. Her heart raced at the gentle contact. Was she nervous? It couldn't be anything else, right?

"Ella!" Bellamy's voice cut through their moment, and Ella jerked her hand away. Her stepsister rushed to her side, practically ramming her out of the way. "Do you know Chaz?"

"We just met." Ella ducked her head. "I've got to go, but it was nice you joined us this morning, Mr. Prince."

She sidestepped Bellamy and walked out the door into the autumn sunlight. The way her pulse continued to pound, she almost worried about having a stroke or heart attack. What was wrong with her? Why had she been so frazzled and frantic the last few days? And why did it always happen when Chaz was around?

* * *

Ella. Well, at least now he had a name for the pretty blonde he kept running into.

Chaz hadn't attended a worship service in far too long. His parents worshipped, but their congregation was small and consisted mostly of older people. During school, Chaz had fallen out of the practice of going. For the last couple years of being back home, he hadn't picked it up again.

But Jake and Kari invited him every week. Chaz couldn't count how many times he'd told them no, and they still asked. Like the story of the persistent widow in the Bible, their diligence had paid off, and here he was. Needless to say, he was blown away when he saw the very girl he was searching for sitting halfway up the auditorium. Would she have given him more time if the other girl hadn't interrupted?

Speaking of ...

The blonde placed her hand on his arm and smiled up at him. "We're *so* glad you're here today, *Mr. Prince*."

For some reason, when Ella said it, he believed it. From this woman, the words came across as insincere. Still, he put on his public face and offered a smile.

"Thanks so much. I really enjoyed the service." And he had. In fact, it had confirmed what he had mentioned to his father a few days ago. He needed to be doing more. To be more useful and purpose driven. He simply had to find what that purpose was.

"I'm so glad. Brother Butterfield sometimes gets carried away with his sermons. You just never know." She gave a shrug and glanced around before returning her attention back to him.

"You about ready to go, bro?" Jake clapped him on the shoulder. Saved by the best friend.

Chaz's neck relaxed. "Sure."

"Hey, Bellamy. How's it going?" Jake winked at her.

She scoffed. "I'm fine, Jake. How's hotel life?"

"Fine and dandy." He saluted her. "If you don't mind, I'm going to steal Chaz. We're headed to lunch."

"Oh? Going out to eat?" She straightened and gazed at Chaz with wide eyes, her lids slowly lowering and then raising again, her lower lip slightly pouted. An expression that was probably supposed to come across as innocent, but didn't quite make it.

"Yep. Out that door." Jake chuckled at his own joke and nudged Chaz into moving.

"Thanks, man." Chaz slapped Jake on the back when they turned to leave. "I feel like I owe you."

"Bellamy is okay, but she had that look in her eye." Jake waggled his eyebrows.

"That look?"

"You know. The one that says she knows you're a very eligible bachelor and she'd like to fix that for you."

"So funny." Chaz shook his head. "Were you serious about lunch?"

"I'm always serious about food." Jake leaned against his truck. "But no pressure. I was just giving you an out."

"Actually, if you're willing to let me pay, I want to run some ideas by you. That sermon got me thinking."

"Sure. Where we going?"

Fifteen minutes later, they were settled at Tudor's Biscuit World, a restaurant known for serving biscuits all day. They settled in with a full spread of biscuits, gravy, and potatoes. Nothing better on a Sunday.

"What did Brother Butterfield's sermon get you thinking about this morning?" Jake forked a bite of potatoes. "Looked to me like your focus was more on a certain blonde about halfway up the rows of pews. And I'm not talking about Bellamy."

"You know that woman I keep running into? That was her. Ella, she said her name was."

Jake choked and took a drink of coffee. "Ella? Bellamy's stepsister?"

"Apparently."

"Interesting." Jake took another large bite.

"You sound like you know something you aren't saying."

"Nope." Jake leaned back and took another drink. "Carry on. The sermon?"

"Right." Chaz pushed a piece of sausage around on his plate. "He was talking about how talented God is and how we're His masterpiece, right?"

"I think that's what I heard, yes." Jake smirked.

"And as he was discussing all the ways God is creative, it hit me that the drawing I found yesterday was an image of God's creation. And it was created by someone local." He froze and glanced at Jake. "Do you think Ella did it?"

Jake shrugged. "I've never seen her draw, but she and Kari don't always invite me to join them when they hang out."

Chaz pursed his lips for a second then decided to table that thought for another time. "Anyway, the drawing is good. And it made me wonder what other local artists live around here who haven't been discovered yet. I mean, West Virginia is sort of known for the arts. We have Blenko Glass Company and Fiesta

Tableware and stuff, too, but why don't we showcase more people who paint or draw?"

"You mean besides all the ones featured at Tamarack? Or the Huntington Museum?"

Chaz frowned. "I mean in our gallery."

"Okay." Jake leaned forward. "So you're wanting a way to showcase more local talent. I can get behind that. But how will you convince your dad?"

"That's the part I'm struggling with. He thinks the talent he already has is the best. And for some reason, he's set against featuring local artists."

"So you need a way to show him how good the local art is." Jake knocked on the table. "Take that turkey drawing in and prove it."

"Only a few problems with that." Chaz crossed his arms. "We're not one hundred percent sure who drew it in the first place."

Jake nodded.

"And it's just a sketch, not a finished piece. Nothing he could hang on his walls. I need to show him something finished."

"So you need to find whoever drew that turkey."

"Right." Chaz tapped his fingers against his biceps. "Though it's not fair to only show him one bit of local art."

"So you need a way to bring in more. Like a contest or something."

Chaz snapped. "Yes. What if we have a contest?"

Jake raised a brow. "We?"

"Your idea. You can help." Chaz pulled a napkin out of the dispenser and grabbed a pen. "This plan has to be perfect."

6

"Why am I here again?" Ella wiped her brow with the back of her hand. "You don't need my help."

"Of course I do." Fae waved from the lounge chair in her backyard. "These old bones don't move like they used to, you know."

"Did you or did you not parachute off New River Gorge Bridge last Bridge Day?" Ella propped her fists on her hips.

"Yes. But, dear one, that was gravity moving my bones for me." Fae smirked. "And it's a far different way of moving than bending down to pull up vines from a garden."

"Mm." Ella leaned down to yank another piece of what used to be a tomato plant from the ground. "I still say you're trying to find ways to pay me for things you could do yourself."

"But why do things myself when I can pay you to do them for me?"

Ella couldn't deny the money would make things easier. And what else was she to do on days the market was closed? She couldn't get another job because Angela seemed to expect her to be at her beck and call all the time. Besides, would anyone hire her when she could only work three days a week?

"After you finish the tomatoes, you can see if there are any pumpkins left hiding among the leaves." Fae sipped her tea as if she had nothing better to do than watch Ella work. Maybe she didn't. Ella honestly had no idea what Fae did most of the time.

"Why do you always plant such a big garden, Fae? You can't eat all this yourself, can you?"

"I put some up for the winter. And what I can't use, I share." Fae shifted on her seat. "What's the point of having a green thumb if I can't use it to benefit others?"

"You have to be one of the most giving people I know, Fae."

"You need to get to know more people, Ella-girl. I'm just a Christian."

"No *just* about it." Ella leaned back on her heels and studied her neighbor for the first time in a while.

Fae's red hair had faded to a soft yellow, which she wore in a loose knot at the back of her head. Most of her wrinkles were smile lines, creasing her eyes and cheeks in a way that made her appear perpetually happy. Her floral top and light-blue pants were flawless, as if she were about to head out to a tea party.

"I want to be like you when I grow up." Ella smiled at her friend.

"And here I thought you already had grown up."

Ella shook her head. "Age-wise, sure. But my life feels like it's on hold. Maybe forever."

Fae rose and ambled over to kneel next to her. "Not forever, sweet girl. Nothing is forever. You know that better than most."

Tears burned at the corners of Ella's eyes. "Yes."

"Sometimes, God uses these in-between moments to prepare us for whatever is coming next. Just like these seeds I planted in the spring took several weeks before they sprouted and grew tall. And then it took several more weeks before they gave me any veggies. If they had rushed, the tomatoes or peppers or pumpkins wouldn't have been worth eating. They had to ripen and mature. Maybe God's letting you ripen."

"You calling me green, Fae?" Ella swiped at the moisture on her cheek before grinning.

"Maybe just a wee bit." Fae hugged her then grunted. "Help an old woman back up, would you?"

Ella giggled but did as she was told. Fae settled back into her lounge chair, and Ella faced the pumpkin vines. Most of the vines had shriveled up into ugly brown pieces, the leaves long gone. The grass was tall around where the vines had grown, because the landscapers couldn't cut any closer for fear of snipping the vines too. Tall grass tended to house snakes and other such creatures, but if Fae wasn't worried, Ella shouldn't be, either.

She waded into the midst of the overgrown patch, glad for the tall garden boots Fae had loaned her. Gloves protected her fingers from the prickles as she tugged the vines up where they had put down roots, following them back to where the plant originated. Several grew over each other, tangling near the middle of the patch. A spot of orange caught her eye.

Her breath whooshed out as she scooped up a perfectly round pumpkin. Even the bugs seemed to have left it alone in its little cocoon of grass. She snipped it free from the vine but then wished she hadn't.

"Mind if I stop a minute to sketch?"

"Of course not."

Ella settled the gourd back into its nest and fetched her supplies from Fae's porch. Sitting in her own patch of tall grass, she quickly pulled out some pastels to draw the pumpkin. It would be the only pop of color, half-hidden among the brown grass. The story of fall in one picture—

where all was glory one minute and brown the next. The changing of the seasons.

Fae's words from earlier echoed in her head as she carefully added in more details. Was God simply using this time to help her grow? But grow into what?

"May I see?" Fae asked as Ella stood.

"I guess it's only fair, since it's your pumpkin." Ella walked over, carrying the sketch pad close to her chest before slowly lowering it.

"My, my." Fae grasped the edges tenderly. "You sure are a talented girl."

"It's not perfect."

"Says who?" Fae shot her a look that stopped any more protests. "Art doesn't have parameters that say it has to look this way or that. Beauty is in the eye of the beholder, and I'm beholding this artwork and saying it's beautiful."

Ella burst out laughing. "Fine. I'm glad you like it. Just imagine how good it would be if I could take a few more classes."

Fae lowered the drawing and studied Ella. "You really are hard on yourself. I wish I knew why. Because if you could see what I see, you wouldn't say such things."

Grabbing hold of Ella's hands, Fae pulled her down beside her. Ella sat while her neighbor studied her for another minute. Most of the time, Ella loved spending time with Fae, but occasionally, moments like this happened, leaving her feeling like a schoolgirl chastised for something she couldn't control.

"Dear heart, God made you just the way He wanted you. Remember what the sermon said yesterday? You are a masterpiece!" Fae squeezed Ella's fingers. "I wish with all my heart that your mother had lived longer so she could teach you to embrace who you are, but I'm doing my best to do that for her. You are like her in so many ways, with a good dose of your daddy's stubborn pride. And all together, you make one absolutely lovely girl, inside and out."

Ella ducked her head.

"If you didn't care, you wouldn't stay with Angela and Bellamy. Wouldn't make sure your mama's dishes went to people who look like they care about them instead of any deal seeker. Wouldn't see everything around you as a piece of art created by the Master Artist Himself. Your soul is sunshine, and you make the world better by being in it."

"Fae—"

"And I'm not only saying that because I love you." The older woman smacked Ella's fingers lightly. "One of these days, something's going to happen to help you believe this. I just hope I'm around to see it."

"I want to believe you."

"Then do. You can say all I just told you over and over in your head while you finish pulling vines." Fae winked.

Ella grinned. What would she do without her spunky neighbor?

* * *

Chaz stood in the dining room, studying his mom's china. He looked back and forth from the gravy boat in his hands to the plates lined up in the hutch. Both had pink roses, but were they the same? How was he supposed to tell if this rose pattern matched that one when all the little roses looked exactly alike to him?

"What are you doing?" Mom startled him, and he almost dropped the gravy boat. "What's that?"

"Oh, um … I noticed you didn't have a gravy boat, and I saw this one the other day. Thought it might be a match."

She lifted it from his hand and ran a finger over the side. "Wow. I didn't even know you could still find this pattern. This china was my grandmother's, and they quit making it years ago."

"So I was right?" He ran a hand through his hair, trying to appear nonchalant.

"You were. It's a perfect match. Thank you."

"You're welcome." He relaxed a smidge. "I'm glad I happened to spot it."

"Where did you find it?" Mom opened the hutch door and set the boat next to a serving bowl.

Not good. If she knew where he found the gravy boat, she might go buy the dishes herself, and his birthday-gift idea would be ruined. But he couldn't lie to her, either.

"I'll have to remember. I went several places the other day."

She lifted a brow but didn't push. As she shut the hutch, his gaze caught on the painting behind her. It had been there as long as he could remember, but he hadn't paid it much mind. Now, his attention zeroed in on it.

It displayed a scene familiar to anyone who lived in West Virginia: rolling mountains covered in trees, a hint of a waterfall off to one side, and a train chugging along near the bottom.

"Who painted that?"

"Hmm?" His mom looked his way.

"That painting. Who is the artist?"

Mom stepped over and ran a finger down the frame. "A dear friend from long ago. She was very talented, I thought. Or maybe I just love our state."

"Does she still paint?"

Mom seemed to wilt. "No. No, she died quite a few years ago."

Chaz draped his arm over his mom's shoulders and squeezed. "Sorry. Didn't mean to make you sad."

"That's okay." She patted his hand. "There are some people in this world who leave a larger hole when they pass away. She was one of them."

"What was her name?"

"Sara Renders."

He studied the painting for another moment. "Too bad she's gone. Maybe she could've helped me with my plan."

"Your plan?" Mom straightened. "What are you plotting?"

"I want to convince Dad to open up the gallery to new artists—local artists. We have so much undiscovered talent around here. But Dad doesn't want to explore the possibilities."

"Your father has built that gallery up to be the prestigious place it is now. I think he's afraid if he changes anything, it might not be as amazing." Mom pressed her palm to his cheek. "But don't give up. You've always had a good eye for art. And a good heart. I think this is a great idea. But don't go in helter-skelter. Make sure you have all your *t*'s crossed and *i*'s dotted."

Chaz nodded. "I thought it might be good to have a contest. We could display the winner's art in the gallery, and it would give Dad a great chance to see all the local artists. But I need something to convince him the local art is good enough to hold the contest in the first place."

Mom nodded. "It's a great start. Something tells me you're going to find what you're looking for. Be patient. And pray about it. God wants to help us achieve our goals if they align with His will. And I don't think there's anything in this that would go against Him—unless you're only doing it for your own glory."

"No. I want this to be about the artists. I want to help

people get discovered. To have a chance for their artwork to reach people far outside West Virginia."

Mom gave his arm a squeeze. "I'm already proud of you. And I'll be praying you find what you're looking for."

Or *who* he was looking for, as the case may be. Chaz studied the painting another minute before heading to the front door. Maybe he should've talked it all through with his mom days ago. She was much better at giving advice than Jake.

"Oh, and Chaz?"

He froze in the doorway. "Yes?"

"If you remember where you found those dishes, let me know. I'd like to replace a few pieces I've broken."

He nodded, afraid if he answered out loud, he might give himself away. Why did she have to make it so hard to shop for her birthday?

At least if he had to snag those dishes before someone else did, it gave him an excuse to return to the flea market. And maybe see Ella again.

Ella placed a picture frame on the shelf above the china. The photograph that used to sit behind the glass now hid in her chest at home. Angela might want the frame filled to "help people see what it looks like with a picture in it," but there was no way Ella was selling her family photos.

She pulled her jacket tighter. Some vendors had heaters in their spaces, which helped warm things up, but in the cool months, the warehouse stayed pretty cold. She cupped her hands and breathed into them, trying to warm her fingers.

Bellamy was a no-show this morning, but Ella couldn't find it in herself to care. Last night at Bible study, Bellamy bragged about Chaz Prince having a crush on her. It made Ella want to gag.

A few of her dad's books fit beside the frame. *The Count of Monte Cristo, Frankenstein, Robin Hood*, and *Robinson Crusoe*. All hardbacks in fairly good condition. Ella had hidden away his copies of *Grimm's Fairy Tales* and *The Wizard of Oz*. Those she counted as her inheritance.

"Not that I believe in fairy tales anymore." She straightened a stack of board games.

"Morning, Ella." Marjorie waved at her as she shuffled

past, a Tiffany lamp under her arm. She must have been shopping at Mr. Simeon's booth this morning.

"Morning," Ella called before the older lady was out of range of hearing.

In some ways, the flea market was like a family. Most of the booth owners knew each other and stopped to chat throughout the day. It was also like a family because as much as they might like each other, they all wanted the customers at their own booths instead of someone else's. Ella pulled a few more books from the box then sliced through the tape to break it down.

"Wait!"

Ella froze, her knife halfway through the tape. Slowly, she lifted her head to confirm who stood behind her.

"Sorry," Chaz huffed. "I just thought I might need that box."

He came back.

Not for her.

For the dishes.

"I have more tape. We can secure it again." Ella slipped her knife into her pocket and straightened. "I take it the gravy boat was a match?"

"It was." Chaz grinned and stepped into the booth, making it feel much smaller than it had a moment ago. "I knew you looked familiar the other day, but for some reason I couldn't place you. I think it was that"—he motioned around his head —"scarf thing you were wearing."

"Oh." Ella touched her hair, which was in a bun today. "Yeah. I use it sometimes to keep the dust out."

Chaz nodded. "Makes sense. I guess I'd only seen you once before, which was that morning. Not sure either one of us was fully awake for that meeting."

Ella turned her attention to a figurine on the shelf next to her. She wasn't about to let him know she'd been awake for several hours when they bumped into each other. "Right."

She'd returned to the Starbright several times in the last week but hadn't seen him again. Maybe it was a one-time thing. Or Kari was doing a better job at making sure they were on separate floors. Either way, Ella wouldn't complain.

Having him here now trying to make conversation had all her nerves firing at the same time. If he got to know her, would it ruin all her chances at having her artwork in his gallery? She was a nobody. Just a girl dependent on her stepmother, working a few days a week at a flea market. How would that recommend her for a prestigious gallery?

And yet she couldn't shake the dream. Maybe she'd come back one day and reintroduce herself after working through several more classes, finishing her degree, and really becoming something. Wouldn't he be surprised then? That the nobody had gone on to exceed her potential?

"Ella?" Chaz's voice pulled her from her thoughts, and she realized he'd said something else to her.

"So sorry. What?"

"I asked about the dishes. You said you had a full twelve place settings, right?"

"Yes."

"I'd like to buy whatever you have."

Her heart dropped. "Are you sure? I mean, you said your mom already had some of them. Twelve place settings take up a lot of room. Maybe just replace the ones she's broken?"

Because that way I still have hope of keeping a few for myself and my future home. Just six, Lord. Is that too much to ask?

Chaz shook his head. "I was talking to my mom about her china the other day. She said it's no longer made. That the set was her grandmother's and she thought she'd never be able to find any again. I want to go ahead and buy all of it so that if anything else breaks, we're covered."

Ella swallowed a lump of grief. "It was my grandmother's too."

She hadn't meant to say the words out loud. But she couldn't take them back now. Chaz stepped closer and placed a hand on her arm. "Why are you selling them?"

"They don't match my stepmother's style." Ella ran her finger across a plate.

"But you could pack them away for your own use."

She shook her head. "No space to store things we don't need."

"A storage unit—"

"No space." Ella stepped away from his touch and moved toward the entrance to their booth. "Let me grab the other box of dishes that's not displayed."

"I could help—"

She waved a hand and quickly walked toward the back side of their booth. The flea market was arranged so the vendors had a little alleyway between their booths where they could store excess inventory. It wasn't well lit, and often the paths were narrow and littered with items that had fallen off the piles. No need to make both of them squeeze through there.

Besides, she needed a moment or two to regain control of herself. These were only dishes. How many times had she repeated that to herself? Why wouldn't it sink into her heart, where she could truly believe it?

Behind the booth, she rummaged through a few other boxes and crates before finding the one marked "china." It was heavy, but no heavier than her heart. And she carried that around all the time.

"Chaz, darling. What a pleasant surprise." Bellamy's voice rang out on the other side of the thin wall.

Great. Ella rolled her eyes, huffed, then hefted the box. Now not only did she have to deal with losing a big part of her mom's history, but she had to do it while someone gloated with pure pleasure as she packed up every last bowl and plate. All while using that cloying, noxious voice on the man buying them.

Maybe she should leave. Pretend like she'd never been here, never seen Chaz today.

No. That would only make things worse. Better to face this head-on and get it over with.

"What were you looking at?" Bellamy purred as Ella walked closer.

Chaz cleared his throat as if embarrassed. "Oh, um. I don't think I was supposed to find it, but it was sticking out from behind this bench and caught my eye."

Ella froze. Her drawing. He'd found her drawing? She didn't know whether to panic or celebrate.

"You're right. You weren't supposed to see that yet." Bellamy's voice held a hint of something that terrified Ella. What was she up to?

"Because it's not finished?" Ella could barely see the edge of Chaz from this angle, so she eased a step closer. "It's amazing. Reminds me of another painting I love."

Her breath hitched. He loved it? Could this be her chance after all? Despite the worrying?

"Really? You like it?" Bellamy moved into Ella's view and fluttered her hands near her face. "You have no idea what that means to me."

To her? Since when did Bellamy care about Ella's artwork?

"You drew this?"

Ella almost dropped the box.

No. No, no, no. This could not be happening.

"I mean, I dabble here and there. Nothing fancy like what's

in your gallery or anything. I just can't *not* draw the beauty God has given us around here, you know?" Bellamy mashed together several phrases Ella had used in the past. She was stealing credit for her drawing, and now she was stealing her words too?

Ella moved closer, eyes narrowed. No. Bellamy had gone too far.

"Wow, Bellamy. I had no idea." Chaz's attention stayed on her drawing.

Bellamy turned as if sensing Ella behind her. She held a finger to her lips then slipped Ella's pad from her bag on the stool. Ella's heart stopped as Bellamy mimicked tearing the pages in half. So, this was her game. Taking credit and keeping Ella quiet about it by threatening the rest of her artwork.

Tears welled in Ella's eyes. It was all too much. To lose her mom's dishes and then her artwork and a chance at the gallery too? *God, how is this helping me grow? How is this going to work out for good?*

* * *

A noise behind him drew Chaz's attention away from the incredible artwork.

"Oh, Ella. That looks heavy. Let me help." He stepped out of the booth and took the box from the girl who looked about ready to collapse. She blinked a few times, her eyes suspiciously moist. Had she been crying? What had upset her?

The dishes. He was taking her grandmother's dishes. And acting like it was no big deal. As if it didn't matter that she was losing a tie to her family.

"Maybe you're right, Ella. Maybe I should only buy six place settings today. I mean, what are we going to do with twenty place settings?"

Ella wiped her eyes and shook her head. "No. You're right. They don't make this pattern anymore. You should buy them all while you can so you have the extras in case any more break."

She rummaged through a corner box and pulled out a tape dispenser, quickly re-taping the box from earlier. "I'll get the ones on the shelf packed up for you. You wanted the serving pieces too, right?"

He nodded mutely. She was so strong. Much stronger than he was.

"Do you really like my drawing that much, Chaz?" Bellamy inserted herself into his personal space again, stroking his arm as if he were a cat.

Ella stiffened but didn't say anything. Was she jealous of Bellamy's artistic skills? That didn't seem to fit the tiny bit of her personality he'd witnessed so far.

Truth was, he loved the artwork. The depth of the valley, the intensity of the colors in the trees, the stark blackness of the coal train chugging through it all. It spoke to him more than anything else he'd seen lately.

This was what he needed. This would prove to his dad that talent was all around them, hidden in the people of their area, just waiting to be displayed.

The only downside was that it belonged to Bellamy. When he found it, he'd fervently wished it was Ella's. That would explain so much. But if it were, wouldn't she speak up? Correct her stepsister?

"Chaz?" Bellamy tapped his bicep.

"It's beautiful."

Bellamy beamed. "Do you think it's good enough to be in your gallery? Could we do a showing? The kind where you wear fancy dresses?"

Chaz swallowed a laugh. Those events were only for well-established artists or those who were rising fast. Not for someone with one good drawing.

"Probably not right away. But, if I have your permission, would you be willing to let me borrow this for a while?" He studied the pencil-and-charcoal piece in his hands again. "I have this idea I want to pitch to my dad, but I need something to help me convince him, and I think this might be just the thing."

"Ooh!" Bellamy hopped up and down, her blonde curls bouncing. "I'd be honored."

"I'll get it back to you as soon as I can," Chaz promised.

"No rush. Honestly, if it helps you, then it was worth every last minute I poured into it." Bellamy leaned even closer, and Chaz stepped back.

A crunch sounded under his shoe, and he winced. *Please don't be one of the dishes. Please don't be one of the dishes.* He glanced down and saw a broken picture frame.

"Oh, Ella. How clumsy of you, leaving that there on the floor." Bellamy set her fists on her hips. Chaz found the gesture odd considering the girls must be about the same age.

Chaz knelt down as Ella gathered up the loose pieces of glass. He clasped her fingers to still their work, but not before he noticed a small drop of blood appear on one.

"You're hurt."

"It's fine." Her voice was so quiet he could barely hear it over Bellamy's continuing rant.

"Do you have any bandages?"

Ella blinked and nodded. "Over in that box where the tape was."

"Don't move." He fished around in the mess until he discovered what he was looking for.

He peeled the wrapper off and returned to Ella. The blood hadn't increased. Probably was already clotting. But the sudden urge to protect her even in this small way was overwhelming.

"Seriously, Chaz. She can do that herself." Bellamy was practically on top of him.

"It's hard to bandage your own right hand. It's no trouble." He winked. "Besides, it's partly my fault she's hurt in the first place."

"Guess I better not tell you I'm left-handed?" Ella's lips turned up a little as she whispered the remark.

"Don't ruin my chivalry now." He tugged the bandage in place and barely kept himself from pressing a kiss to the tip of her finger. "There. All better."

"I'll have your dishes packed up in a few more minutes." Ella's voice was breathy.

"Please add this frame to my total."

"Oh, no—"

"Seriously. I'm the oaf who stepped on it. It's fine."

With a nod, she grabbed a piece of newspaper to wrap another plate. She stroked the edge before covering the dish and placing it in the box with the others. His heart twinged. While making one woman happy, he was breaking another's heart.

"So, Chaz. Want to tell me more about this big idea of yours?" Bellamy's voice grated, and he almost regretted discovering the drawing.

"Not yet. I've got to get some more pieces in place before I can tell anyone." He rose to his feet then helped Ella to hers after she packed away the last dish.

The shelf now stood half-empty, ready to be filled with more items. Were they all from Ella's family, or did some come from other places too? What was the rest of this story that didn't seem to add up all the way?

Ella tallied his total and handed him the paper receipt. As

he passed her his credit card, her fingers caught his eye again. Now that they were standing out of the shadow of the shelf, he noticed her fingernails had a distinct bluish tint. Not like a manicure. Something else. And he couldn't blame the newsprint like he'd done with the black smudges the week before. Almost like ... ink, or paint.

He glanced between the stepsisters, his mind whirling. Something fishy was going on here. And as excited as he'd been to find the dishes and the drawing, discovering the truth about Ella sounded even more intriguing.

8

Ella barely survived the rest of the day. Why had Chaz come so early? Why couldn't he have come later in the day so she wouldn't have to stare at those blank shelves for seven hours and know what was missing? And with Bellamy sprawled across her daddy's chair, gloating, Ella was barely able to breathe.

At exactly 6 P.M., she tore out of the flea market as if her life depended on it. Maybe it did.

"Ella." Bellamy's voice added to the fire in her gut. "Rendersella."

From the moment Bellamy had heard Daddy's silly take on the classic tale, she hadn't ceased to use that name to mock Ella. What had once been funny and lighthearted now turned a knife in Ella's back every time she heard it. She clenched her fists, counted to ten, then slowly turned.

"In case you didn't pick up on my message earlier"—Bellamy ran a finger down the bag strap hanging from Ella's shoulder—"if you say anything about that drawing being yours, I will destroy every other piece of art you have. Including the ones your precious mama drew."

Ella's lungs wouldn't fill. Couldn't. She was going to suffocate right here in the parking lot, surrounded by the oxygen she needed so desperately.

"Do we understand each other?" Bellamy lifted a brow and pursed her lips.

Ella simply nodded. What else could she do when her lungs weren't working? Bellamy sauntered off to her fancy little car and slid inside as if she hadn't just completely ruined Ella's life. Ella's legs shook, and she forced herself to turn and walk the rest of the way to Dad's old truck. The wind whipped around her as if furious on her behalf.

Swiping at the tears now running freely down her cheeks, she started the vehicle and put it into gear. But where to go? She couldn't go home right now. Couldn't risk spending more time with her evil stepsister.

Kari? No. This time of day was always extra busy for her. And besides, she ran the risk of running into Jake at the hotel. And possibly even Chaz. No way.

Fae. Fae would understand. She pointed the truck toward home with the plan of running next door instead.

As the sky opened and fat raindrops hit her windshield, she couldn't even bemoan her wipers that needed replacing. This weather fit her mood perfectly. Soggy, damp, gloomy, and gross. If Fae wasn't home, Ella would sit in the yard and let the storm wash over her.

As she drove through her neighborhood, several lights shone from Fae's windows, beckoning her inside. Ella pulled her hood up over her head, grabbed her bag, and ran through the hedge. Skipping up the two back steps, she pounded on the door. Fae whipped it open almost immediately and ushered her inside.

"What's wrong? What happened?"

"Fae—" Ella's legs finally gave out, and she sank to the floor.

"Dear girl! What do you need? A doctor? A drink?" Fae fluttered around her, touching her hands, her head, shoulders, arms.

Ella couldn't stop sobbing long enough to answer. She shook her head and braced her hands on Fae's immaculate kitchen floor.

Fae sat next to her and pulled her into her arms.

This. This was what Ella needed most right now.

After a few minutes, the words Fae whispered penetrated Ella's hazy mind. A prayer. A petition for God to cover Ella with peace and strength and comfort. Her sobs began to calm, and her tears began to dry. The fire inside her slowly burned down.

"Now, how about we move somewhere more comfortable, and I'll serve you something warm. You're chilled through. Don't you know it's raining?" Fae wiggled her body back and forth a few times before finally pushing off the floor. She held out a hand and pulled Ella up, too, steering her into the living room to a spot on her comfy sofa.

"Give me five minutes." She wrapped a blanket around Ella's shoulders and scurried back to the kitchen.

Ella blew her nose and wiped her face as best she could while she waited. Fae's cat, Rufus, meandered over and forced his head under her hand to demand some pets. She complied, his purrs extinguishing a bit more of the storm inside her chest. He curled into her lap and closed his eyes.

Oh, that comfort would come as easy as to a cat. Not to mention having fewer problems.

"One bowl of hot soup, some bread, and a cup of tea. This should help at least a little." Fae set a tray in front of her, filled with a whole dinner spread.

"This is too much."

"Nonsense. Eat up. I'll fetch mine." Lickety-split, Fae returned with her own tray and settled beside her. "Let me know when you're ready to talk. I'm here."

How did Fae always know the right thing to say?

Little by little, Ella told Fae what happened, starting with the dishes and Chaz's interest in them last week. How she'd sent them all away with him in boxes today. She swiped at another tear.

"There's more, isn't there?" Fae squeezed her arm. "I think we need chocolate too. Hang on."

Ella drew a shuddering breath. The next part hurt worse. Strange, considering how much she'd dreaded the part she'd already told.

"Okay. Now we're ready." Fae plopped down, almost overturning a large platter of brownies in the process. Rufus glared at her over his shoulder before moving to a less bumpy spot.

Ella took a brownie and placed it on her plate. "Chaz found one of my drawings."

"Ooh!" Fae sat up straight and clapped. "Which one? The pumpkin?"

"No. The train in the valley."

"Perfect. And he wants it in his gallery." Fae was practically beaming.

"Not exactly." Ella picked her brownie into a pile of crumbs. "Bellamy was there."

Air hissed through Fae's teeth.

"She told him it was hers."

"She did *not!*"

All Ella had to do was look at Fae, and her neighbor slumped. "That girl!"

"He has some sort of plan. But he needs local artwork to

convince his dad to do it, evidently. He said the piece was perfect."

"And why didn't you speak up? Claim that gorgeous drawing as your own?"

"Bellamy told me if I said anything, she'd destroy all my other artwork." Ella choked on the rest of the words. "And my mom's too."

"What are you doing sitting here?" Fae shoved her lightly. "Get home and hide those treasures. You can't let her do that!"

"Some of those pieces are still hanging in the main rooms of the house." A small miracle, Ella had thought. Now, she wasn't so sure. "Angela was too cheap to buy something else to replace them."

"Surely Bellamy won't destroy the artwork decorating her own house."

"I'm honestly not sure anymore. And I have no idea how I'm going to protect my other pieces. What if she claims them too? I could turn into her own personal slave, providing her with artwork that should have my name on it."

"No, ma'am. You will not." Fae crossed her arms and gave a sharp nod. "We will not let her win."

Ella let her head fall back against the sofa. "She already has."

"Pish posh! She has not and will not. You're still alive, aren't you? Your fingers still work?"

"What?" Ella frowned. "Of course they do."

"So you keep drawing and painting and creating. And then you show Chaz Prince your artwork and let him decide for himself. And you keep it out of the filthy hands of that conniving stepsister of yours."

"I lock my door, but I know one day she's going to pick the lock or something. I'm doing the best I can."

"I'm not sure you are."

Ella straightened, her fire roaring back to life. She'd come over here for comfort, and Fae was chastising her? Was the world completely against her today?

Fae clasped her chin in her fingers and squeezed. "You are a child of the King, and you are better than what you've let yourself become these last few years. Your daddy would cringe to see you like this."

A new tear ran down Ella's cheek.

"You are beautiful, and your artwork is too. And you need to start living up to your potential instead of using that stepmother of yours as an excuse."

Ella squeaked but wasn't allowed a full protest, because Fae rushed on.

"If you have to hide everything over here, be my guest. You know neither of them visit me." Fae motioned to her overstuffed living room. "Besides, they'd have to hunt for it amongst all my things."

A giggle escaped despite her sadness.

"Create the best painting or drawing you can. We'll fix this. Because you and I both know there's no way on God's green earth that Bellamy could ever draw something half as good as you."

Ella let a full laugh burst through.

"And the problem with lying is that you always get found out." Fae raised a brow. "So while we wait for that to happen, we prepare to take advantage of it when it does."

* * *

Chaz entered the Prince Gallery the next morning with the drawing in a portfolio under his arm. His stomach was tight, like a wound-up spring. He had to get this right. Something told him his dad wouldn't listen to any more ideas if this one wasn't up to par.

A painting to his right gave him pause. The artwork portrayed a meadow with sunlight streaming through clouds onto a shepherd and a lamb. A perfect reminder that he had a Shepherd watching over him too. One who wanted to help him as he faced his battles. Right. If he was going to make a change in his life, he needed to start now. The right way.

God, You know the desires of my heart. You know I want to live up to the good works You have planned for me. Please bless the words I use when I speak to my dad in a few minutes. Help him see what a blessing this can be. And if this is not from You, and not Your will, please ... help me be okay with that. Amen.

He nodded toward the artwork as if it somehow portrayed the One he had petitioned. Man, he was going a little crazy. This didn't bode well.

"Chaz?" Dad strode through the gallery. "What are you looking at?"

Deep breath.

Okay. Now or never.

"This picture of the meadow."

Dad nodded. "I'm sad to see that one go."

"Sold it?"

"No." Dad studied the picture another moment. "No, the artist is pulling out. Said they found a gallery closer to home that wants to showcase more pieces."

"Wow."

"Yes. It happens from time to time, but not often. Only twice before." Dad shook his head. "Too bad. Leaves me with quite a few gaps to fill."

Chaz stilled. *Okay, God. Thanks for the opening.*

"I might have an idea of how to do that."

Dad turned his full attention on him. "Let's go talk, then. I'm at a loss."

Chaz refrained from pumping his fist, but just barely. He still had to pitch the idea and get his father to agree to it. But this was the most promising chance he'd had thus far. Dad motioned to the couch then, in a rare move, settled in a chair right next to him.

"What's your idea?"

"Hear me all the way out before you make any decisions. It's not going to be an automatic fix, but I think it's going to bring excitement and stir up a lot of interest."

Dad raised a brow but stayed silent.

Chaz pulled out the drawing and held it up for his father to see.

Reaching out, his dad fingered the edges while he studied it. "This is quite good. Did you draw this?"

"No," Chaz huffed. "I only wish I had this much talent. A local artist did. I discovered her the other day at a flea market."

"You want to feature her work?"

"Yes and no." Chaz set the drawing on the table and pulled out a bullet-pointed action plan he had worked on until the small hours of the morning. "I want to feature local artists. Several of them."

His father glanced up sharply from the page he'd been skimming. "You've discovered more than one with this talent?"

"Not yet." Chaz held up a hand as a reminder to hear him out all the way. "But I want to. This drawing proves there is undiscovered talent of this caliber in our area. That it's worth pursuing the rest of my idea."

"Wouldn't that put us in direct competition with places like Tamarack? We're not that far from them. It's one of the reasons I never sought out local artists before. They'd all rather go there or to Huntington."

"Right. There are a lot there. But not everyone gets a spot at those places. This would be only for artists who haven't been discovered yet."

Dad leaned back and crossed one leg over the other. "I'm listening."

"I'd like to host a contest. Everything anonymous, so we don't know who entered the artwork. We can set it so that entries have to be here by the middle of November, then we can display all the artwork in that empty room for a couple weeks, then host a gala to announce the winners."

"And the winners would receive ..."

"A chance to display several pieces at our gallery."

Tapping his fingers together, Dad pursed his lips. "It definitely has potential. I think we can up the ante a bit, though. What if we invite a few other gallery owners to our gala too? Let them see the artwork on display? And maybe offer a chance to take some art courses for the runners-up."

He liked it! Chaz wanted to jump up and down. His dad not only approved of his idea but also offered ideas to expand it.

"Those are great ideas."

"All right. Let's get Gertie in here to start working on the marketing for this. We'll need to make sure it's in all the state papers. Maybe fliers around the universities?" Dad pulled out a pen and started scratching ideas on the edge of the page.

Chaz tamped down his elation and worked up a bit more nerve. "And Dad?"

His father paused and glanced at him over his glasses.

"If this works out well, I'd like a larger role in the management of the gallery."

"You really want to hinge your management potential on this one event?" Dad raised a brow.

Chaz swallowed down a niggle of doubt. He had to trust. Had to believe God had answered his prayer.

"I do."

Dad stuck his hand out. "All right."

Chaz clasped it firmly.

"Now, go grab Gertie, and let's get this ball rolling."

Chaz headed out the door to fetch their marketing guru. Did all dreams come true so quickly? He had no idea, but this was all rather surreal.

9

F ae was right, of course. Several days later, Ella sat cross-legged on a desk staring out the fourth-floor window of the Starbright Hotel. She couldn't let Bellamy win. Not this time.

She'd come here for more inspiration. But rain poured from the sky this morning, muddling any view she might have had even if the deer had braved the weather to show themselves. They did not.

With no sign of a break, Ella gave up. Time to get on with her real life, anyway. Or close enough to time. Maybe Kari would let her sneak a cup of coffee on her way out.

After making sure everything was straightened in the room again, she left. And bumped right into ... Chaz Prince.

"We've got to quit meeting like this." Wrinkles formed at the corners of his eyes as he smiled, his arms on her elbows steadying her.

"Agreed. I'm so sorry. Again." She tucked a strand of hair back behind her ear.

"On your way down?" Chaz motioned toward the elevator.

Ella nodded, afraid to speak.

"Have you had breakfast yet?"

"Oh, no. But I'm fine." Ella moved to the side of the elevator farthest from him as the doors slid shut.

"You should join me. I know for a fact that on Thursdays the hotel has fresh blueberry muffins from the bakery downtown."

The little lift in her tummy was from the movement of the machine—not his words. Definitely not his welcoming smile or how bright his eyes appeared this morning.

"I shouldn't. But thank you."

"Not a breakfast eater?"

She smothered a sigh. He would not let the conversation die.

Shaking her head, she watched the number above the door change. Was the elevator descending more slowly than normal today? Maybe the rain decelerated the gears or something.

"You could at least grab a coffee and sit with me a few minutes." He was several steps closer than he'd been a moment before.

"Oh, I—" The door opened before she could protest again.

"They have this really good hazelnut flavor. Have you tried it?" He cupped her elbow and steered her toward the dining area.

A glance toward the desk revealed Kari wearing a smirk on the verge of a laugh. Was she okay with this? Did Chaz make a habit of spending nights here and staying for breakfast? Was it a perk of being friends with Jake?

Kari would more than likely do the same for her if she needed it, but she'd never asked. She already pushed their friendship boundaries by requesting so much time staring out their windows. But months before, she'd been helping Kari straighten some rooms while one of their maids was out, and when she had seen the majestic creatures, she couldn't resist. Kari had agreed immediately.

Breakfast, however, was a different matter altogether. More like stealing. Kari made a shooing motion with her hands and winked.

Maybe just this once.

"You should at least try these. They're my favorite." Chaz pressed a plate into her hands and plopped a muffin onto it.

"I'm sorry. Do you live here?" The words burst from her mouth before she could stop them.

Chaz grimaced and served himself a muffin, as well as sausage and eggs. "Sometimes."

Ella frowned. What did that even mean?

"My dad and I don't always see eye to eye. On our rough nights, Jake lets me crash here. It gives Dad and me both a chance to cool off before we see each other again."

Ella would end up here every night if she left every time she and Angela didn't get along. When she accepted the cup of coffee he handed her, his fingers lingered an extra second.

"You okay?"

"Sure." She glanced back at the seating area. "I assume you also have a favorite table."

His chuckle warmed her middle. "Nah. What looks good to you? It's a nasty day. How about over there by the fireplace?"

"Sure." She followed him to a table with two chairs to the right of the blue-and-yellow flames.

A television displayed the local morning news show above them, but Ella tuned it out and carefully peeled the wrapper from her muffin. As she tore it in half, one of the berries dripped onto her fingers. Real berries. She licked the mess and realized Chaz was watching her.

"Guess I'm a bit of a klutz." She wiped the tiny bit left on a napkin. "Always making messes."

"I make quite a few of my own." Chaz focused on his own breakfast. "Remember that frame the other day?"

"Guess we're a matched set." The moment the words escaped her lips, she wished them back. But it was too late.

"Mmm." Chaz sipped his coffee. Maybe he hadn't heard her. "A matched set, huh? Now we just have to figure out what we're a set of."

So much for hoping her words were inaudible.

"Chaz Prince is here to talk with us this morning." The television drew her attention. She looked back and forth between the screen and the man across from her.

"Prerecorded." He rubbed the back of his neck. "Didn't even cross my mind that it was set to air this morning. Maybe we can get Kari to change channels."

"No." She covered his hand before he could stand but quickly jerked back. "I mean, what's it about?"

The grin filling his face was more charming than any he'd given her before. "The contest we're launching next week."

A contest. An art contest. Her gaze glued to the screen as she listened to his spiel explaining all the details. Wow. This. This was what she needed.

"Bellamy's drawing helped me talk my dad into it." The Chaz sitting across from her turned her muffin into stone with his words.

Right. He still thought Bellamy drew her train. She could tell him right now. Not prolong it. Bellamy didn't have to know how he found out.

Her mother's painting of Ella as a three-year-old popped into her head. What if Bellamy destroyed it? It could be sliced. Burned. Painted over. She blinked a few times.

"My dad would never have agreed to this scheme without proof of local talent. That drawing was like a gift from God. I'm hoping she'll enter it into the contest." Chaz continued talking while Ella warred with herself in her head.

"Right. What are the rules?"

"Do you have your phone?" Chaz held out his hand. "I can show you the website."

"Um, I do, but it doesn't have internet." She ducked her head, wishing she hadn't bumped into him again. Why did he always catch her in humiliating positions? Why couldn't he have found that drawing when Bellamy wasn't around to ruin everything?

"Hey guys. What's up?" Kari pulled another chair over.

"I was just telling Ella about the contest." Chaz pointed over his head, but the segment was over, and all that showed on the screen was a weather radar predicting more rain.

"Ooh. What kind of contest?" Kari leaned forward and snitched a bite of Ella's practically untouched muffin.

"The Prince Gallery is hosting a contest for local artists. All artwork is due by mid-November. We'll display it all for a couple of weeks and then have a gala in early December to announce the winners."

"Will they win a spot in your gallery?" Kari's eyes widened, and she nudged Ella. Ella hadn't told her about Bellamy's conniving from the week before.

"They will. And the runners-up will receive a certificate for some additional art courses from the local university."

Ella's breath caught. A dream come true. More courses would help her get past this lull in her drawing. Would maybe even help her reach her mom's level. Help her with movement and faces and other little details that she grappled to master. All she had to do was place as a runner-up.

* * *

Something passed across Ella's pretty face, wrinkling her fair skin before it smoothed out again. Struggle? Encouragement? Excitement?

"Do you draw, Ella?"

Her blue eyes widened. "Oh, um—"

"Does she?" Kari exclaimed before Ella elbowed her in the ribs. Kari frowned at her friend. Looked like Kari understood Ella's actions as well as he did—which was to say, not at all.

"I ... dabble a bit. Sometimes." Ella ducked her head, her blonde hair falling around her face like a curtain, hiding her. What was she hiding from? Him? Or was she hiding something *from* him?

"Well, your contest sounds amazing, Chaz." Kari stood, rubbing her side. "I'll be sure to let my artist friends know about it. The ones who admit to being artists, at least."

Kari sent one more look Ella's way before marching back to her counter. Ella picked at her muffin, setting all the blueberries to one side and the crumbs to the other. Her fingertips held a blue tint once more, but this time he understood why. Maybe she'd simply been working with blueberries last week.

Chaz took a deep breath. "Listen. I've been wanting to talk to you ever since I walked out of your booth last Thursday."

Ella lifted her eyes slightly.

"I tried to catch you Sunday, but you snuck out somehow."

The corner of her pink lips twitched. Interesting. Had she left like she did because she'd been avoiding him? All the more reason to finish his apology.

"I wanted to apologize." She brought her head back up again.

"Why?"

"Those dishes—"

She held up a hand. "Not another word. It's done. Over. They're yours now. I hope your family enjoys them for many years to come."

"But I swooped in and bought all of them, acted like it

didn't mean anything to you for me to walk away with a piece of your family heritage."

"You're not very good at the 'not another word' thing, you know." Ella leaned back and crossed her arms.

"I've been told." He rested his elbows on the table. "But it's been bugging me ever since that day. I wanted to make sure you were okay. That's why I was so glad to see you this morning. Why I insisted on breakfast."

She tucked a piece of hair behind her ear, and his fingers twitched, wishing he'd been the one doing it. Where did that thought come from? With so many girls seeking him out in the last year—ever since that stupid article about him being one of the most eligible bachelors in West Virginia—he'd developed an aversion to the female population in general.

Interesting that he wanted to get closer to Ella.

"It's fine. Seriously. I knew they'd be sold eventually." She set her plate aside. "At least because you took them all, I didn't have to see the set broken up. I know it will be cherished and enjoyed. That helps."

"Is all the stuff in that booth from your family?" His hands reached out to cover hers of their own volition.

She didn't pull away. "Most of it. A few things I think belonged to Angela's first husband."

"Why do you have to sell all your stuff?" He shook his head. "That's such an uncouth way for me to put it. *Stuff.* As if it's not important."

"No. It is just stuff. Worldly possessions. I do still have a few pictures and pieces of them tucked away. And I have the memories. Those are more important."

"Still … it can't be easy." He squeezed her fingers.

She gave a tiny shake of her head, as if emerging from a trance. "I've got to go."

"But the market isn't open today."

"I have to be somewhere else." She pulled away, leaving his hand feeling emptier than it ever had before. "Thanks for the muffin."

As she rushed out into the rain, he sighed. "Yeah. Real big spender, Prince. You could have at least taken her somewhere that meant something."

"Talking to yourself?" Jake flopped onto the chair Ella had vacated.

"I have to find intelligent conversation somewhere." Chaz lifted a brow.

"Hmm." Jake leaned his chair back on two legs. "Looked like Ella was offering up at least a semi-intelligent conversation."

"How long were you watching me?"

"Long enough."

Chaz stacked their trash to prepare to take it to the bin. "Every time I talk to that girl, I get more confused."

"I find that happens with women in general. It's like they speak a totally different language." Jake chuckled.

"This is different, though. Like a mystery to solve."

"It's just Ella. Ask Kari. They've been friends forever."

Except evidently, Kari didn't know everything there was to know about the elusive Ella, either. And as the thought crossed his mind, he realized he didn't even know her last name. He needed to find more ways to bump into her.

10

"Psst." Ella hid behind a column in the Starbright Hotel lobby a few days later. "Is it safe?"

Kari lifted a brow. "You tell me. You're the one keeping secrets."

Ella flinched and jogged over to the counter before ducking down behind it. "Look, I didn't get a chance to fill you in. I'm sorry, okay? I promise I'll tell you everything now."

"Tell *me* everything, or tell the other person you're misleading?" Kari propped her chin on her fist. "Because it seems like you don't want him to know you're an artist. And I can't figure out why."

Ella scrubbed her hands over her face. "It's not that I don't want him to know. It's that I *can't* let him know."

"Explain."

"Bellamy."

Kari groaned.

"No, I need to start before that." Ella let her head fall back against the wall with a thump. "Chaz came in last week and bought my mother's china." She blinked against the rebellious moisture trying to return to her eyes. No time for that.

Kari lowered herself to the floor and squeezed Ella's hand. "I'm so sorry."

"It went to a good home. I'll be okay." Ella glanced in the direction of the dining room. "It's why he insisted on having breakfast with me the other day when we bumped into each other. ... And how did that happen? Didn't you promise we wouldn't accidentally end up on the same floor again?"

Waving her hand in the air, Kari huffed. "We'll deal with that later. I don't see what buying your dishes has to do with him not knowing you're an artist."

"While I was grabbing the other box of dishes, he discovered my drawing."

"Your drawing?"

Ella nodded. "The train."

"I love that one. Did he hate it?"

"No. He loved it too."

"I don't understand." Kari rubbed a spot on her forehead.

The bell rang above their heads, and Kari jerked, wrinkling her nose. She crouched to all fours and then straightened. Why? Kari lifted a pen as if it had been on the floor and tucked it behind her ear. Ah. To make it look like she'd been looking for something under the counter. She helped the customer who needed to check out. After answering what seemed like twenty-five questions, Kari ducked back down beside Ella and finally returned to their conversation.

"So, tell me how Chaz loving your drawing is a bad thing."

"He thinks it's Bellamy's." Ella buried her head in her bent knees.

"I still don't understand."

Ella explained what had happened, shushing Kari when she started throwing a fit. "I agree. It's not fair, but it's the way it is, and now I have to deal with it."

"So what are we going to do?"

Ella's heart lifted a bit at her friend's question. *We.* A reminder that Ella wasn't doing life alone, no matter how much it felt like she was at times.

"I am going to make the best art I can and submit it to the contest. I want to win that runner-up prize. Then, if they host another contest down the road, I'll have a better chance at the grand prize."

Kari blinked. "Did you or did you not just say he loved your drawing?"

"I did."

"Then why are you only aiming for runner-up? Submit something as good as the train, and you'll prove that the other one is yours too. If he liked that, you're a shoo-in."

"Just because he liked something doesn't mean it's the best. He's inviting artists from all over the state. And I really want those art courses. So I'm fine with being a runner-up."

"Ella." Kari squeezed both her arms. "I wish you could see how amazing you are like the rest of us do. Your artwork is already wonderful. Better than runner-up."

Ella shook her head, but Kari wouldn't let her say anything more.

"When you get more than you're expecting, maybe you'll see."

Blinking away more moisture, Ella hugged her friend. "Well, you better start praying those deer show up soon, then. I need models."

Kari laughed, stood, and handed her a room key. "And Chaz isn't even here, to my knowledge. Sometimes Jake lets him in instead of me, which is how he ended up on the same floor as you the other day."

Ella nodded, gave her friend another hug, then headed up to the third floor. *Okay, God. You know the desires of my heart. Please, bless my hands and my abilities. Let me use my drawing to showcase what You've already created. And please let there be a few deer out this morning.*

There were. She took it as a good sign and got right to work. Sketching quickly, she contemplated the best way to showcase the deer. In a fall meadow with colors all around? Near one of the local waterfalls? What would make the best background to catch the judges' eyes?

She stilled as an idea popped into her head. There was a place about an hour away that her mom used to love to draw and paint more than any other. That's where she'd go for her background. A hint of a waterfall trickled down a cliff, a stream danced across rocks and roots, and a bit of meadow grew wildflowers surrounded by trees. The spot was close to where her grandparents had lived when her mom was young. The Gauley River National Recreational Area, if her memory served her. Perfect.

Now she just needed to find time to get over there.

Chaz hadn't seen Ella in several days. It shouldn't bug him, considering he hadn't even known she existed until a few weeks ago. But now that he was aware of her, he wanted to spend as much time with her as possible. To learn more of her secrets and history. To find out why her fingers were always stained different colors.

The timing was off, though. When his dad agreed to Chaz's plan, he also gave most of the responsibility of running it to him. Which meant more hours working at the gallery. It was exactly what he had wanted, but he wanted to spend time with Ella almost as much.

"How's it looking?" Dad strode into Chaz's office Friday morning. "Got many entries?"

"More than I expected in under a week since we announced the contest." Chaz motioned to several pieces on his desk. "We may have to find a way to hang more paintings than normal in that room. If the entries continue to come in at this rate, we're going to fill the whole space."

Dad stroked his beard. "I had no idea there were so many undiscovered artists in this area. We've been confirming they're West Virginia residents? And they don't have anything hanging in other galleries?"

"They're required to show an ID when they drop off their entry and fill out the forms. Including a waiver that swears their art isn't displayed in any other galleries." Chaz pulled another painting from behind his chair. "Look at this one."

A long whistle escaped his father's lips, and Chaz's lifted into a smile. The piece wasn't necessarily one he'd buy for himself, but it was stunning. More modern, with sharp angles and colors slightly off from what could be found in nature. But the beauty of the model still came through in the portrait.

"How many are we up to?"

"Fifteen already." Chaz motioned out the door. "Here's what I'm thinking."

They walked to the center of the room now emptied of the previous artist's work. The blank walls called to him.

"We can sort by style, if you think that's a good idea. Modern over to one side. Landscapes here. Portraits. Still lifes. I'm thinking I'll sort of lean them against the walls until we get a better idea of how many to expect total. Once we have an estimate, we can start hanging them."

Dad nodded as he studied the space. "Okay. But we have to make sure they're not damaged before they're hung. You're ensuring they're framed properly, right?"

"Yes. It's in the rules, and we make sure everything is in order when the pieces are dropped off. I guess I need to get ahold of the first artist and make sure she brings a frame if she wants to enter the contest. I snagged hers before it was behind glass."

"Good idea."

It was a good idea ... except it meant talking to Bellamy on purpose. No telling what she'd make of that—probably would encourage her to continue pursuing him.

Dad rubbed a finger under his chin. "We can set up some easels, too, if we need to. Or even bring in a couple of those temporary walls to put in the middle and hang more."

"You think we'll get that many?" Chaz ran a hand through his hair.

"You said we're up to fifteen, right? It's only been three full days. Next week is the end of October, so they have almost three more weeks. Better to be ready for more than not."

Chaz nodded. "True."

"Need some help moving those entries in here?"

"Sure." Chaz followed his dad back into his office, and they each grabbed a piece.

After several more trips, all the entries were scattered around the space, a few already hanging on the remaining nails. This was really happening. And his father seemed almost as excited as he was.

"This was a great idea." Dad clapped him on the shoulder. "I'm proud of you."

Chaz's chest expanded. "Yeah?"

"You saw something I didn't. Saw a need, an opportunity." Dad nodded while looking around at the artwork again. "Even if we only have these fifteen pieces, this is already a success."

A lump lodged in Chaz's throat. Words he'd never expected to hear, especially not this early in the process. Exactly what he needed. Hopefully it would continue to give him the boost necessary to be able to endure another conversation with Bellamy.

Maybe if he promised himself a reward ...

Bellamy and Ella both attended church services with Jake. He could catch Bellamy there, where it should be easy to get away quickly if needed. And maybe have a chance to catch Ella. Should he ask her to lunch? Would she agree?

He lifted his lips into an uncontainable grin.

Worth a chance.

11

S ettled into their normal pew the next Sunday, Ella was telling Fae about wanting to go to her mom's favorite spot for her background when she felt someone sit down beside her. She froze before slowly looking over her shoulder. Chaz.

"This spot wasn't saved for someone, was it? Jake's not here this morning." His black peacoat looked dashing against the green sweater underneath.

"Of course not, young man. You're very welcome to join us." Fae stretched out a beringed hand. "I'm Fae."

"Chaz." He pressed a kiss to her fingers like a proper gentleman. "Pleasure to meet you."

Ella pushed her hands under her skirt so she wouldn't be tempted to see if he'd kiss her fingers too. What had gotten into her lately? She was supposed to be avoiding Chaz Prince, not looking for more opportunities to spend time with him.

Angela and Bellamy sauntered down the aisle. Bellamy glared over her shoulder at Ella, one brow raised. She held two fingers to her eyes, then pointed them at her to indicate she was watching Ella. Right. As if she needed the reminder.

"Is it okay with you too?" Chaz's voice was low and right next to her ear.

She jerked around, almost bumping noses with him. "What? Oh, of course. No need for you to sit by yourself. I wonder where Jake and Kari are today."

"No telling. Maybe something came up at the hotel."

She nodded.

"Good morning."

Saved by the announcements. No need for more conversation now. And hopefully he wouldn't expect any after the services, either.

Chaz turned out to have a rich tenor, and his voice blended well with Fae's alto on Ella's other side. She had to remind herself several times to join in the singing and not just listen. Her daddy had sung tenor, and Chaz's was close to the same tone. She swallowed against a lump in her throat. Nice as it was to hear those notes again, it also reminded her of what she no longer had.

Fae reached over and squeezed Ella's hand during the prayer. On the other side, Chaz's fingers twitched her way before he jerked them back. Once more, Ella hid her free hand beneath her skirt. Did he want to hold her hand? Or was something else going on? They barely knew each other.

The sermon was about telling the truth. Ella squirmed. She hadn't actually told an outright lie in regard to her artwork. But wasn't hiding the truth just as bad? It was, according to Brother Butterfield.

She sighed, and Fae squeezed her fingers once more. Sometimes it was scary how well Fae could read her mind.

She knew Fae was right when she said Bellamy would be discovered. Ella's plan was to make sure the truth came out as soon as possible without losing anything dear to her.

"Let's stand and sing." Brother Butterfield finally finished, and Ella gratefully pushed the truths of his lesson to the back of her conscience.

"You okay?" Chaz asked quietly after the closing prayer.

"Fine." She offered a tight smile.

"Ella, I need you this afternoon." Angela stopped at the end of the aisle, tugging at the cuffs of sleeves that couldn't possibly keep her warm during this cold snap. "We need to box up a few more items for the market."

"Hi." Chaz thrust out his hand. "I'm Chaz Prince. I don't think we've met."

"Mr. Prince," Angela practically purred. "Bellamy has told me so much about you."

Ella barely kept from rolling her eyes.

"Hi, Chaz." Bellamy fluttered her fingers at him. Her dress didn't appear any warmer than her mother's.

"Bellamy." Chaz nodded. "I'm glad you're here. I actually needed to talk to you about that piece you let me borrow. If you want to enter it in the contest, we'll need a frame, and I'll need you to come sign the entry forms."

"Oh." Bellamy shot a glance at her mother before turning back to him with a huge smile. "Of course. Is there a particular day this week that works? I'm completely at your disposal."

"Contest?" Angela raised her brows. "What contest?"

"The Prince Gallery is hosting an art contest," Chaz said. "Bellamy was kind enough to allow me to borrow one of her drawings so I could show my dad the talent we have in this part of West Virginia. Your daughter is very talented."

"Of course she is." Angela glanced back and forth between Ella and Bellamy, as if putting together all the pieces. Would she out her own child? "I'll make sure she stops by with a frame. Do you remember the size of the piece?"

Chaz blinked. "I'm sorry. I didn't think to measure it."

"No problem. We'll take care of it." Angela turned back to

Ella. "Ella? I expect to see you home this afternoon. You have a bad habit of disappearing on Sundays."

"I'll—"

Chaz touched her arm. "Actually, I asked Ella to have lunch with me. I hope you won't mind. She did me a favor last week, and I wanted to thank her."

Ella closed her mouth. What was he up to? Not only had he not asked her to lunch, he obviously hadn't listened to the sermon, either, because he was lying.

"Oh." Angela pursed her lips.

"Maybe we could join them." Bellamy pouted and batted her eyes. "We were planning to eat out too. It only makes sense. We could talk more about the contest."

Angela narrowed her eyes. "Perhaps another time."

Bellamy squeaked. She was rarely told no. Especially in situations like this.

Angela lifted a brow as she stared at Ella another moment. "I'm sure Ella will tell us all about it when she comes home in a little while."

A knife twisted in Ella's gut. Chaz might have postponed the inevitable, but he hadn't eliminated it completely. She would have to face her stepmother. And there was no telling how that would go down. What was Angela up to now?

"I'll try not to keep her out too long." Chaz squeezed her bicep, sending a shot of warmth through her torso.

"We'll hold you to that, young man. It was a pleasure to meet you." Angela smiled.

"Bye, Chaz." Bellamy tromped after her mom.

"Ready?" Chaz motioned for Ella to follow.

She turned to hug Fae one more time. "Enjoy your lunch, dearie. I like him," the older woman whispered in her ear.

Ella playfully swatted her neighbor. The woman was trouble. But also a blessing.

She turned and joined Chaz in the aisle. What was going through Chaz's mind? Breakfast last week. Lunch today. What was his endgame?

* * *

Chaz's Jeep warmed up quickly. He'd talked Ella into riding with him, promising to bring her back to her truck after lunch. She'd wavered a few seconds, but then agreed, lifting her booted feet up into his car. He'd poked the edge of her flowery skirt in after her so it wouldn't get caught in the door.

"What are you in the mood for?" Chaz steered them toward downtown. "Italian? Steak? American?"

"This was all your idea." Ella clasped her hands in her lap. "I assumed you had a plan."

"The plan was simply to spend more time with you." He tilted his head as he thought through possibilities. "Chinese?"

Her cute little nose wrinkled. "No, thank you."

"Anything else sound good?"

"Italian is always yummy."

He nodded and drove to Pasta La Vista. The name was a little strange, but the food was always satisfying. It wasn't everywhere you could find an Italian restaurant run by a Latino family.

Ella was already climbing down from her seat when he came around to her side. He swallowed his pride and simply offered his arm. Maybe she wasn't used to having someone open her door.

Seated in a booth with water glasses on the table, Ella set down her menu. "So, want to tell me what this is all about?"

"This?" He looked up from where he'd been deciding between the ravioli and the Alfredo.

"This lunch. Seemed rather spur of the moment to me. I

didn't even get a chance to turn you down." She crossed her arms.

"Did you want to turn me down?" He lifted a brow.

"I don't know." She tilted her head, her blonde waves cascading over one shoulder. "We barely even know each other."

"What better way to fix that than to eat together?"

The waitress came by to take their orders and left them with a basket of breadsticks. Ella snatched one and took a bite.

"What exactly were you wanting to know?" Ella wiped her fingers on her napkin. "More about Bellamy?"

Chaz choked on his sip of water. "No. I'd never invite a woman to a meal and then ask her to talk about someone else. That's just ... wrong."

She blinked then studied her bread.

"I wanted to get to know *you*."

"I'm not that interesting. Just a girl. I work at the flea market and ..." Her voice trailed off, and she looked out the window.

"And?"

She shrugged. "Friends with Kari."

It wasn't what she'd started to say originally. He'd bet his dream on it. But what wasn't she saying?

He'd let it go for now. "How long have you known Kari?"

"Since shortly after she and her brother moved here. When their aunt needed them to take over the hotel, they started worshipping with us. We were in the same Sunday school class."

"Jake and I met at college. We were in the same fraternity." Chaz leaned back as the server brought their food. "When he settled here, he remembered I lived here too and sought me out. He spoke way too loud in the gallery the day he came to find me. Demanded I show him all the great hunting spots."

Ella giggled. "Sounds like Jake."

He held his hand toward her, palm up. "Shall we pray?"

She bowed her head, but her hands were safely tucked out of reach. So much for finding a way to hold them. He focused and said a quick blessing for their food.

When he finished, he picked the conversation back up. "Kari and Jake are great friends to have."

"The best."

When she offered nothing else, he chose a different topic. "You've lived here your whole life?"

"Yes."

"Funny we never ran into each other before now." He twirled fettuccini around his fork.

"You were a few years ahead of me in school. And we moved in different circles." She stared at her pasta, not meeting his eyes.

"So, you did know who I was."

"I didn't recognize you at first. But Kari reminded me. Then, yes. I knew you."

"Seems like you're one up on me, then. You know all about me, but I know very little about you. Only that you work in the flea market, you lost your parents, and you're a Christian."

She finally lifted her gaze. "That's mostly all there is. Seriously."

He didn't believe her. She was like a coal mine, full of hidden depths and riches waiting to be discovered. But would she let him in? Not today, evidently.

"Will your stepmother be terribly mad when you get home?"

She grimaced. "Hopefully not. She doesn't usually care where I spend my Sunday afternoons. Not sure what the urgency is today. The flea market isn't open again until Thursday."

"Hmm." He finished off his last bite of chicken. "Need me to come with you? In case there's something heavy to move?"

"No!"

He blinked.

"Sorry. Just thinking what a mess the house is right now. Angela is constantly redecorating and rearranging things. I never know where the sofa will be from one day to the next. Not something I want anyone to see who isn't already family."

Her excuse sounded only somewhat legitimate. Was she afraid he'd get to know her better if he saw where she lived? Or were things worse than they seemed?

He was reading too much into this. Just because Angela was her stepmother didn't make her evil. This wasn't a fairy tale, after all.

"All right. Well, can I at least treat you to some tiramisu before I take you back to your truck?"

The corner of her mouth turned up. "Twist my arm, why don't you?"

Aha! She had a sweet tooth. He'd learned at least one thing today. If he found a few more opportunities to be around her, maybe he'd learn other things, like her favorite color and her birthday. It was worth trying, at any rate.

He waved the server down and ordered their dessert and two cups of coffee. Judging by the expression on her face, he'd done that right too. Progress.

But the meal was going far too quickly for his taste. When his coffee arrived, he sipped as slowly as possible. He hated to take her back to her world. Even taking small bites didn't make the tiramisu last long enough. He stood and helped her shrug into her coat. When would he be able to get away to see her again?

12

"What did you say to him?" Bellamy barely let Ella in the door before getting in her face.

"What?" Ella stepped back as far as the doorway would allow.

"You had to have told him something." Bellamy punched her arm. "What did you say to Chaz?"

"I told him thank you for the lunch." Ella rubbed her bicep. "That hurt."

"Good. Maybe it will help you remember that you're not supposed to be talking to him."

"Believe it or not, I've been trying to avoid him. He's the one who sat next to me this morning. I wasn't expecting it."

"A likely story." Bellamy crossed her arms. "Why would he sit next to you for no reason?"

"He said he needed someone to sit with since Jake wasn't there. He recognized me from when he bought the dishes." No way was Ella going to admit she'd seen him since then. If Bellamy found out about their little breakfast tête-à-tête, nothing good would follow.

"He could've sat with me." Bellamy's pouty face wasn't becoming at all.

"You arrived after he'd already found a seat." Ella inched to the side, hoping to make a break for it and escape this conversation.

"So?"

"So, he's the kind of guy who doesn't want to be rude." Ella shrugged.

"And you're sure you didn't say anything about my drawing?"

Ella froze. "*Your* drawing? You mean *my* drawing that you claimed?"

The slap hit before Ella even knew it was coming. "My drawing."

"Girls, girls." Angela sauntered into the foyer. "What's going on here?"

Bellamy should've tried out for the school play, considering the way she could turn from vicious to sweet in the snap of a finger when her mom came around. Too bad it was all an act.

"I was just reminding Ella of a promise she made to me. Sometimes she forgets things."

Ella rubbed her cheek but didn't say anything. Angela always took Bellamy's side, no matter what. It didn't signify that Ella was right in this case. She wasn't related to Angela by blood.

"I'm sure Ella will keep whatever promise she made to you, Bellamy. No need to make her stay here in the cold entryway." Angela rubbed her hands together. "Besides, we've got work to do this afternoon. Ella, why don't you go change? Then we can get started."

Ella brushed past Bellamy, wishing she could retaliate. If she thought she could get away with it, she'd engage in a real fight, one in which she didn't have to stand there and take everything Bellamy dished out. But until she could save up enough to move out on her own, she was stuck. Especially with Bellamy's threats hanging over her.

It's why she had started storing more of her artwork and supplies in her truck instead of her room. No need to tempt fate—or her stepsister, as the case may be. She moved past the dining room, then stopped and backed up.

"Where is it?"

"What?" Bellamy was right behind her, obviously waiting for this reaction.

"Where is my mother's painting?" Ella raised a shaky finger and pointed to the blank spot on the wall. "What did you do?"

"We needed the frame." Bellamy shrugged.

Ella's heart pounded against her chest. "And the painting that was in it?"

"I threw it away. We didn't need it anymore."

How Ella kept from screaming, she had no idea. "Where? Which trash can?"

"It doesn't matter, Ella. It was a dumb picture of a bird."

"My mother painted that bird." Ella clenched her fists. "Where did you throw it away?"

"In the kitchen." Bellamy's voice dripped with false innocence.

Ella rushed past her, not caring that she knocked into her arm on the way. She was beyond the point of caring if she hurt Bellamy or not, because in no way could it hurt as much as Bellamy hurt her. The kitchen trash overflowed, as usual. The painting had been shoved in, the top bent over and crushed into what looked like leftover spaghetti.

A sob broke free as Ella pulled the artwork from the mess. Pieces of noodles clung to the bird's beak, making it looking like he was feasting on worms. Sauce marred his wing feathers.

Where the top had been bent, some of the paint had broken, and now tiny white lines ran through the once-rich leaves of the tree.

Tears poured down Ella's cheeks. In all the ways Bellamy had abused her through the years, this topped the list. Ella picked the noodles off, patted the canvas with a paper towel to remove most of the marinara, and carried it up to her room. She needed a better plan. Her mother's artwork wasn't safe here any longer.

"Aren't you changed yet?" Angela passed her in the hallway.

"I had to rescue my mother's painting first. I'll be down in a couple minutes."

"You dug something out of the trash instead of doing what I told you?" Angela straightened.

Ella matched her pose, inch for inch. She lifted her chin and stared at her stepmother, daring her to say one more thing. If all else failed, Ella could live in her truck. Fae would feed her until she could figure out something else.

Angela lifted a brow but didn't speak another word. Ella stepped into her room and shut the door. She laid the painting on her desk and wiped away her remaining tears. She would mourn more later.

And while she did whatever it was that Angela wanted her to do, she would plan. Bellamy could call that drawing hers as long as she wanted to, but it would never be truly hers. The piece held too many parts of Ella—the waterfall and trees for Mama, the coal train for Dad, the pencils and charcoal to combine everything in her world into one landscape. And the more Ella thought of her original plan for her new art piece, the more she realized it was missing some of those elements. She reworked the ideas in her head. It would be different than the one Bellamy stole, obviously, but maybe she should include some similarities.

Ella pulled on a hoodie and a pair of jeans. Good thing holes in the knees were in style. Otherwise, she'd look a lot poorer than she already did. She stepped lightly down the stairs and through the hallway until she found her stepmother.

"There you are." Angela straightened from where she'd been searching through the bottom shelves in the living room.

"Dad's records?" Ella had been wondering how much longer those would remain in the house.

"Now that we have space in the booth where those dishes used to be, we can start setting these out. There's good money to be had in records. They're coming back into style in some circles, you know." Angela waved a hand. "Go find some boxes, and we'll decide which ones to move first."

Right. Ella spun on her toes and headed to the garage. What Angela didn't know was that everything Ella took to the market she also went through herself, saving out a few special pieces. Angela would never know they'd not been sold, because she never followed up with what was put on the shelves.

Ella's stash sat near the front of the garage, the area hardest to get to due to all the junk stacked between it and the kitchen door. Her old chest was full of ornaments, books, a few clothing items, and some family pictures. Now, she'd sneak in a few records too. The ones Daddy played over and over again, dancing with Mom in the lamplight during the evenings. Maybe someday Ella would find someone to dance with in her own living room. Someday.

An image of Chaz tugging her hands and then spinning her around flitted through her mind, accompanied by one of the old melodies. Ella chased the thought away. Chaz Prince was out of her league. She'd be happy to simply work for him someday.

At least, that's what she told her heart.

* * *

Chaz stared at the three new entries on his desk. Amazing. He knew art filled these mountains, but he never ceased to be awestruck by the caliber. Each piece made him wonder how they would ever decide on the winners.

His favorite, though, was still the train in the valley. But Bellamy ... Much as he hated the idea of not having that piece in the gallery, he hoped she'd forget to bring a frame and fill out a form.

"Chaz!"

No such luck. Bellamy waved at him from outside his door, a large frame in her arms.

"Just like you asked." She held the gilt frame as if it were a dress to be modeled.

"Great. Is it the right size?"

"It should be." She stepped into his office as if invited.

No getting out of it now.

He motioned to a table against the wall. "Let's put it here and see if we can get it situated. I'll have Gertie bring in the entry form for you to sign."

"Perfect." Bellamy tittered. He had no idea girls actually did that in real life. Huh. He learned something new every day.

He stepped to the door and waved Gertie over. "Can you bring an entry form in?" He lowered his voice. "And then maybe stick around until this guest leaves?"

Gertie studied Bellamy for a second before giving a brisk nod. "Be back as quick as I can."

Thank you, God, for Gertie!

"Where's my drawing?" Bellamy looked around as if expecting it to be on the wall already.

"Here. I put it away so it wouldn't get damaged." He pulled out a bottom desk drawer and lifted the piece.

"Yay. I can't wait to see how it looks in the frame."

Chaz frowned as he studied the structure. The back piece had obviously been pried off. Staples and tiny nails remained around the edges, bent at odd angles. He carefully lifted the wood and set it aside before positioning the drawing in the center of the glass.

"There's going to be a gap. Did you bring a mat?"

"A mat?" Bellamy frowned. "I didn't know I needed one. You said I needed a frame."

"Right. A mat is a piece of ... well, mat board, that goes around the picture to cover the gap between the picture and the frame. See here?" He pointed to the glass still visible around the picture. "Your picture doesn't go all the way to the edges of this frame, so you'll have this random space where you can see the wood backing it. Not the best way to display something. We need a mat about three inches wide to cover that up so the focus is on the drawing and not the framing."

"Oh." Bellamy slumped.

"Here we are." Gertie waved the papers in her hand. "If you'll sit over here, we can get this all filled out."

"Sure." Bellamy pulled a purple pen from her tiny purse. "I came prepared."

"Great." Gertie smiled and patted a chair.

"I'll see if I can find a mat while you do that. We might have some extras around here somewhere."

"Perfect, Chaz. Thank you so much! I don't know what I'd do without your expertise and experience." Bellamy batted her eyelashes at him.

"Right." He quickly stepped out of his office. Whew. That girl was something else.

"Something wrong?" Dad stepped out of his office as Chaz marched past.

"The artist of that first drawing is here. She brought a frame, but it's too large. I'm checking to see if we have an extra mat board lying around that would work."

Dad frowned. "That's a pretty amateur mistake."

"She seems like an amateur. Like she's never framed one of her pictures before." Chaz tugged at the front of his hair. "I don't know. Something feels off about this whole thing."

"Here." Dad pointed toward a closet. "I think there's some in here."

Sure enough, he pulled out several that appeared the right size. Chaz gratefully accepted them. Anything to keep Bellamy from having to come back again.

Dad followed him back to his office. "I want to meet her."

Chaz nodded. This might not be the best idea. But too late now.

"Hello." Dad strode in, one hand extended to shake Bellamy's. "I'm Kingston Prince."

"Oh!" Bellamy popped up and offered a sort of curtsy. "So good to meet you."

"I hear you're the artist who created the beautiful piece that started this whole shindig."

Bellamy tittered again. "You flatter me, sir. I just like to draw a bit."

"Hm." Dad rocked back on his heels. "Well, we're honored to have your piece in this contest, young lady. Best of luck."

Bellamy smiled. "Thank you so much. You have no idea how much this all means to me."

Chaz had worked one of the mats into place and situated

the back onto the frame once more. He carefully held it up so they could see if it looked okay. "What do you think?"

"Perfect!" Bellamy clapped. "Wow. I never imagined how great it would look in a frame. Thank you so much for your help, Chaz."

He'd picked a maroon-colored mat. It was completely wrong for the piece, clashing with the oranges and greens of the trees. Wouldn't a true artist be able to see the contrast and how the mat distracted from the drawing?

"You're happy with it this way, then?" Chaz met his dad's eyes and saw the same caution.

"I love it. Thank you so much."

"Ms. Bellamy, we need you to finish filling out the form too." Gertie tugged at Bellamy's sleeve.

"Right. Of course. Let's see. Where was I? Oh, yes. 'Medium used.'" Bellamy tapped her pen to her lips. "That's the size?"

"No, honey." Gertie narrowed her eyes. "That's what you used to make the piece. Was it acrylics? Watercolors? Oils? Charcoal? Pastels? Pencil? Mixed?"

Bellamy's eyes grew larger with each option. She blinked a few times before she scrawled "oils" across the page. There was no way this was done in oils. It was obviously pencil with possibly charcoal for the train. What was going on? If this wasn't her drawing, whose was it? And how had she obtained it?

Chaz and his dad exchanged another glance. Neither one of them were impressed with this show. Chaz secured the back and propped the artwork against the wall. Dad meandered closer and studied it, then tapped his hand in the lower corner.

Leaning closer, Chaz looked to see what his dad had noticed. Nothing looked off to him. Train tracks and a small stream rode off the page. No smears or tears or anything to mar the picture.

"No signature," Dad whispered.

Chaz wasn't about to bring that up to Bellamy. Whoever she'd stolen this from needed the opportunity to reclaim it—which was harder to do when it was signed. But would the real artist show up to claim his—or her—piece?

Chaz thought back to where he'd originally found it and started connecting some dots he should've seen before. The paper Ella had been focused on. Smudges on her fingers. Her elbowing Kari. But if all that meant what he thought it did, why was Ella allowing Bellamy to claim her drawing?

13

This vista never grew old. Ella sat on a blanket on the hood of Dad's old truck, parked at the Gauley River National Recreation Area overlook. It took her about an hour to get there, but it was worth it. Overlooks were a dime a dozen in this state, with all the mountains and hills, but Ella always wanted to stop anyway.

This particular space, however, was extra special. Her mom had always loved it, even more after Dad proposed here. Ella hugged her knees to her chest and breathed in the crisp autumn air. Just what she needed after the last few days of sorting through Dad's records, looking up how much they cost online, and labeling them at the highest prices possible, per Angela's orders.

Well, all except the few she'd snuck into her hidden stash in the garage. Some things were worth going against her stepmother's orders for. Dad's books and records fell into that category.

Beside her, a canvas dried in the breeze, the first two layers of paint already finished. On her other side, a sketch pad fluttered, more pages of the same view flickering back and forth like a flip-book. She couldn't decide which medium was her favorite, so she was testing them both.

Thank you, God, for this beautiful view. For these few moments of peace.

A chirp from her phone reminded her time was up. If she were to make it back to the house before dark, she needed to leave now. And considering how the lights on her truck didn't shine as brightly as she wished, she'd better get on the road.

She quickly gathered her things and stashed them safely in the old toolbox behind the cab. It had taken a while to get all the coal dust out of the toolbox after Dad's death, but now it was clean enough that she didn't worry as much about her artwork getting smudged. She climbed in and turned the key.

Nothing.

Not even a click or a chug or a cough.

Ella's heart beat faster. Maybe she hadn't turned it far enough. She pulled the key out, inserted it, and tried again.

Silence.

"Not funny, God." She leaned her forehead against the steering wheel. Now what?

She could handle this. She was a grown-up. The truck had gasoline. She hadn't left anything on, so it couldn't be the battery. Right? She could pop the hood and look inside, but it wouldn't do her any good. While she knew how to check the oil and change a tire, this was beyond her ken.

Pulling her phone out, she sent up a prayer of thanksgiving when she saw 50 percent battery and four bars of service. Okay. Who to call?

No way was she dragging Fae down here this late in the day. Fae wouldn't be any more help, anyway. Ella scrolled further through her contacts—not that there were many. Kari. She probably didn't know anything about trucks, either. But Jake might. And Kari could ask Jake.

She pushed the call button and waited.

"Hey, girl. What's up? Haven't seen you in a few days."

"Yeah." No way was Ella about to tell Kari she'd been avoiding the place in case Chaz was around. "I've been busy. Listen. I've got a situation."

"What's wrong?"

"Humphrey died."

"I'll come jump you. Where are you?"

"That's the other part of the situation." Ella stared out the windshield at the view she loved most. "I'm about an hour away from you."

"Oh man. Hmm." Muffled sounds filtered through Kari's end of the phone. "Let me see if I can find that brother of mine. He was around here a minute ago."

"Do you think he'll mind?"

"Nah. If he does, I'll give you a call back and we'll figure something else out together, okay?" Kari's voice was strong and assured—just what Ella needed.

"Okay. Thanks."

Did Jake have her number? If not, he had Kari's, and Kari could either pass it on or be their go-between.

Ella would've climbed out of the truck for a better view, but with the sun going down, the temperature would be dropping. No need to freeze while she waited for Jake. Assuming Kari could find him.

Right as Ella was tempted to call Kari back, her phone rang.

"Help is on the way. I just need to tell him your location." Kari's perky voice was music to Ella's ears.

Ella quickly explained how to find her. Then she pulled out the blanket she'd been using earlier and tucked it around her arms. This old truck still had a lot of life in it, but it wasn't as insulated as some. And she couldn't run a heater even if she wanted to.

Knowing Jake, it wouldn't take him an hour to get here. He drove fast. And for the first time, Ella didn't mind the thought of him speeding.

* * *

"Jake?" Kari called through the open hotel-room door, where Jake and Chaz were elbows deep in fixing a bathroom sink. Chaz met his friend's gaze in the mirror, knowing Kari seeking him out usually meant something else was wrong.

"In here." Jake wiped his forehead with the back of his arm.

"Hey." Kari stepped into the bathroom. "Oh." She stopped and took in the mess before her. "Not good."

"Nah. Almost got it fixed. Just have to put everything back together."

"Not what I'm talking about." Kari tapped her phone against her leg.

"What's wrong?" Chaz wiped his hands on a towel, wincing when it left a black streak across the white. "Sorry. If this doesn't come out, I'll pay for it."

She waved him off. "Jake has ruined more towels in the last couple years than you can count. What's one more?"

"Way to throw me under the bus." Jake grabbed the towel from Chaz. "What's wrong?"

"Ella's truck broke down."

Chaz's gut tightened.

"Okay," Jake said. "Give me another half an hour and I can go get her." He flipped a wrench into the air and caught it behind his back. "Wouldn't be the first time I've jumped her off."

"I don't want her out there by herself for that long," Kari huffed.

Chaz frowned. "Where is she?"

"Gauley River National Recreation Area."

Chaz whistled. "That's quite a drive. Any idea what's going on with her truck?"

"It usually needs a jump." Kari rubbed her forehead. "I'd offer to go myself, but someone needs to man the desk while this Jake-of-all-trades cleans up his mess."

"I'll go." Chaz unrolled his sleeves and grabbed his jacket from the towel hook. "She doesn't need to sit out there any longer than necessary. I've seen that truck."

"Are you sure?" Kari followed him into the hallway.

"Of course. Not a problem." Chaz slid his jacket on.

"Don't do anything I wouldn't do." Jake's taunt followed him down the hall.

Kari rolled her eyes. "I'm sort of glad you're going instead of him."

Chaz chuckled but also hustled. The thought of Ella stranded on the side of the road all alone didn't sit well with him. What had she been thinking driving so far when she knew her truck was unreliable?

Didn't matter now. All that mattered was that he get to her as quickly as he could. The sun hovered over the horizon as he stepped outside, and a cold breeze ruffled his hair. He slipped into his Jeep and pointed it east. Time to rescue the damsel in distress. Though something told him Ella would hate to be called that.

On a hunch, he swung by his house and grabbed his tow dolly. If she'd needed Jake as many times as he indicated, she might need more than an easy fix tonight. Better to be prepared.

Everything grew darker as he followed the highway to the spot Kari said Ella was. What had drawn her out here? Had she meant to stay so long? Was she warm enough?

He had to back off the accelerator more times than he

wanted to. There was pushing the speed limit, and then there was reckless driving. And when the grade became five percent, he needed to slow down, even though his heart argued otherwise.

Finally, signs for Gauley River told him he was close. Following the directions for the overlook, he spotted the old truck in the small gravel lot. He pulled in next to Ella with his headlights facing her vehicle. He'd need the light to assess what was going on, if nothing else.

She stepped out, shielding her eyes against the light. The headlights made her blonde hair appear silver as the breeze blew loose pieces around her head. Her flannel shirt and vest had probably been warm enough earlier, but now the temperature was close to thirty. Where was her jacket?

He met her near the hood of his vehicle.

"Chaz? I thought Jake was coming." Was that disappointment in her voice? The thought shot regret through his chest.

"Kari didn't tell you?"

"She said help was on the way." Ella tucked a strand of hair behind her ear.

"Well, sorry to surprise you, but Jake was fixing a sink and needed to finish."

"No." Ella ducked her head. "Sorry. I'm not ungrateful. Just … surprised."

So, not disappointed. Okay.

"Well, let's see what's going on. Is it making any noise at all?"

She shook her head and handed him the keys. He pursed his lips after checking several things. He'd almost bet it was the battery, and at this point, it might not even have enough life left to jump-start.

"Think we can jump it?" Her voice held hope he hated to squash.

"Let's try."

With the cords hooked up, he revved his engine and let it run for a bit, willing at least a little life into hers. She tucked her hands under her arms and bounced on her toes. Some knight in shining armor he was. He reached into the back seat of his Jeep and found an old sweatshirt.

"Here. It's not super thick, but maybe it will help a little." He handed it to her before telling her to try starting the truck.

Nothing.

Okay. Time for a new plan. No way were they going to go find a battery and bring it back at this time of night. And something told him she couldn't afford a tow truck—nor be willing to allow him to pay for one. Time to put his four-wheel drive into action.

"How do you feel about letting me tow you back?"

She faced him, mouth slightly ajar, and all he wanted to do was erase the uncertainty and worry from her pretty face. He gently clasped her upper arm. How could he assure her that everything would be okay?

"I've actually towed Jake's truck with this thing a time or two." He motioned to hers. "Yours isn't nearly as big. I'll back my Jeep around, and we'll get things hooked up. Are you okay with that?"

"I guess I don't have much of a choice, do I?"

He smiled. "Not much. Unless you want a real tow truck to come get you."

She shook her head.

"Right. Let's do this, then." He backed up to her truck and lined up the dolly with her wheels. Now came the hard part. "How strong are you feeling tonight?"

She was a tiny slip of a girl. Would they be able to get her truck on this thing without more help? He stretched his neck back and forth. They'd soon find out.

"Why?"

"We have to push the truck up onto the dolly."

Her mouth formed an adorable little O. She nodded and moved to the other side of the truck. Attagirl.

With the truck in neutral, they pushed on the count of three. It budged a few inches, but not enough. Chaz blew out a large breath and counted again. *Please, God.*

After several more tries, the truck was on the dolly. He strapped the wheels in place and made sure all was secure and ready to go. It would have to do.

"Ready? It could take us a while, because towing always needs extra brake time. You gonna make it?" He held open his passenger door.

She stepped up and slid onto the seat. "I'll be okay. I really appreciate this."

He turned the heater up and slowly pulled out with his emergency flashers on. Time to pray his way back to town. Ella glanced back as if to confirm her truck was still there. She pulled one leg up, tucked her hands underneath. A minute later, she twisted and looked out the back window again, her fingers picking at a frayed spot on his old sweatshirt.

"It's okay." He reached over and clasped her hand, giving it a squeeze before letting go. She was too skittish for him to try holding it longer. "What were you doing all the way out here, anyway?"

"Oh." She glanced away. "It was my mom's favorite spot. I like to come here every now and then. To remember her."

"How often does Jake have to come jump your truck?"

She ducked her head and tucked her hair again. "Sometimes."

"If you're hungry, there are some granola bars and stuff in

the glove box. Nothing fancy, but it's better than starving."
Past experience said her pride wasn't about to accept. "And
will you grab me one too?"

Slowly, she reached forward and dug through old napkins
and receipts until she found a couple wrapped snacks. She
handed him one, and once he opened it and took a bite, she
followed suit. They were stale, but until they got her truck
taken care of, he couldn't offer her better.

A couple hours later, he pulled into an auto shop.

"What are you doing?" Ella roused from the light sleep
she'd fallen into half an hour earlier. "I can't—"

He touched her arm. "I've got this."

Before she could protest again, he climbed out of the warm
vehicle and headed into the store. The manager didn't look
happy to see him come in five minutes before closing, but he
didn't care. Ella needed trustworthy transportation. In less
than fifteen minutes, they had a new battery installed in her
truck, and he had it unhooked from his dolly.

"I'll pay you back." She crossed her arms over her chest as
he folded his straps and put them in the back of his Jeep.

"We can discuss that later. Right now, I just want to make
sure you have a way to get where you need to be. You okay to
drive home?"

She nodded. As she reached to tuck back a piece of hair, he
intercepted and did it for her. Silky soft. So was the ear his
fingertips brushed.

Her breath caught, and she lifted her eyes to his. Much as
he wanted to linger, he lowered his hand again, though he
didn't back up. What was the rest of her story? How else could
he earn her trust enough to let him in? She shivered as the
wind whipped around them.

"I guess we should go, huh? It's getting late." He stepped
back first, although everything in him protested.

"Yes." She pinched her lips together. "Thank you."

He waved with a shrug, as if he hadn't tried to be her hero tonight. "Glad to help. Be careful driving home."

And just like that, he let her drive away again. Would she continue to avoid him? He needed to find more of the places she spent time at. He could only bump into her so many times in church, at the hotel, and at the flea market. Would Kari be willing to help him find ways to see Ella more often?

14

It was late in the day, and Bellamy had abandoned the booth hours before. Ella soaked in the peace and quiet. Ever since she'd come home late a couple days ago, Angela and Bellamy had been watching her more than ever.

She hadn't dared tell them who had rescued her. Simply that she had car trouble and had to get help to fix it before she could come home. Angela looked like she wanted to know more, but she'd kept quiet. Ella wouldn't complain.

Now that Bellamy was gone and the customers had thinned to almost none, Ella pulled out her sketch pad. With a charcoal pencil in hand, her fingers started forming a shape without her thinking about it. She couldn't do this at home any longer. Too risky. In moments like these, she gave in and allowed herself to truly relax.

"Are those records?" A man squinted at the shelf from the doorway of the booth.

"They are. Feel free to look." Ella waved her hand at the vinyl section, knowing he probably wouldn't buy any. The way Angela made her price the albums, they were too high for this market. But Angela didn't understand anything except the desire for more money.

While he browsed, she filled in an eyebrow on her drawing. Wait. Was she sketching a face?

She blinked a few times and focused on the paper in her lap. A familiar set of eyes and nose stared up at her. The profile she'd snuck glances at more often than she should've on the way back to town several nights ago. After he rescued her.

"Any chance I could talk you down on some of these prices?" the browser asked.

"Unfortunately, they're set for now. My stepmother insisted on those prices."

He nodded and pushed back to his feet. "Thanks anyway."

"Have a nice day."

She couldn't be upset that she'd sold only one today. After already losing so much, maybe it was a blessing to have these priced too high. It kept them here longer.

She feathered in Chaz's hair, then his ear and chin. Not quite perfect, but close. Had she ever been able to capture a face this well before? She'd given up long ago on noses. With the shading and random bumps and ridges, they never looked right. But this one ...

She shaded in a bit more around his right nostril. Added a few lashes to his eyes. A bit of stubble around that strong chin.

Her breathing picked up pace as she worked. What was going on? She never had a reaction like this to anyone who wasn't making her mad. Never remembered all the little details of how they looked. Or the scent that lingered in their clothing —one she was extra familiar with after hours of wearing his sweatshirt.

Was it because he had rescued her? Because she so desperately needed him to find out her secret without any repercussions? Was there truly something to him being the most eligible bachelor in West Virginia? Did that add an extra allure?

She shook her head. Ridiculous.

After a few more swipes of her pencil, she forced herself to stop. She was supposed to focus on finishing a piece to enter in the contest, not moon over the man running the competition.

The pieces she'd worked on at the overlook a couple days before were still safely tucked in the toolbox in the truck. No way to get them now. The light in here wasn't great, anyway. Maybe she could find some time early next week to sneak over to Fae's and use her extra room, where sunlight poured through the windows.

"Didn't I see dishes in here a few weeks ago?" A woman entered the booth and looked around.

"We sold the whole set last week. Is there anything else I can help you find?" Ella rose to appear more helpful.

"No." The woman spun around and walked away. "Never mind."

"Right." Ella reclaimed her stool and stared at nothing.

Her mind was unfocused tonight. Actually, she'd been unfocused since Chaz had rescued her two days ago. When he gently tucked her hair behind her ear, she wasn't sure she'd ever breathe normally again. How did one gentle touch turn her mind completely to mush?

And how could she undo it?

He was out of her league, beyond her reach. So why did he keep acting like he wanted to reach out for her? Her hand mindlessly moved over the new page in her sketch pad, and she once again drew Chaz's eyes.

Enough.

She put it away and dusted off her fingers. Daydreaming about him wouldn't change things. Until Bellamy's lies were discovered, being around him was more dangerous than good —even if it was really, really good—the way he had treated her at the restaurant and taken care of her sad, old truck. The way he'd tucked her hair behind her ear. She sighed. How did she even get into this mess?

The smell of food reached her before she could see where it was coming from. Had someone brought their dinner into the flea market? It happened frequently, but normally it didn't smell this good. Her tummy rumbled. When was the last time she'd eaten a real meal?

"Hi." Chaz appeared in her doorway, and she jumped up.

"Hi." She brushed her fingers on her jeans. Were they covered in charcoal? Why had she chosen that medium tonight?

"I thought I'd make up the lousy dinner from Tuesday night." He held up some to-go containers. "This should be way better than a granola bar."

"You don't owe me—"

"A man has to redeem himself when all he was able to offer were stale granola bars." He moved into her space and motioned for her to sit. "It's nothing fancy. Just pepperoni rolls."

She hummed in appreciation. She hadn't eaten those in a long time. Despite being a state staple, her stepmother thought them lacking in sophistication. She banned them from her house, claiming they could eat better than some rudimentary coal-miner lunch.

"I take it you approve?" He smiled and perched on her dad's old chair.

"I always approve of pepperoni rolls." She lifted the lid and breathed in the aromatic steam. "Yum."

He handed her a water bottle then dug into his own container. When she took her first bite, she closed her eyes in bliss. Memories of helping her mom make these while Ella stood on a chair to reach the counter mixed with memories of packing up a bunch and going out for a picnic and art session.

"Are these your favorite food?"

She opened her eyes again and caught his grin—the one that made a dimple appear in his right cheek. Had she remembered to include that in her drawing? "Not necessarily, but they're *a* favorite. And wrapped up in lots of family memories from when I was little."

He nodded and chewed for a few moments. "I can see that. Can I ask ... Would you tell me what happened to your parents?"

She pulled a piece of pepperoni out of her roll and tossed it into her mouth to give herself an extra minute. Had anyone ever asked her that? When was the last time she'd told this story?

"Mom had cancer. We lost her when I was eight." Ella studied the container in her lap. "She fought for several years, but ... it was too much."

Chaz moved to the floor in front of her, a hand on her knee. "You don't have to tell me if it's too hard."

"No." Ella shook her head and blinked away tears. "It's actually nice to talk about it. I don't get many chances."

"Okay."

"Dad married Angela about a year later. I think he hoped it would help both of us not be so lonely anymore. It was okay for a while. He helped maintain the balance in our household."

Ella took a deep breath. "But he was injured. He worked in coal. Had gone to help inspect a mine. They're so much safer now than they used to be, you know?" She shook her head. "But there was an accident. By the time they got him back up to fresh air, he'd lost so much blood."

Chaz's hand covered hers. "How old were you?"

"Fourteen."

* * *

Chaz's heart sank to his belly. So young. Ella had lost both of her parents when she was still a child. And though she still had her stepmother and stepsister, they didn't act like they viewed her as family. How had she stayed strong for so long?

"I'm sorry."

"It's all right." Ella swiped at the tears running down her cheeks, leaving behind a black smear under her right eye.

He clasped her hand and studied her fingers. The tips were stained black. Newsprint? Or something else?

"Oh." She jerked away. "I meant to wash that off earlier."

"What is it?"

She pinched her lips together, as if ashamed.

"Newsprint? From when you wrap things up in here?" He motioned around them.

She shook her head, a strand of hair escaping her scarf. "Coal."

He blinked. "Coal."

"What can I say?" She ran a sleeve over her cheek, only smearing it worse. "I'm a coal miner's daughter."

A grin tugged at his lips. "Let me help."

He pulled a handkerchief from his pocket—a habit his mom insisted he learn at an early age. With a bit of moisture from his water bottle, he had a makeshift washcloth. He gently smoothed it over her cheek, wiping away the remaining tears and the coal.

Her story still didn't make sense, but he'd let it slide for now. He had a feeling if he pushed, she'd only rebuild some of the walls she'd let down. Instead, he'd find more excuses to see her again, especially considering how well tonight's plan had worked.

"Your dinner is getting cold."

She nodded and took another bite. He moved back to the chair, and they ate in silence for a while. He took the opportunity to look around him. Records now lined the shelf where the dishes had sat. There were a few mugs, some books, a desk, and the chair he sat in. None of the items were antiques, but they all appeared loved. How much of this did she wish she could keep? How many memories were wrapped up in these items?

"Thank you." Ella's soft words broke him out of his runaway thoughts.

"For dinner?" He closed his now empty container.

"And for the rescue the other night." She ducked her head. "I knew the truck was having a rough time, but I figured it was from the weather. It gets finicky when the temps change so quickly."

Chaz nodded.

"But I should've known it needed something more. Jake warned me the last time he had to come ..."

"How old is the truck?"

She shrugged. "It was my dad's. Angela didn't want it, but she decided it was okay for me to have when I turned sixteen. That way I could drive myself to school and work. I learned how to change the tires and check the oil in high school. The boys in the mechanics class thought I couldn't handle it, but I pulled a higher grade than any of them."

He chuckled. "I would've liked to see that."

"I should've recognized the signs that it needed more. And I do mean to repay you—"

Holding up a hand, he shook his head. "I'm sure you'll get your chance. Someday, maybe you'll need to come rescue me."

"I can't imagine your Jeep dying on you."

"Maybe not. But there are more things a person can be rescued from than a dead car." Chaz shrugged. "Especially with Jake as a best friend."

Her giggle sent bubbles of joy through his chest—effervescent and spirit lifting. He couldn't help but join in.

"I think it's past time to close." She gathered her trash and flung her bag over her shoulder.

"I'll walk you out." He'd parked next to her truck with this possibility in mind. "Did you have a good day?"

"Didn't sell much." Ella locked their gate and headed for the main door. "I imagine things will pick up more after tomorrow."

"Tomorrow?"

"Halloween." Ella glanced at him. "People start Christmas shopping earlier each year. The serious ones start right after Christmas while the sales are still on. But the next level of shoppers usually start after Halloween."

"Good to know." He nodded. "Guess I need to get busy. What would you like for Christmas?"

She jerked her head around, eyes wide. "Don't you think you've already given me more than enough?"

He shook his head. "Is that even possible?"

When she started to shiver, he clasped her elbow and steered her the last few feet to their vehicles. "Where's your coat?"

"I forgot to grab it this morning." She stashed her bag in the cab and turned back to face him. "But I'm going straight home. No worries."

"Be careful, Ella." He grabbed her hands and gave them a squeeze. "I'll see you soon?"

"You do keep finding ways to run into me." Her sweet lips tilted into a smile.

Leaning closer, he whispered in her ear, "Make it easier, and I'll do it more."

In the moonlight, her wide eyes practically glowed.

He pressed a kiss to her cheek then backed away before she could protest. Or before he could claim more than a simple peck, which tempted him more and more each time he saw her.

15

Ella's door was open. Her pulse stuttered. Why was her door open? She slowed as she neared her room, her heart beating harder. What exactly was she about to discover?

Bellamy stood on the other side of the bed, studying something Ella couldn't see. But it was something she hadn't wanted Bellamy to find. Because it came from her trunk, where she stored her personal things.

"What are you doing in my room?" She tried to control her voice, but a slight waver tinged the question anyway.

Bellamy turned slowly and held up a drawing. "What is this?"

"It's called artwork. I know you don't understand much about it, but something you should understand is that it's mine and you're not supposed to be in here."

"I thought you were told not to do any more *artwork*." Bellamy spat it out like a curse.

"No. I was told to not tell Chaz that the artwork now hanging in his gallery is mine and not yours. I have done what you said." Ella crossed her arms over her chest as Bellamy twisted the cardstock in her hands.

"And how are we supposed to keep it a secret that you're an artist if you're still going around drawing?" Bellamy jerked her hands wide, and a corner of the paper tore. "Oops."

Not a hint of remorse was within touching distance of her stepsister. Ella needed Bellamy out of her room—and fast. But how to make that happen when she was on the other side of the bed from the door? On the side that held Ella's artwork?

"Bellamy ..." Ella held out a hand as if she were calming a wild animal. "Let's be reasonable."

"Reasonable? How can I be reasonable when you're obviously trying to steal my chance at winning the most eligible bachelor in West Virginia?" Bellamy grabbed both sides of the drawing and ripped it in half.

Ella's heart lurched as if it were part of the paper. "No. Please."

"Too little, too late, Rendersella." Bellamy spun and started grabbing more items.

"Bellamy, no! These are *my* things. You can't just come in here and take away all my stuff." Ella was frozen in place, afraid if she moved, things would only get worse.

Bellamy glanced over her shoulder with an evil scowl. "Watch me."

She started throwing all sorts of papers and canvases into a garbage bag. Then brushes, paints, pencils, and anything else she could find. Ella jerked forward to intervene, to stop her, but Bellamy lunged like a wild cat anytime she came close. She scratched, hit, even gnashed her teeth at Ella. Then, Bellamy did the worst thing possible—she opened a jar of primer and dumped it into the bag, then gave the whole thing a few good shakes.

Ella slumped to the hard floor, her heart a puddle around her.

"That'll teach you not to sneak around and do art behind

my back. You can't steal this moment from me, Ella Renders. Because I'm a better choice than you, and he needs to see it through all this paint and pencil mess you're always in." Bellamy stepped on Ella's leg, where she'd collapsed on the floor, before marching out the door.

Surprisingly, her eyes were dry. Nothing. No sobs. Not even a prickle behind her lids.

Instead, something hot bubbled up inside her. She clenched her fists and set her jaw. She still had the two pieces she'd started, but now she had no paint or pencils to finish them. And no money to buy more, because every dollar she earned needed to go toward paying Chaz back for her battery.

She had to do something. She couldn't let Bellamy win. Did God not want Ella to prove Bellamy's lie by entering another piece in the contest? Everything had seemed to point that way —Fae's and Kari's encouragement, the beautiful start she'd gained while at the overlook, even how well she'd been able to capture a face in charcoal this evening.

She crawled over to the open chest and groaned when she looked inside. A few tiny nubs of charcoal and one lone pastel lingered in the bottom. Years of work—gone in a matter of minutes.

"No more."

Bellamy's car had screeched out of the driveway a few minutes earlier. Ella jumped up and started through the house, lifting her mom's last few paintings from the walls. Bellamy could destroy Ella's work, but Ella wouldn't let her touch another one of her mom's pieces. And Bellamy would do anything to keep Ella from finishing what she started. Time to be more proactive.

Ella pushed through the kitchen door and out into the cold night. Through the hedge, up the porch, where a warm light shone through a back window. She knocked with her elbow, hoping it was loud enough for Fae to hear.

"Ella. What in the world?" Her neighbor ushered her in, then took a few of the paintings from her before they slipped. "These are Sara's."

"Bellamy destroyed all my artwork and supplies tonight. Except for the few pieces in my truck and bag, everything is gone." Ella laid the portrait of herself as a girl on Fae's table. "I need you to hide these for me, please."

"Ella, your work—"

"I'm not giving up. I'm just going to have to figure out another way to do it. I can't afford more supplies." Ella held up a hand. "And you are *not* buying them for me. I need to do this on my own."

Fae set her chin at a stubborn angle. "I'll agree ... for now. But you come to me if you decide to let me help. Sometimes God wants us to allow others to help instead of trying to do everything on our own."

Ella shook her head. "I brought these to you. I let you feed me several times a week. I'm not alone."

"You're never alone, dear one." Fae wrapped Ella in her arms. She was just the right amount of pudgy to be comfortable and soft. Ella burrowed into her warmth for an extra minute before straightening once more.

"I have no idea what to do about my pieces, though. Where to find free art supplies?"

"Well, a long time ago, people didn't have all these fancy supplies you have now. They had to make their own paints. Wonder what we could use to do that."

Ella plopped into a chair. "Make my own paints? Out of what?"

"Earth. Spices. Vegetables." Fae pulled her laptop off the

kitchen counter and settled beside Ella. "Let's research, shall we?"

After perusing several pages, Ella shook her head. "Most of these are more like watercolor paints. I am absolutely horrible at watercolors."

"And when was the last time you tried it?" Fae regarded her with a raised eyebrow and pursed lips.

"I don't know. Once I figured out I couldn't do it well, I set watercolors aside for something else."

"Then it's time to start playing with them again."

"Fae, the contest deadline is just over a week away. I don't have time to play."

"Tomorrow is Saturday, is it not?"

"Yes. And you know very well that I have to work the booth on Saturdays."

"Then on Sunday afternoon, we'll start hunting and gathering." Fae pressed a button, and a page started printing from a printer across the room. "I'll have plenty of ideas by then. And this isn't considered buying you supplies. I'm simply providing the Wi-Fi, dear."

Ella hugged her fiercely, Fae's plan settling over her shoulders like a shawl. "You're the best."

As soon as the cake was eaten, Chaz couldn't wait any longer to reveal his mom's birthday surprise. He set the box on the table, proud of his find despite the wonky wrapping job. Mom protested but dug in and gasped once she lifted the flaps.

"Wherever did you find a full set of these dishes?" Chaz's mom ran her finger around the rim of a serving bowl. "You were supposed to tell me if you found more pieces so I could go buy them myself."

"And lose out on the perfect birthday present for you?" Chaz scoffed. "No way."

"So, where?"

"At the flea market. One of the booths had all of them." Chaz stared at the lacy pattern of Mom's tablecloth as Ella's sadness over losing the set washed through him again. If only there was a way to make both women happy.

"What aren't you saying?" Mom covered his hand with hers.

"The girl who runs the booth—Ella—her stepmom is basically making her sell all her parents' things. This set belonged to Ella's grandmother and then her mother. It was supposed to be hers. It about killed me to walk away with it."

"So, why did you?"

Chaz looked up. "Because if I didn't buy them, someone else would've. Maybe piece by piece. Or one place setting at a time. At least this way, all the dishes stayed together. And she knew you'd appreciate them since you already had some of your own."

Mom shook her head. "I've never seen you act like this about a girl."

"Act like what?"

"Like you care about more than what she looks like."

Chaz grinned. "Maybe this is the first time I do. She's worked her way under my skin, I guess. I want to know everything about her, but she barely gives me any details when I ask. I know her mom died of cancer and she lost her dad a few years later. Her stepmom and stepsister ..." Chaz shuddered. "I don't know. They don't treat her like family."

"Sounds like you've already uncovered quite a bit. Where did you meet?" Mom leaned back and took another sip of her coffee.

The sounds of Chaz's dad and brother washing the dishes

in the other room filtered through the closed door but didn't disturb the peace of the moment.

"We bumped into each other at the hotel."

Mom sighed. It drove her crazy that he sometimes spent the night there instead of talking things through with Dad. But his way worked for now.

"I thought maybe she was a guest from out of town, but it turns out she's Kari's friend. They met at church."

"I like her already." Mom smiled.

"Anyway, then I saw her at the flea market. And again at … Well, you may never believe this, but she was in the meadow when Jake and I went turkey hunting a few weeks ago."

"Sounds like God wanted you two to meet."

"I'm beginning to hope that's true." Chaz leaned his elbows on the table. "I took her out for lunch after church one week. And rescued her the other night when her truck wouldn't start. And I can't stop thinking about her."

"This may be the best birthday gift you've ever given me."

Chaz blinked. "If I'd known all these years you wanted dishes—"

"No, silly." Mom leaned forward and grinned. "You talking like this about a girl."

With a shake of his head, Chaz blew off her statement. "Doesn't matter yet. I have to get through this contest and see if Dad will give me a raise so I can find a place of my own. And I think she's hiding something, but I can't figure out what. It's like everything she says comes across as truthful but isn't quite the whole story."

Mom frowned. "Well, that puts a damper on things."

"But I don't think it's anything bad. It's like she's not allowed to say something." Chaz shoved his fingers through his hair. "It's hard to explain."

"Maybe Dad and I need to come with you on Sunday.

Check out this new place that's bringing you back to Christ." Mom waggled her eyebrows. "Maybe see this girl."

"Please don't scare her off before I've even convinced her to be my friend."

Mom crossed her heart. "I would never."

"Mm-hmm." Chaz chuckled. "Right."

"What? I have two boys. Can you blame a mom for wishing one of her sons would go ahead and get married so she can finally have a daughter?"

"Oh, I see how it is." Chaz shook his finger at her. "You're trying to replace us."

"I would never replace my boys. I love them all." Mom rose and pressed a kiss to his forehead. "But sometimes it would be nice to have someone to watch a rom-com with. Or go shopping."

"You're going to make us watch a rom-com tonight, aren't you?" Chaz stood too.

"Me? Would I do that?" Mom blinked as if innocent. "I would never force my guys to watch a romantic comedy. But if they happen to ask what I want to watch *on my birthday*, I might have one in mind. And if they happen to sit in the room with me, *since it's my birthday*, maybe they can watch it, too, and come up with some ideas for how to start something romantic of their own."

Chaz groaned. "I'll go warn the others."

"Love you too." Mom patted his cheek.

He paused and wrapped her in a hug. Her head came only to his shoulder now, but she was and would always be his favorite person to talk through his problems with. She squeezed him back then looked up with a furrowed brow.

"You okay?"

"Just appreciating what a great listener you are." He smiled. "Will you pray for me as I try to figure all this out?"

"I pray for you every day." She brushed his hair back. "But it's always nice to have specifics."

He nodded.

"You're a great guy, Chaz. And not just because *West Virginia Life and Times* magazine says so." She penetrated him with a gaze that had always been able to see more than he liked. "Somewhere out there is a girl perfect for you. If it's this Ella, we'll welcome her with open arms. If not, I'm praying the right one comes along. Just continue striving to be a man after God's own heart. That's the right way to win a girl's heart too."

He saluted his mom. Perfect advice. Now to find more ways to implement it.

16

Ella dashed into the church building and up the aisle. Fae sat in her normal spot and had left an opening at the end for Ella. But today, Ella needed to make sure there wasn't room for anyone else to sit on her other side.

She tapped her neighbor on the shoulder.

Fae turned and beamed. "There you are."

"I need you to switch places with me." Ella glanced back over her shoulder.

"What? Why?" Fae frowned.

"Fae, *please*." Ella widened her eyes, hoping to convey the necessity of the switch.

"Ella Marie Renders, what is going on?"

"I don't have time to explain right now, but I promise I have a good reason."

Fae narrowed her eyes but stood so Ella could scoot past her and sit on the inside instead of by the aisle. As Ella settled into place between Fae and the youngest Matthews kid, Chaz approached. There was no way he didn't see them switch places.

She lowered her gaze as if completely enamored with her bulletin, but she could sense him standing there. Fae nudged

Ella, but she pretended she didn't notice. When she felt a sharp pinch on her leg, she whipped her head around with a glare.

"Ella, Chaz is here." Fae lifted a brow.

"Oh. Good morning, Chaz." Ella gave a half-smile then looked back at her lap.

"Rude," Fae hissed in her ear before she turned her attention to Chaz. "How are you today, young man?"

"Okay, Fae. I thought there might be room for me here, but it looks like I arrived too late." His voice faded at the end of the statement. "Guess I better wait near the back and see if Jake shows up."

"I bet he will. So sorry we didn't save you a spot. We'll know better next time." Fae elbowed Ella.

Ella grimaced but still refused to look in Chaz's direction.

Bellamy's perfume wafted over before her shrill voice broke the awkward silence. "Why, Chaz Prince. What's wrong? Nowhere to sit today?"

"I was just greeting Fae and Ella while waiting for Jake to arrive." Chaz's tone took on a more formal tone.

"No need to wait for him. You can join us. There's plenty of room on our pew over here." Out of the corner of her eye, Ella saw Bellamy give Chaz's arm a tug, but he remained fixed in place.

Ella swallowed the urge to scoot over a tad. The Matthews family had spread out, but they didn't really need as much of the pew as they occupied. But she couldn't. Not with Bellamy right there, able to see every little motion. She had to stay away from him as much as possible until after the contest. Until Bellamy's threats would no longer hold sway. No matter how much it hurt.

"Chaz, my man." Jake's greeting caused several heads to turn as he walked up the aisle to where Chaz stood.

"Thanks for the offer, Bellamy, but I'll sit with Jake today." Chaz moved toward the back of the auditorium.

Bellamy growled loud enough for Ella to hear. Ella refused to look her way. Ever since Friday, a thin thread of tension remained between them, just waiting to be broken. Sunday morning right before services started was not the time to risk a blowup with her stepsister.

All through worship, Ella swore Chaz's gaze was on the back of her head. How she would escape without him talking to her again, she had no idea, but she had to try. Even though Bellamy had destroyed most of her art stash the other night, there were still other ways she could make Ella's life more miserable.

Better play it safe. As safe as possible, anyway.

Which was even harder to do since earlier in the week when he had fed her pepperoni rolls and left her with a kiss on the cheek. She ran a finger over the skin where his lips had pressed. How was she supposed to avoid a guy when she wanted to spend more time with him?

Fae nudged her as she stood for a hymn. Oops. The whole service had flown by, and now it was almost time to leave. And she had no plan for how to get away without Chaz stopping her where Bellamy could see.

"Are you going to tell me what's going on?" Fae poked Ella's arm immediately after the final "amen."

Ella glanced over and caught Bellamy's glare. "Not here."

Fae looked in the same direction and *tsked*. "That girl. I need to pray harder for her soul."

Chagrin filled Ella's gut. She should be praying for Angela and Bellamy too. But it was next to impossible to pray anything more than, "Please get me away from them." Not exactly good Christianity.

"We already have plans for this afternoon. Might as well

come prepared to talk." Fae slid her fur coat on and buttoned it. "Are you coming straight over?"

"I'm going to change into something I can get messy in first." Ella shrugged into her mom's old, thin trench coat. "It shouldn't take me long."

"I'll have the roast ready." Fae left without another word. So much for using her as a shield.

"Ella." Chaz touched her arm as she passed the back row.

She couldn't ignore him now. Slowly, she looked up into his face. His expression conveyed bewilderment and hurt—hurt she'd caused. "Hey, Chaz."

He raised a hand as if trying to grab an answer out of the air. "What's going on?"

"I—" Ella looked back toward where Bellamy stood surrounded by her friends. "I can't talk about it right now."

"Have I done something?" He leaned closer, and she caught a whiff of his cologne.

She shook her head. "It's not you. But I do need to go. I promised Fae I'd spend the afternoon with her."

Chaz looked as if he wanted to say more. Over his shoulder, Jake and Kari frowned, confusion all over their faces. Kari had already scolded Ella for lying once. What would she think about this situation? She hadn't lied today, but what she was doing felt just as wrong.

"See you around?" Ella offered a half-smile, which was all she could muster.

"I hope so."

She nodded then stepped out into the cold Sunday afternoon. Bellamy's voice reached her before the door swung all the way shut. "Chaz! Hey, Chaz! Are you busy? Would you like to join us for lunch?"

Ella squeezed her eyes against the idea of him spending time with her stepmother and stepsister. No telling what they'd divulge about her. He didn't seem to want to hang out with Bellamy, but would that change if Ella kept pushing him away?

* * *

It took much longer than it should have, but Chaz finally extricated himself from Bellamy and her mom. His head reeled from the whole morning. What had happened? Why had Ella avoided him? She very obviously made sure he couldn't sit with her. What had changed since Thursday?

"Dude." Jake clapped him on the shoulder. "What was all that?"

"All what?" Chaz rubbed the middle of his forehead.

"With Ella, obviously. I'd never expect you to explain Bellamy."

"So much help, Jake." Kari patted her brother's arm on the other side. "Come on, boys. Take me to lunch before I have to go back and man the hotel desk."

Chaz prepared to protest, but Kari's narrowed eyes quelled him. Right. Well, at least maybe she'd have some insights into Ella that he couldn't glean by asking himself the same questions over and over.

Ten minutes later, they sat around a small table in a Chinese restaurant. Chaz pushed the salt and pepper shakers into a straight row, then started organizing the sugar packets. Kari reached over and scooted everything out of his way.

"Spill it. What did you do to my girl?"

"What?" Chaz glanced up sharply. "I thought maybe you could tell me. Last time I saw her, we were good—great."

Kari lifted one of her brows. "She sure didn't look great this morning."

She'd looked wonderful to Chaz. Except for the part when

she wouldn't let him near her. Her light-blue dress was wide at the bottom so that it swirled a bit when she walked. But that obviously wasn't what Kari meant.

"I'm completely confused. I honestly don't know what changed between Thursday and now."

"Thursday?" Kari crossed her arms. "It was Tuesday that I sent you to jump her truck."

Chaz rubbed the back of his neck. "Right. I ended up towing her back because her battery was dead. We got it fixed. Then on Thursday, I dropped by the flea market and brought her some pepperoni rolls. We ate and chatted."

At least, that's all he was going to tell the siblings. No need to mention the cheek kiss. Or how he couldn't find enough time to spend with her.

"Why do I feel like that's not the whole story?" Kari pinned him with a stare.

When the server brought their meals, he couldn't help but be grateful for the interruption. It might've been easier to go to lunch with Bellamy. At least she wouldn't be giving him the fifth degree about his recent interactions with Ella.

After Jake led them in a prayer, he ripped into his chopsticks packet and pointed them at Chaz. "So why exactly did you take pepperoni rolls to the flea market the other day? Not that I don't love a good pepperoni roll. But you never bring me any."

Kari swatted her brother. "I don't think that's pertinent to this conversation."

"Look." Jake flicked a few pieces of rice her way. "If I'm about to lose my best guy to a girl, then of course it's pertinent. And who uses words like *pertinent*, anyway? Just because you're all smart and stuff doesn't mean you have to act like it."

Kari rolled her eyes.

"So?" Jake turned his attention back to Chaz.

Sometimes, eating meals with these two was like watching a tennis match.

"So nothing." Chaz bit into an egg roll and chewed for a minute. "I brought her dinner because I felt bad that all I had when I rescued her were a few stale granola bars. I was making it up to her."

Jake scoffed. "Again, I say—you've never done that for me."

"I've never fed you stale granola bars?"

"Well, no, but that jerky a few months ago was pretty tough, man. And what about that time you tried to grill the fish we caught and ended up cooking it so long it basically disintegrated into the fire and we had only a few bites left? Or—"

"Point taken. I will bring you pepperoni rolls sometime in the future. Or at least pay for your lunch today."

Jake sat back and smirked.

"Now that we've appeased my brother ..." Kari leaned forward.

"*Appeased*," Jake muttered under his breath.

"... we can get on to the real issue. What could have happened between Thursday and today to make Ella so skittish?" She popped a shrimp into her mouth and stared into space.

That was the real issue. It couldn't have been anything he'd done, because he hadn't seen her since Thursday night. Unless that tiny little kiss ... But surely not. It was nothing.

"What?" Kari narrowed her eyes.

"What *what*?" Chaz focused on his lunch and tried to school his expression so he wouldn't look guilty.

"Uh-uh. You were thinking of something. I could see it in your expression." She drew a circle in the air around his head with her chopstick.

"You can't read my face," Chaz scoffed.

"Wanna bet?" Kari motioned toward her brother. "The only other person in the world I can read easier is him."

"Hey!" Jake flicked more rice at her.

"You were thinking of something that might've upset Ella. What was it?"

Chaz's cheeks heated. Did he really have to do this? Now? Here? Ever?

Kari and Jake both stared at him, waiting.

"I mean ... Well, it's nothing really. Can't be. I barely even ..."

"Did you kiss her?" Kari's eyes widened.

"No! Yes?" Chaz grimaced.

"Which is it?" Jake laughed. "Obviously nothing memorable."

Chaz glared at his friend. "I walked her to the car. Squeezed her hands. Leaned in and kissed her cheek, but just barely. I mean, it hardly even counts, right? Surely something like that wouldn't have upset her?"

Kari rocked her head back and forth. "I honestly don't know. Ella hasn't dated anyone in the four years we've lived here. Not even expressed interest in anyone. I have no idea what her stance is on relationships or guys in general. Did she know you were thinking along those lines?"

"*I* didn't even know I was thinking along those lines. Not really. It was sort of spontaneous." Chaz ruffled his hair. "Every time I'm around her, I want to be around her more. But it's hard, you know? I'm swamped with the contest thing. And she works those weird hours at the flea market. And then today, she avoided me like the plague."

"She has been acting sort of weird lately." Jake popped a bite of broccoli into his mouth. "Hiding behind the counter. Bursting out of random hotel rooms. What's that about?"

Kari glared at her brother.

"What?" Jake shrugged. "Am I not right?"

"She was hiding?" Chaz pushed his plate back, not really hungry anymore.

"It was before she knew who you were. She was embarrassed." Kari waved down a server and asked for to-go boxes.

"It's still weird," Jake muttered.

"I don't think it was the kiss." Kari squeezed Chaz's arm. "I'm not sure what it was. If I figure it out, I'll let you know."

"Thanks, Kari." Chaz packed up his leftovers and paid the bill.

Lunch hadn't solved any of his problems, but at least he knew his friends were on his side in this strange situation. If only he could quit worrying about whether or not he'd done something wrong.

17

"I'm not sure this is worth it." Ella studied the colors tinting the tips of her fingers. "Do you think I could enter my hands as artwork?"

"They're lovely hands." Fae stirred a pot whose contents were turning a pink hue. "But I think it would be hard to leave them at the gallery."

"True."

"How're your colors coming?" Fae glanced over at the various containers Ella had all over the table. "I like that purple one."

"Blueberries." Ella pointed to a yellow. "Dandelions." Then a green. "Kale. I still can't understand why you had kale in the first place, but it seems to be working. It's a great hue."

"And the spices? Are they turning out?"

"The paprika makes a nice orange. Not sure about this turmeric color."

"Maybe you need to add more?"

"I don't want to use up your whole spice cabinet." Ella dipped a brush into her bespoke turmeric paint and spread it across a piece of paper. Not as bad once it wasn't concentrated. Maybe.

"Please. When was the last time I used that spice? I can't even remember what recipes call for it." Fae waved a hand in the air. "It's probably expired. At least this way it's getting some life."

Ella shook her head. If she let her, Fae would give her everything in the house if she thought it would help. But that would defeat the purpose of doing this on her own.

Ella laughed silently. Alone. She wasn't alone. If it weren't for Fae's well-stocked garden and pantry, she wouldn't have half these colors. Though she still wasn't sure how she'd use them. Somewhere, she'd read that natural dyes tended to fade faster than chemical ones. Would a painting created with these colors last long enough to be judged?

"I see that frown wrinkle over there." Fae pointed a wooden spoon at her. "Stop worrying. God gave you all these natural ingredients to make paint. He'll ensure it works."

Ella huffed. "So He's going to suddenly endow me with the ability to paint with watercolors?"

"I never said that." Fae shook the spoon, splattering pink dye across the kitchen floor. Rufus meandered over, sniffed the drops, turned up his nose, and wandered off again. "I said He's going to work it out. Trust Him."

Ella sorted through the colors again. Walnuts had been a lot of work but made a lovely brown. Onion skins produced a darker, more purply brown. They had oranges and yellows. Pink. What might produce a deeper red?

Back to the spice cabinet. Pepper flakes? Maybe. Saffron? Too expensive to waste on something like this, even if it were the right color. Did Fae even remember she had some of these spices in here? *Hmm.* Chili powder?

She grabbed another jar and mixed in water and spice, giving it a good shake. Time was not on her side in this process. This was the third day she and Fae were concocting and experimenting with various ingredients and hues. She only had one more day off this week, and then she had to work the next three days. When would she have time to paint?

The contest deadline was next week. And she needed to turn it in before the actual deadline, because she'd be working that day. She squeezed her eyes closed and whispered a prayer that God would give her faith like Fae's. Even just a little bit like hers. Half?

Fae's arms came around her. "Dear one, God gave you amazing abilities and talents. We've created almost every color in the rainbow. You found enough paintbrushes in your bag and in the bottom of your trunk, so you can still paint. This is going to work."

Ella nodded, but a tear dripped down her cheek.

"Father God, please wrap Your strength and wisdom around this dear child." Fae whispered the prayer right into Ella's ear. "Show her what to do, and help her use her talents to glorify You, most of all. We praise You for Your amazing creation that gives us so many colors and so many beautiful things to paint and draw. We praise You for Ella's mom, who taught her how to see Your creation through an artist's eyes. We praise You for listening to us. In Jesus' holy name, amen."

"Amen," Ella breathed.

"Let's finish up these last few that we're working on and see what we still need. But I think we're about there." Fae shuffled back to the stove and drained the pink water into a jar. The avocado pits had given their all for the beautiful fuchsia color. Who knew they could create such a shade?

Ella sorted the jars by pigment, in order of the rainbow. Every single color was represented, some in more than one tint. Fae added her pink and grinned before starting to clean up some of the mess scattered over the table.

"What are you going to paint with all these gorgeous colors?" Fae's question echoed through Ella's head.

"I honestly don't know. I meant to use Mom's favorite overlook as my background with some deer. But I can't do that with these. I wouldn't know where to begin. It needs the richer and darker tones I get from acrylics, oils, or pencils."

"Okay. So think of something else that inspires you. You're so good at all you do."

Ella shook her head but closed her eyes and thought back through different times and places that had taken her breath away. Almost every one of her favorite moments had two people in them. Two people who obviously needed to be in her painting.

She pulled out her sketch pad and started penciling in the silhouettes. Where should they be standing? The fuchsia caught her eye again. Sunset. Or sunrise. Either way, that pink needed to streak across the sky. Mountains, obviously. She had a few pencils with her. Maybe she could afford a few more to work in details and let the paint be the background.

"There's my girl." Fae squeezed her shoulder. "You work. I'll make dinner."

Ella's lips turned into a grin. *Okay, God. Let's do this. Take my idea and show me how to pull it off.*

* * *

"It's looking great." Dad clapped Chaz on the shoulder as he stood in the contest room and studied the landscape wall.

"Yeah?"

"I wouldn't say it if it weren't true." Dad grinned, his goatee twitching. "I had no idea there were so many amazing artists in the state yet to be discovered. Why didn't you talk me into this sooner?"

"In my defense"—Chaz raised a finger—"I did try."

"I know, son. I know." Dad turned and gazed over the portraits next. There weren't quite as many of those. Then the still lifes, and finally, the more abstract pieces.

"How will we choose the top three?" Chaz spoke the question that had bothered him for a couple weeks now. "There are so many styles. I'm beginning to think I should've given more specific parameters."

"Too late for this year." Dad nodded. "But we'll get through and maybe tighten things in the future."

"So you think this is something we can continue?"

"I'm thinking we may need to add a wing to the gallery dedicated to artists from the state." Dad stroked his beard. "I did some research. While other galleries in West Virginia feature local artists, a lot of them have limited space. We can really make something of this."

Wow. To go from his dad barely listening to singing the praises of his idea was intense. But Chaz wasn't about to complain. This was exactly what he wanted. Mostly.

A week had passed, and he still hadn't seen Ella. Hoping to catch her at the hotel, he'd stopped by there each morning. But no Ella. And she was the one he wanted to share with about his success. He glanced around at all the artwork surrounding him. Something told him she'd understand.

"You looked like you were still waiting on something when I walked in." Dad's voice brought Chaz back to the present.

"I don't know. I mean, I'm sure a few more entries will come in over the next week. Some people wait until the last minute." Chaz scratched his chin. "It seems like something is missing, but I have no idea what."

"*Ooh!*" A voice Chaz had hoped not to hear again until Sunday at the earliest sounded right behind him.

"Bellamy." He turned and gave her what he hoped was a pleasant smile. "What can we help you with today?"

"I just wanted to come by and see how my picture looks hung on the wall. It makes it so real, ya know?" She waved a hand toward the abstract wall.

"Yours is just over there." Chaz motioned the opposite direction. "But contestants—or anyone else—aren't supposed to be in here until we've received all the entries and have them set up. New pieces are still arriving every day."

"Really?" She scrunched her nose. "I had no idea there were that many artists around here."

"Neither did we. But we're thrilled at the outcome." Dad moved over and motioned her back toward the entryway. "Let's save the excitement for the gala in a few weeks, though. It makes it more fun."

"I'm so excited." Bellamy clapped her hands. "I've already picked out my dress."

"Great." Chaz cleared his throat.

"It's blue. Now you know." She touched his sleeve. "In case you, you know, you wanted to look for me. Or even match."

Chaz tugged at the collar of his sweater. "I'll probably just wear my suit. I mean, we're calling it a gala, but it's not like a fancy masquerade ball or anything."

"Oh! A masquerade be so much fun. We could all wear masks, and you wouldn't know who the artists were until after you announced the winners." Bellamy spun in a circle. "Can we do that? I've always wanted to go to a masquerade."

"That might be too much to pull off for this party. Maybe for the opening of the new exhibition." Dad smiled. "That will be a fancier occasion, for sure."

"And just think." Bellamy clasped her hands together. "My artwork will be displayed for all to see."

"If you win," Chaz couldn't help but remind her. "The

contest isn't over yet. There are hundreds of great entries. And we'll only pick three to receive a contract with the gallery."

"Right." Bellamy simpered. "But I know how much you love my train, Chaz. It's a shoo-in."

Chaz cleared his throat. "I'm only one of the judges."

"I'm sure you can"—Bellamy lowered her voice to a whisper—"use your good influences on the others."

"Anyway, as lovely as it was to see you again, we've got more work to do to prepare for the contest." Chaz motioned toward the door. "I'm sure I'll see you soon."

"Sunday, right?" Bellamy lifted her brows. "And maybe you can have lunch with me this time? I'm asking early enough that surely you don't have plans with anyone else already."

"Actually ..." Dad stepped over, rescuing Chaz once more. "He's supposed to eat with his mom and me on Sunday this week. We haven't had him for a Sunday lunch in a long time."

"Oh." Bellamy pouted. "Maybe next week."

"We'll have to wait and see." Chaz refused to make any promises. This girl would not take a hint.

After she finally left, Chaz turned to his dad and groaned. "Why couldn't I have been born ugly?"

"You take after your mom." Dad shrugged. "And I married a beautiful woman. Blame her."

Chaz groaned again before returning to his office to work on the advertisements for the viewing sessions and the gala. As good as it was to have more work to do, sometimes he missed being able to get out and ignore his responsibilities here.

This is what I asked for. And he loved it. He'd just love it more if it left more time for seeing Ella. And if he wasn't trapped here where Bellamy could keep finding him.

18

"I need you to do me a favor." Ella held her phone to her ear and crossed her fingers, hoping Kari would agree.

"What kind of favor?" Though Kari's voice held caution, she didn't outright turn her down.

Ella released a pent-up breath. "Do you think you could get Jake to distract Chaz? Maybe even lure him out of the gallery for an hour this afternoon?"

"What's going on, Ella?" Kari lowered her voice as if she didn't want to be overheard.

"I finished my art piece. It's ready to be submitted to the contest. But I ... If Bellamy finds out that Chaz knows I'm an artist, it could be bad. She's already destroyed—" Ella swallowed a lump of emotion.

So far this week, she'd been able to avoid her stepsister. Good thing, considering her fingers were still stained.

"Has she hurt you?"

Ella shook her head. "No. Not physically. But she destroyed several of my drawings. And threw away most of my supplies."

"Ella." Kari's reply came out like a gasp.

"It's okay. I figured it out, and now I need to get this

submitted. But Chaz can't know. Not until the truth about Bellamy is exposed and she has no way to retaliate."

"Well, good news. Jake is actually at the gallery already. I think he's hoping to try and talk Chaz into hunting in a few weeks. Opening day and all that." Kari tapped something on her end. "Let me see if I can talk him into convincing Chaz to leave for a bit. No telling how much time it will buy you, but I'll let you know as soon as I find out."

"You're the best." She set her phone aside and focused on the task at hand.

Ella wrapped the frame in some brown paper Fae had given her, taping the edges closed. It didn't completely disguise it, but at least it hid the details from prying eyes. She carefully laid it on the floorboard of her truck and climbed in. While waiting for Kari's go-ahead, she could drive over and park at the restaurant across the street.

The text came before she arrived, so she sped up a bit and whipped into a spot in front of the gallery. Deep breath. She could do this. All her hard work the last weeks would not be for nothing. She had to at least try—for Fae, if for no one else.

"You'll never win anything if you don't enter, dear heart." Fae's words rang in her head.

She nodded, hopped out, and gathered her painting. Time was wasting. Kari hadn't been sure how long she could keep the boys away.

"Can I help you?" An older lady with bright-green glasses hanging from a chain around her neck greeted her.

"I have an entry for the art contest." Ella shifted the heavy frame.

"Of course. Right this way."

Ella followed the woman to what must be Chaz's office. His name was on a plaque beside the door, and his cologne lingered in the air. She forced herself not to take a deep whiff.

"We'll need you to fill out these forms." The lady motioned to a sofa and handed her a pen. "Let's see what you've got."

Ella tried not to watch while she unwrapped it, but she couldn't help but sneak peeks between entering her information. Last name: Renders. First name: ... Ella paused. If she wrote her first name, Chaz might figure out it was her. Not that she was the only Ella in West Virginia. And he didn't know her last name, as far as she was aware. But it was a risk.

She'd signed her painting as "E. Renders." Surely that would work here too. She wrote the initial and moved on.

The woman gasped, and Ella glanced over. Her painting leaned against the wall, the afternoon sun acting like a spotlight to highlight the sunset in the frame. If they could capture this lighting, she might have a chance.

"This is stunning, young lady." The woman nodded. "What medium did you use? Watercolor?"

"Yes. Natural watercolors and some pencil for the details. With a bit of charcoal." Ella filled the information in on the form as she said it out loud. The charcoal was for her daddy.

"Well, it's a great combination. Good job."

Ella's heart soared. *Okay, God. It's up to You now.*

She handed her forms to the nice lady and shook her hand before pulling her coat tighter and heading back out into reality. Just being in the gallery motivated her, even though it was daunting. So many amazing pieces had already been submitted. Did hers really deserve to be among them?

I'm just in it for the runner-up lessons, she reminded herself. *God, You hear me? That's all I want. Thanks.*

"Ella."

She froze. Chaz stood right in front of her, directly between her and the door. Now what? She fiddled with the belt on her jacket. She hadn't seen him since Sunday when she'd hurt his feelings. Wrapping her arms around her middle, she tucked her hands under her elbows to keep them from fidgeting. And yet he was still talking to her. Sort of. She swallowed. If only she knew what to say in response.

"You're here?" A frowned wrinkled his forehead.

"Um, yes." She played with a button on her trench coat. So much for keeping her hands tucked. "Hi."

"Did Bellamy send you for something?"

"Oh. No." Ella shook her head, her ponytail whipping her cheek. "No. Bellamy and I ... We're not really talking right now."

"Oh." He took a tiny step closer. "Why are you here?"

That was the question she'd hoped he wouldn't ask. How to answer? She couldn't tell the truth. Not yet. She ran a hand over her mouth.

"Were you looking for me?" He spread his hand across his chest.

"Well ..." She ducked her head. She'd been trying not to see him, but she couldn't deny a surge of happiness that he'd shown up before she left. How had he worked himself into her life in such a large way in such a short time?

"I missed you this week." His words came out soft.

"Me too." She couldn't have held back the admission if she'd wanted to.

"Come to dinner with me." He reached out to grab her hand and squeezed it. "Please. I'll even buy you pepperoni rolls, if that's what you want."

Her lips turned up of their own volition. But she should probably say no. What if Bellamy saw them?

"Chaz ..."

"Please, Ella. Only dinner. I'll even make sure you get home early since I know we both work tomorrow."

She pinched her lips together but gave a quick nod. "All right."

"Yeah?"

She nodded again. "Yeah."

"Don't go anywhere. I'll be right back. I just have to tell Gertie I'm leaving." He hopped a bit as he moved past her but then spun around and pointed. "Seriously. Stay right there."

She giggled and confirmed she wasn't moving. Oh, she was in trouble. But how could she bring herself to hurt him again?

"What are you doing?" Jake's voice startled her.

She glanced over her shoulder and caught her breath as he stepped out from behind a pillar. "Jake. You scared me."

"Good." He crossed his arms over his chest. "Because that's my best friend you're messing with."

She shook her head. "I'm not trying to mess with him. Honest, Jake."

"Really?" Jake lifted a brow and reminded her of a look Kari liked to give—usually to him. "Because he was pretty upset on Sunday after you pulled that little avoidance stunt. I just want to make sure that's not going to happen again."

"Look, it's complicated, okay?" Ella tugged at the end of her ponytail. "I don't want to hurt him. Maybe I should just go—"

Jake grabbed her arm as she started to leave. "Oh no, you don't. You said you didn't want to hurt him. Disappearing after promising him a dinner together ... What do you think that's going to do to him?"

"What's going on?" At Chaz's voice, Jake loosened his hold on her arm, though his expression told her she better remember what he said. As if she could forget.

"I was just telling Ella about something that happened earlier this week." Jake stepped back and brushed off Ella's sleeve.

"To Kari?" Chaz frowned. "Is she okay?"

"Yep. You know her. She can take care of herself."

Chaz nodded but didn't appear convinced.

"I'm guessing I'm being ditched." Jake thumbed Ella's direction.

"Don't take it personally." Chaz rubbed the back of his neck.

"I get it, man. See you soon. The deer are calling." Jake backed away, but not without pointing at Ella one more time.

* * *

The lighting at King Tut's drive-in cast funny shadows on Ella as she stared out the windshield while they waited on their burgers. Why she wanted to come here on such a chilly night, he had no idea. But at least the heat in his Jeep worked.

The carhop rolled out with their tray and smiled as she delivered their meals. "Can I get you anything else?"

"Need any ketchup or anything?" he asked Ella.

"I'm good."

"That's it. Thanks." He passed her a tip then rolled the window back up to keep out the cold air.

He put a hand to Ella's to stop her from unwrapping her food. "Pray with me?"

She nodded, and he intertwined their fingers before offering up a simple prayer. It didn't cover half of what he wanted to discuss with God. Though he did throw in a "thank You" for allowing him to bump into Ella this evening. He still wasn't sure why she'd been at the gallery, but he wasn't about to throw away this opportunity.

He tugged Ella's hand over and pressed a kiss to it before she could pull away. Her fingertips were ... blue? Green? He caught them and turned them this way and that in the dim light, baffled.

"What is this?"

She tugged free. "I was helping Fae with a project earlier this week, and it left our fingers stained for a few days. It's almost gone, honestly."

"This is almost gone? I can't imagine how bright the colors were right after your project." He chuckled, then paused. "It's nothing toxic, right?"

"Nope." Ella slurped her drink. "All natural. Just takes a few days to fade."

"I never know what color your fingers will be. Black, blue ..." He motioned to her hands, now wrapped around her burger. "Green."

Almost like paint or ink ...

Another piece of the puzzle that was Ella nearly wiggled into place.

She stilled and turned wide eyes his way. "Are they dirty that often?"

"No, not dirty." He stroked her cheek. "But it keeps me curious. About what you do when you're not at the flea market. When you're spending time with Fae. What is she having you do that leaves your fingers mimicking a rainbow?"

Ella chewed her bite for a minute before wiping her mouth. "Dyes. Made from natural ingredients. It took a lot of trial and error to get the shades we wanted."

"Natural dyes." He blinked. "Fae sure is an eccentric soul, isn't she?"

"She is." Ella nodded. "But she's like a mother to me. I couldn't ... well, couldn't really do anything without her."

"She seems amazing. I didn't mean anything bad by what I said." He popped a fry in his mouth.

"No. You were accurate. She's eccentric. And sometimes flamboyant. But always authentic and loving and strong and faith-filled." Ella rested her head against the seat and glanced his way. "She reminds me often of things I'm tempted to forget."

"Like?"

"Like how God made me exactly how He wants me. Like I am still loved even though my parents are gone. Like if God wants something to happen, He will provide a way."

"I was reminded of something like that recently." Chaz picked an onion off his burger and took another bite, chewing slowly to give himself time to figure out how to express what he wanted to say. "Before this contest, my dad was against every idea I had for so long, I wondered how I was ever going to convince him to go along with this."

Ella listened, her focus on him.

"Then I found that drawing in your booth."

Did she cringe at that? When he looked again, her face was clear of emotion. Maybe it was the lighting.

"And then, another artist who had space with us backed out of his contract and left a large area to fill. Just the right timing to suggest this idea for filling it."

"That's amazing." Ella gently touched his hand, and his heart skipped a beat. It was the first time she'd reached out to him.

"I've offered lots of thanks for it. God and I haven't been on speaking terms much over the last few years. But Jake kept bugging me to join him at church. And you were there too. And that sermon the first week ..." Chaz shook his head. "It's like He was trying to get my attention."

"He does that." Ella smiled before turning back to what was left of her food.

"I'm figuring that out." Chaz glanced at her out of the corner of his eye. "I don't suppose you'd be willing to explain what happened Sunday?"

Ella stilled. "I can't, Chaz."

His heart sank a degree. He'd half expected that answer, but it still stung. As if she didn't trust him enough to open up all the way. They remained quiet for several minutes, tension thick between them.

"I'll be pretty busy over the next few weeks," Chaz said, breaking the silence. "There's only a few more days for artists to submit their work to the contest. Then the judging begins, and the gala right after Thanksgiving so we can announce the winners."

"Did you receive many pieces?" Ella's question sounded more than casually curious. Was she excited on his behalf?

"Way more than I expected. I think it blew my dad away. He had no idea our state had so many undiscovered, talented artists." Chaz wadded up his trash and stuffed it back into the bag. "We've completely filled up that empty room. Even had to bring in a few moveable walls to hang more. It's surpassing my dreams, for sure."

"That's ... great, Chaz." Ella added her trash to his.

"You okay?" He reached out and clasped her hand again. "You sound a little down."

"I'm fine. Just dreading going back to the flea market tomorrow." She closed her eyes. "I don't mind the place or the people. It's ..."

"Having to see pieces of your past walk away."

"Yes." She met his gaze. "Yes. It's like I'm losing my parents over and over again."

The console didn't make it easy, but he pulled her as much into his arms as he could, cradling her head to his shoulder. "I'm sorry."

"It's not your fault."

"But I added to it."

She shook her head. "Those dishes would've sold

eventually. Better for them to go to someone like you than a stranger."

He pressed a kiss to her temple. "Well, I'm glad you deem me worthy of owning your mom's dishes. My mom was thrilled with them, by the way."

"Of course you're worthy." She sat back and wiped her cheek. "Definitely out of my league."

"What?" He grabbed her chin and gently turned her face his way. "Says who?"

"Isn't it obvious?"

"All I see is someone amazing and kind and beautiful. Probably more so in all those categories than I am. Maybe you're out of *my* league."

Her breath hitched, and his gaze dropped to her lips. What would happen if he closed the few remaining inches between them? Would he chase her away again? Would she welcome his kiss?

A car horn blared nearby, and they both jumped, moving back to their separate sides of the car. He cleared his throat, and she smoothed her jacket.

"I promised not to keep you out late, didn't I?"

She nodded.

"Okay, then." He pulled out and drove her back to her truck at the gallery.

Before he could climb out and open her door, she had done it herself. She had her truck unlocked before he reached her.

"Ella."

She paused, still facing her vehicle.

"Please, don't stay away so long this time."

"You said yourself that you're about to be very busy."

"I still have to eat dinner." He tugged her fingers. "And, would you possibly consider attending the gala? It would mean so much to me …"

Ella spun around, her lips parting. "You want me there?"

"More than anyone else." He stepped closer, willing her to realize how important she had become to him. "Will you come?"

"I'll—" She glanced to the side, as if fighting with herself. "I'll try."

"That's all I can ask." He squeezed her arms before stepping back once again. "See you Sunday at worship?"

She nodded and climbed into her seat before he could press another kiss to her cheek. It was progress, right? She had come to dinner with him. He stuffed his hands in his pockets and leaned against the cold metal of his Jeep. They'd just have to see how things went on Sunday and go from there.

19

"What are you wearing to the gala?"

Ella froze as she climbed into her truck and turned to face her neighbor. She'd put this moment off for over a week now, knowing Fae would try to go all fairy godmother on her. Good thing she'd already worked out a plan.

"Kari is loaning me a dress."

"Kari is six inches taller than you." Fae propped her fists on her hips.

"That's why God gave us safety pins." Ella winked and grinned, knowing Fae wouldn't let it slide that easily, but hopeful anyway.

"Ella Marie, you really want to attend one of the most important events of your life thus far in a dress held together with pins? Is that really the image you want to project as you accept your award?"

"Fae, the only place the dress doesn't fit is at the bottom. It's a very pretty dress. I'm not going to look like some orphan off the street." Not that she wasn't one, but that was beside the point.

"I'm sure it's a pretty dress, but I want you to look your best."

"I promise not to embarrass you." Ella raised her fingers in a scout symbol.

"And your shoes?"

Ella glanced down at her hand-decorated Converse. She was quite proud of them, honestly, but knew Fae wouldn't consider them appropriate for something like this. Good thing she had that covered already too.

"I'm wearing Mama's boots. My dress is long enough no one will even notice my footwear, and the boots have a slight heel, which will hopefully keep me from tripping on my hem." Ella tapped her wrist as if there were a watch there. "Now, are we done? Because I'm supposed to meet Kari to get ready."

Fae crossed her arms over her chest. "You're sure you won't let me help you come up with something nicer?"

"Fae, I'm not going to be one of the grand prize winners. No one will even notice me. I'm in it for the class vouchers they're giving to the runners-up. That's all." Especially after she heard how many entries there were in total. Over a hundred!

"You don't give yourself enough credit, dear one." Fae tugged her into a hug. "I just want you to be ready for whatever amazing things God has planned for you."

"It's okay, Fae." Ella burrowed her head in Fae's shoulder, breathing in her familiar floral scent. "Besides, it's too late for you to fancy me up. There's no time."

"You'd be surprised what I can do in no time." Fae pushed her back and held her shoulders. "But fine. I can see you're just as stubborn as I am. Go on. Wear Kari's dress. I'll just make sure you let me help you get ready for the ball when they open the new exhibit. In the meantime, I'd better get myself ready so I can see you win."

Ella shook her head but accepted what Fae meant as a blessing. Fae was wonderful, but she had much more faith in Ella's abilities than Ella did. Hopefully Fae wouldn't be too upset when Ella didn't win the grand prize.

Ten minutes later, she rushed into the Starbright Hotel. Kari grabbed her and yanked her down the hallway toward her personal apartment.

"Where were you? I thought you'd changed your mind."

"Fae intercepted me before I could leave. She didn't think a pinned-up dress was good enough, but I assured her it was." Ella slipped off her shoes and set them, along with her bag, in a chair before grabbing the dark-blue gown and heading to the bathroom to change. Shutting the door, she hung the dress on the hook. "Sometimes she acts a little too much like she's my fairy godmother."

"I could use one of those every now and then. Where do I sign up?" Kari's voice came through the door a bit muffled.

"Something wrong?" Slipping the velvety fabric over her shoulders and hips, she almost felt like a princess.

"No. I just don't think you realize how great you have it sometimes."

Ella tugged at the zipper, but it wasn't cooperating. "Hey, can you help me with this?"

Kari poked her head in and finagled the zipper into place before stepping back and nodding. "Beautiful."

"If you say so." Ella flipped her hair over her shoulders. "Hair down? Or up?"

Kari tilted her head back and forth. "Up. I can braid it into a coronet."

"You don't think I'll look like I'm trying to be uppity? Like royalty?"

"You sort of look like royalty in that color." Kari dragged a chair in and pushed Ella into it. "Besides, we're going to the Prince Gallery."

Ella smiled and let her friend do her hair. Kari wore a red dress with slightly puffy sleeves. Ella's dress was sleeker, with a bit of sheer fabric over her shoulders. Too bad she didn't have a fur to wear with it. Mom's old trench coat would have to do once again.

"Voila." Kari stepped back and motioned to Ella's head. Her blonde hair now sat braided in a crown around her head, tiny tendrils framing each side of her face to soften the look.

"Are you sure it's not too much?" Ella touched a bobby pin digging into her scalp.

"It's just right." Kari slapped her hand. "Now let's go, or we're going to be late."

Ella slipped into her boots and followed her elegantly dressed friend back out to the lobby. Jake turned where he'd been pacing in front of the door. He let out a whistle and bent both elbows.

"I guess I can't complain too much about how long it took you to get dressed. Not when I get to escort two of the prettiest girls. Let's go."

Ella rolled her eyes but played along.

"You better not let Chaz hear you say that." Kari poked her brother.

"Why's that? I can't imagine he'd disagree." Jake smirked.

They piled into his truck—thankfully he'd cleaned it out after hunting last weekend—and were on their way. The gallery's parking lot overflowed, but the businesses to each side had opened their lots for the event. Jake found a spot on the far side of the CPA's office. Considering the way more cars continued to pour in, the businesses farther down might have to share some space too.

"Ready?"

Ella blinked and realized both her friends were waiting for her to climb out of the truck.

"I guess?"

"That doesn't sound very certain." Jake lifted her out of the truck and shut the door before she could change her mind. "Now that Kari finally told me about your art, I want to see it."

Kari had spilled the beans after that day Chaz took her to dinner. Jake had apparently come back to the hotel all in a dither over how horrible Ella was to treat Chaz as she had. Kari's explanation helped some, though Jake still didn't know everything about Bellamy's threats. Even Kari didn't know *everything*.

How Ella would avoid Bellamy tonight, she had no idea. But it was too late now. Her artwork would be displayed with all the others—one with her name on it, and one without. What would she do if the piece Bellamy had claimed won but her other entry didn't?

She froze and reminded herself to breathe.

"You okay?" Kari squeezed her arm. "Because your painting is amazing, and you have no reason to be ashamed."

"Just dreading what may happen when Bellamy finds out I entered the other piece."

Kari exchanged a look with her brother before tugging Ella's arm to get her moving again. The crisp, early-December wind cut through her thin coat, but the warmth of the gallery spilled out and wrapped around them. The noise of laughter and conversation buzzed through the air as they entered the lobby and gave up their coats.

Ella placed a hand to her belly and took a deep breath. This would be the first time she'd see the other pieces. Was she ready for this?

People were everywhere, leaning close to see details, glancing up to view the pieces hung higher. The room was large but full. They had moved the temporary walls out to the lobby to provide more space for people. Near the entry to the office wing, refreshments were set on a black-clothed table. Fancy dresses and men's suit coats, perfume and cologne, sparkling jewelry ... it all overwhelmed Ella. She didn't fit here.

"Let's find yours." Kari grabbed Ella's arm as if she knew Ella was about to make a break for it.

Into the throng they strode. Ella scanned each piece. Where was her silver frame? Ironically, it hung right next to the piece Bellamy had claimed. How had that happened when they entered them so far apart?

A hand settled on her shoulder, and she spun to see who was there. Chaz. Her lips parted in a smile before she could hold it back.

"Ella?" Chaz reached out and clasped her hands. "You look beautiful."

She ducked her head. "Thanks."

"Are you admiring Bellamy's piece?" Chaz glanced over his shoulder at her first drawing.

Kari stepped forward. "Actually—"

A loud screech tore across the room.

Ella braced herself. So much for avoiding Bellamy.

* * *

Was that sound even human? Chaz searched the crowd for the source, wondering if a wild animal had somehow snuck in through the open door. People parted left and right, making room for ... Bellamy. What in the world?

Ella's stepsister shoved her way through the people. Would he need to have her escorted out? That could make things interesting. Where was his dad? Was he seeing this too?

"How dare you?" Bellamy poked a finger into Ella's chest so hard even Chaz flinched.

Still holding her hands, he pulled her behind him to shield her from her stepsister, who he now faced. "What is going on?"

"She stole my painting."

Gasps sounded all around them. He needed to diffuse this situation, and fast. But how?

"You must be mistaken." Chaz shook his head. "Your artwork is right here."

"I'm talking about that one." Bellamy pointed to the one next to hers, one brow lifted. "She found it in my room and signed her name to it. And then she entered the contest."

Chaz blinked. Murmurs rippled through the room. He glanced behind him at Ella. Her eyes were hard to read, as multiple emotions flitted through them at lightning speed.

"You've got to be kidding me, Bellamy." Kari stepped forward. "Enough of this charade."

"Charade?" Bellamy looked Kari up and down as if she weren't worth her attention. "I don't know what you're talking about. I'm not the one pulling a charade here. Ella is, with her borrowed dress and fairy-tale hair. Who does she think she is?"

"Someone worthy of being here, unlike you." Kari moved closer to Bellamy so that Bellamy had to look up at her.

"Says her best friend. I supposed you believe all her lies?"

Ella stiffened behind Chaz, jerking her arm away from his light grip.

"Bellamy, what's going on?" Angela moved into the circle of tension. "You're making quite a scene, darling."

"Mom, she stole my painting." Bellamy pointed once again. "Signed her name to it and entered it in the contest."

Angela lifted a brow and peered at her stepdaughter. "I see."

"I'm sure there's a misunderstanding." Chaz glanced

between everyone around them. "Ella didn't even enter the contest."

"Then why is her name scrawled across the bottom of that painting?" Bellamy crossed her arms. "Why is she here?"

"I invited her." Chaz stared steadily at Bellamy while conflicting thoughts raced through his head. Was that the only reason she was here? She hadn't ever shown fondness toward her stepsister, so she couldn't be here to support her. He glanced over his shoulder at the woman in question, her fingers a normal hue tonight. Had she entered the contest without him realizing it? But he saw every single piece, every name. He didn't remember seeing an Ella.

"Here you are." Fae approached, sizing up the situation and wrapping an arm around Ella's other side. "I see I'm just in time."

"Can I have your attention, please?" Dad's voice sounded through the room.

Not good. Chaz needed to let his dad know about this situation before he announced the winners. What if this affected the outcome?

"As you all know, I'm Kingston Prince, and I own and manage this gallery." Dad scanned the crowd until finding Chaz and motioning his way. "My son Chaz, however, is the genius behind this event—an event we're definitely going to continue in the future."

Applause and cheers sounded throughout the room.

"You have all blown us away with your talent. West Virginia is well represented here tonight and will be from now on. This gallery will leave this room open for local artists, which will be chosen each year during the contest. Tonight, at our inaugural gala, we're going to announce the first three artists who will have a display here for the next year."

Everyone around Chaz stiffened, and he couldn't blame

them. He reached back until he found Ella's fingers and squeezed. She clung to his hand as if the outcome of tonight would change her whole life. Why was this so important to her? Had she really entered the contest?

"First up, we have promised to award two runners-up with a voucher to take an art class at the local university." Kingston opened the envelope in his hand and studied the crowd for a heavy moment, letting the suspense build. "The runners-up are: Wyatt South, for his acrylic of a black bear, and Katie Hammonds, for her pencil drawing of her grandmother."

Applause once again filled the space, and the two artists moved to the front to accept their vouchers and have pictures taken. Ella's fingers went limp in Chaz's hand. When he turned to glance her way, it was as if the sun had gone out. She blinked away tears.

"Are you okay?"

"Now, for the moment we've all been waiting for." Dad started again before Ella could reply. "The top three pieces chosen from this year's entries."

The air was thick with suspense. Bellamy bounced a bit, her hands clasped in front of her chest, all earlier strife seemingly forgotten. Ella stayed quiet and still behind him, but her grip tightened once more. Everyone held their breath.

Chaz had a bad feeling he was going to have to upset the apple cart after his dad announced the winners. Because Bellamy had claimed one of the winning pieces was hers.

20

Why wouldn't he announce the winners already? Ella waffled between wanting to know and wanting to run away before she found out. Her stepsister didn't seem bothered at all by the earlier turmoil. Maybe because Bellamy had been the cause?

Ella had been sure Chaz would believe Bellamy over her, but instead, he'd protected her and held her hand. Had anyone treated her like this since her father passed? Sure, Fae tried, but it wasn't the same. She gripped his fingers tighter, and he tugged her closer, pulling his hand free long enough to drape an arm around her shoulders. Fae released her on her other side but stayed close.

As laughter tittered around the room while Kingston Prince drew out the suspense even longer, Ella's heart pounded against her ribs. She wasn't even going to be able to hear the announcement over her pulse. She buried her head against Chaz's shoulder.

"First up, for his still-life charcoal drawing of boots and other work equipment, Frank Douglas." Another interminable moment stretched out as Mr. Douglas moved forward to accept his praise.

Finally, the applause died down, and Kingston held up his hands. "Now, for our next winner. A beautiful piece that sums up our gorgeous state quite nicely—Bellamy McIntyre, come on down. Her painting is of a coal train running through a valley."

Bellamy let out a shrill scream and jumped up and down like a cheerleader. Angela placed a hand on her daughter's shoulder as if to keep her from continuing her little show. Bellamy pranced up to Kingston and then actually curtseyed to the crowd.

Ella couldn't help the tears that ran down her cheeks. The world might never know, but that "painting" Kingston Prince loved so much was *her* drawing. Her name wasn't on the line, but it was still hers. She'd won, and the world would never know.

"Ella?" Chaz whispered right in her ear. "What's wrong?"

She shook her head. There was no way to let him know. No way to show him the truth without Bellamy throwing an even bigger fit.

"And the third winner, though in no way coming in last place, has captured the subject of her piece in a ... very unique way. She used all-natural watercolors and pencils ..."

Ella stiffened. No way.

"... to showcase one of the most stunning sunsets I've ever seen. E. Renders, please come up here."

She blinked slowly. Had he really just said her name? Her painting—a winner?

"Ella!" Kari tugged her arm. "Ella, go!"

"What?" Chaz looked from Kari to her.

"Darling!" Fae squeezed her other side. "I knew it!"

"You won!" Kari finally pulled hard enough to get Ella to move her feet.

Away from the shelter of Chaz's arm, the room was cold, though not as icy as the daggers thrown her way from her stepsister's eyes. What blizzard was she about to unleash on the world when she stepped up on that dais? Somehow, through the fog in her head, she realized Chaz followed close behind.

"Are you Ms. Renders?" Kingston held out his hand, a warm smile tipping up his goatee.

Ella nodded. "Ella."

"Ella." Kingston's gaze moved to Chaz then back to her, his grin widening. "Congratulations, Ella Renders."

"She didn't win!" Bellamy shoved between them, ripping the certificate he was handing Ella.

"Excuse me?" Kingston's smile vanished in an instant.

"She couldn't have won. It wasn't her painting." Bellamy crossed her arms, her face stony and fierce. "It was mine."

More gasps sounded. This could not be happening. Both of their pieces had won. Couldn't Bellamy simply accept that she'd won a battle and not continue to wage war? Why did it matter so much to keep up this charade?

"That's a very serious accusation, young lady." Kingston motioned with his head toward the office wing. "How about we go chat where it's quieter?"

Ella gulped. She'd been so close. The certificate was literally in her grasp. At least, part of it. One piece had fallen to the floor after Bellamy's fit.

"Come on." Kari was tugging her again. "You need to defend yourself. We cannot let Bellamy win again."

"We're here for you, Ella." Fae straightened her shoulder as if going into battle. Appropriate.

"Again?" Chaz's question reminded her that he was witness to everything going down. What must he think of all this? Did he believe Bellamy? All this time, Ella had hidden her art from him.

Angela and Bellamy waltzed into Kingston Prince's office as if they were co-owners. Kingston stopped at the door and motioned to the rest of their party. They filed past, pausing as they surveyed the room. Angela and Bellamy claimed the couch, which left two stiff chairs and the large chair behind the desk, unless someone sat with them. Ella wasn't volunteering.

Ella moved toward one of the chairs but didn't sit. Too much nervous energy. Kari and Fae remained beside her, a calming presence in the midst of the storm. Chaz hovered just inside the door, while Kingston leaned against his desk.

"Now"—Kingston rubbed his hands together—"let's start at the beginning. How do you two know each other?"

Bellamy glared at Ella but didn't say anything.

"She's my stepsister," Ella finally broke the standoff. "Her mother married my father."

"So, you live in the same house?" Kingston looked back and forth between them.

"We do."

"Did you two connive this plan to ruin my son's contest and gala?"

"No!" Ella straightened, glancing Chaz's way. He frowned, as if unsure what to think of any of it.

"I would never do anything to hurt Chaz." Bellamy pouted and purred his name. Her attitude sickened Ella. Bellamy's selfishness *was* hurting him, but she couldn't see it past her own wishes.

"And you're the mother?" Kingston pointed at Angela.

"I'm Bellamy's mother." Angela straightened. "Ella was mostly raised when I came into her life. I can't take any responsibility for how she turned out."

True enough, though the words still stung.

"Mostly raised?" Fae hissed. "At ten?"

Angela glared at Fae for a second before schooling her expression to appear placid again. "Some traits one can't out-train from a child."

Kari lunged, but Ella held her back. She was used to such "love," but Kari had never witnessed Angela at her worst. Now their family dynamic was on full display for the people Ella had hoped would never discover it.

Kingston pointed at Fae. "Who are you?"

"Her neighbor and sister in Christ." Fae raised her chin and met Kingston's stare straight on. "And I'm not leaving."

"I wasn't asking you to." Kingston glanced at Kari and nodded. Apparently, they knew each other through Jake and Chaz's friendship, because he didn't ask who she was.

"Meddling old fool," Bellamy muttered just loud enough to be heard.

"Enough." Kingston sliced his hand through the air. "I am not here to hear about your family issues. What I want to know is why this artist thinks the other stole her painting."

Ella swallowed. What could she say? If she protested, it would only make her look guilty. But remaining silent didn't exactly scream innocence, either. What was the best move here?

"I said it because it's true," Bellamy offered. "I had that painting in my room, and Ella stole it and signed her name to it because she knew I entered the contest and would most likely win. Chaz has been paying attention to her lately, and she probably wanted to keep his attention from transferring to me."

Angela glanced at her daughter but didn't refute anything she'd said.

"In fact," Bellamy continued, jabbing a finger Ella's direction, "the frame she used was stolen from a painting that used to hang on our living room wall. If you saw our house now, you'd think we had no artwork, because Ella has stolen all of it in the last few weeks. Probably pawned it somewhere."

"Pawned the portraits and landscapes my mother painted?" Ella pinched her lips tight for a second. "More like I saved them from you."

"Now, girls." Angela held out a hand to each of them.

"Saved them from me?" Bellamy pressed her fingers to her chest. "As if I would hurt a piece of art."

Ella's chest burned. Lies upon lies. When would it end?

"Can you prove without a doubt that you painted that landscape with Ella's name on it?" Kingston asked.

Ella waited, barely breathing. How would Bellamy get out of this? There was no way she could prove it, because it wasn't true. What story would she come up with?

The last few puzzle pieces Chaz hadn't been able to fit together before now slid into place at a rapid pace, showing him a picture he should've fully recognized earlier. Ella was the artist. Not only that, but she was the daughter of the artist whose painting he loved so much in his own dining room.

It was why her fingers were always stained. It was why he'd found that turkey drawing in the meadow after she ran away. It was why she'd been so conflicted during the awards ceremony a few moments ago.

But why hadn't she told him?

"How exactly am I supposed to do that?" Bellamy crossed her arms over her chest. Her answer didn't surprise him, because she couldn't prove it.

But they couldn't let this slide. Not considering so many guests heard her accusations about Ella's piece. There had to be another way besides this disaster of a meeting to solve the issue.

Dad met his gaze and nodded, giving him the floor.

Chaz stepped out of the doorway and stood next to his dad. "We can't necessarily do it right now, but there is a way to prove who the real artist is."

"How? Do you need to see my art supplies?" Bellamy shot a look Ella's way that said she was up to something beyond the craziness she'd already started tonight.

"No. No need for you to prove which supplies you used on the ... paintings we've already seen." Chaz folded his arms and tapped his fingers against his elbow. "I think we need to have a paint-off."

"A what?" both girls asked at the same time.

"We'll hold another competition. Whoever wins this one will be *the* winner, and the one who doesn't win will no longer be eligible to enter our contest or have anything to do with our gallery ever again."

Ella gasped.

"Brilliant." Fae nodded.

"I need to bring you another art piece?" Bellamy frowned. "By when?"

"Actually, to make it fair, I think we need to see you in action." Chaz fought a grin as Bellamy straightened and paled. Angela grasped her daughter's arm.

"You want us to paint something for you here?" Ella's voice was quiet, but he heard the fear. Why was she so afraid if she was the real artist?

"Right." Chaz glanced at his dad. "Don't you agree?"

"I do. In fact, I'll even provide the supplies. If you will both let me know what you need in the next few days, I'll purchase it all and have it ready to go by the end of next week. Then you can come in and work as many days you need to. We have those little studio rooms we never use—I think those will be perfect. We can lock the doors when you leave and unlock them when you arrive."

Chaz did grin this time. Gaining his father's support in his original crazy scheme had been amazing. But to see him have his back in this chaos? Priceless.

"What are we supposed to paint?" Bellamy narrowed her eyes.

"Whatever you want. You can paint or use pencils or pastels or whatever you prefer. And your subject matter is completely up to you, just like the first painting." Chaz stood straight. "Any other questions? Concerns?"

"Will we have a deadline?" Ella rubbed her throat.

"How long does it usually take you to complete a piece?" Dad asked.

Bellamy remained silent, watching Ella. Ella pursed her lips, took a deep breath, then sighed. "It honestly depends. I like to do a few sketches first, to get to know my subject matter. Then I do the background and pencil everything else in. Build it up from the bottom. Depending on how many days I have to work, it can take me a month to do one drawing. But this last painting I worked on more consistently so I could enter it before the deadline. So it took only a week."

"If we set everything up in the next week, would Christmas be too soon for you to finish?" Chaz asked.

Ella shook her head. "I think that will be okay. Will we only be able to come here during the hours the gallery is open? I work at the flea market Thursday through Saturday."

Angela scoffed but didn't offer to release her stepdaughter from the obligation, either.

"If you're willing to try and do most of it during open

hours, we can work with you if you need to come after hours once or twice," Dad answered for Chaz.

Ella nodded. "I'll make sure and get a list to you Monday."

Chaz turned his attention to the couch. "Bellamy, does that work for you?"

Bellamy stood, standing as straight as she could in her ridiculous heels. "I guess it's going to have to work for me, since you won't take my word for it."

"If you're telling the truth, there's nothing for you to worry about." Chaz raised a brow. "Right?"

"I don't work well under pressure." Her voice came out as a whine.

"I'm up for better ideas if you have suggestions." Dad pulled open the door.

"No. She'll follow your instructions." Angela grabbed Bellamy's arm and yanked her out of the office.

Ella paused in the doorway, Kari just outside the office. "Thank you."

"For what?" Chaz moved to stand beside her.

"For this chance."

Chaz opened his mouth to let her know she had nothing to worry about.

Ella was gone before he could reassure her.

"Interesting girl you have there." Dad remained by his desk, now flipping through papers.

"More like a girl I *want* to have. I don't think she believes she's good enough for me. And I can't figure out why." Chaz ruffled the front of his hair. "She's obviously the real artist."

Dad jerked his head up. "Why do you say that? Besides the obvious reasons."

Chaz ticked off the facts that had fallen in line for him earlier.

"It would have been a lot easier for you to tell us this

information beforehand instead of presenting this new contest idea. Why didn't you?"

"Ella needs to believe in herself. And I think the only way that's going to happen is if she wins on her own." Chaz stared off in the direction she had gone. "Besides, this will prove Bellamy a liar once and for all. She made enough of a commotion in front of the other guests. We need to make sure everything is very public when we announce the real winner. I just can't figure out why Ella never told me any of this before."

"Strange."

"I think we have one of her mom's paintings hanging on our wall."

"What?" Dad looked around as though the piece would appear before him. "No way."

"Not here. In our dining room." Chaz motioned with his hands as if outlining a frame. "The big landscape. I asked Mom about it a few weeks ago. She told me it was done by Sara Renders. And Ella's last name is Renders. Both of their pieces had a train. Coincidence?"

"Sara was your mom's friend. I tried to convince her to display some of her work here, but she never would. Said she painted for God's glory and not her own."

"I think there's a lot of her in Ella." Chaz sighed. "I just have to get Ella to see how talented she truly is."

Dad nodded. "But before we move on to all that, we better go through these judging forms one more time. You basically eliminated one of our winners, and we need to pick a new third."

Chaz slapped himself in the forehead. "That didn't even dawn on me."

They went through the results again until they finally reached an agreement. But even as Dad announced the newest winner to the crowd and explained about the paint-off, Chaz's mind remained on Ella. She'd disappeared with the Whites right after their meeting.

And while his gala was a success, all he wanted to do was disappear with them. To learn more about the intriguing artist and why she was so secretive about her drawings.

21

"I need to know how to do"—Bellamy motioned to Ella's sketch pad—"all that."

Across the flea market booth, Ella slowly lifted her head and fixed her stepsister with a stare. "And how does this concern me?"

Fae's voice in her head scolded her for her cold attitude. Not a very Christian way to react. But she was human, too, and the human inside her was fighting the urge for revenge.

Bellamy huffed and flipped her hair over her shoulder. "I just need to know what supplies to ask for. What did you use to do the painting I entered?"

"So you admit it was mine?" Ella kept her face as passive as possible, though one of her eyebrows twitched. "Funny how you told a different story last night."

"Come on, Ella. We both know how this is going to go down."

"Do we?" Ella shook her head. "Maybe you should enlighten me, because I don't think I see the same future as you do."

Bellamy crossed her arms. "You're going to give me some

quick lessons on how to do the art thing, then I'm going to go in there and win so I can have Chaz."

"You realize he's not actually being offered as one of the prizes, right?" Ella shifted on her chair, closing her sketch pad but not letting it go. "He's the one in charge of the contest, yes, but the prize is having your artwork hung in the gallery."

"Yeah, yeah." Bellamy brushed Ella's words aside with a flick of her wrist. "But if I have artwork in the gallery, I can be at the gallery and see Chaz all the time. By the way, I noticed you asking to come after hours. Brilliant. I'm totally taking advantage of that."

Ella squeezed her eyes closed and counted to ten. Would this girl ever learn anything? How had she come out of last night completely unchanged? What would it take for her to see the error of her ways?

"So, tell me how to do the things. And what to tell them I need." Bellamy flopped into Dad's chair and leaned forward, pulling out her phone. "I'm taking notes."

"Write this down." Ella leaned forward too.

Bellamy smiled expectantly.

"I'm not helping you."

With a huff, Bellamy threw herself back in the chair. "You can't leave me like this. Don't you understand what this means to me?"

"No, actually. I know what it means to me, but I have no idea what it means to you. You never indicated any interest in art until a few months ago when Chaz showed up. You aren't really interested in learning now. Otherwise, you'd at least know my piece you stole was a drawing done in pencil and charcoal—not a painting like you claimed. And you definitely wouldn't be treating it so flippantly."

"I haven't flipped anything," Bellamy scoffed. "Don't be stupid. I just want someone to notice me for once. Like they notice you with your stupid little drawings and innocent little smile."

"Then maybe you need to do something you're actually good at instead of taking credit for something someone else did." Ella raised a brow. "Ever think of that?"

"And what am I good at? I don't have artsy ability like you do."

"Surely you're good at something." Ella rubbed her forehead. How had she ended up being the counselor for her evil stepsister? "Baking? Fashion? Party-planning?"

"See? I'm perfect already." Bellamy bounced and beamed once more. "Chaz should choose me no matter what. I'm exactly what he needs."

A full-body massage wouldn't relieve Ella's oncoming stress headache. Just when she thought she might be reaching Bellamy ... this! Ella kneaded her temples to no avail.

"Besides, you gave me what I needed. Pencils and charcoal." Bellamy nodded. "I'll look up YouTube videos on how to use those to draw ... things ... where there's mountains and stuff. Whatever that's called."

Ella barely stifled the urge to growl. Was Bellamy for real? How could they believe she was a true artist after all this? Wasn't it obvious she had no clue about art? That mat she'd chosen for the landscape had almost ruined Ella's picture. Amazing that Bellamy had been chosen to begin with, considering how she'd displayed the drawing.

"YouTube is the best." Bellamy flashed her screen at Ella. "Over a hundred videos. Perfect."

"You can't really expect this to work." Ella leaned her head back against the flea market booth wall.

"Why not?" Bellamy shrugged. "YouTube is a way better teacher than any of my college professors. They're so boring. All these videos have music in the background."

The smell of pepperoni rolls wafted to Ella from somewhere nearby, taking her mind back to the night Chaz had shown up with them and sat and talked to her for over an hour. What did he really think of everything that had happened the night before? Did he consider his gala ruined? Would he ever speak to her again about something besides this contest? Did she still want him to, or was she too embarrassed?

"You know, even if you somehow pull off a miracle and win the art contest, Chaz still isn't going to be interested in you." The words escaped Ella's mouth as Bellamy was preparing to leave.

"Why not?" Her stepsister spun, her face no longer displaying anything but rage. "Because he's in love with you? Please. How could he like anyone who walks around with dirty fingers all the time? Just like the fairy tale your dad used to read to you. Rendersella." Bellamy shook her head. "I supposed you think he's your Prince Charming, come to rescue you from your evil stepsister?"

Ella had a million replies, but she bit back most of them. "I suppose you think just because you're a stepsister, you have to be evil? That's not the way it works, you know?"

Bellamy rolled her eyes.

"Besides, I have nothing to do with Chaz not wanting you. He isn't in love with me. There's no way. But he isn't the kind of guy who's going to want someone fake and pretentious. He'll marry someone real and down-to-earth, who doesn't try to pretend to be something she's not to get his attention. He's going to want someone comfortable in her own skin—not trying to wear someone else's."

"You don't think that's you?" Bellamy crossed her arms again.

"No. I've never been comfortable in my own skin." Ella

looked away, focused on the shelf full of records across the booth.

"Whatever. I have videos to watch." Bellamy stormed out of the booth, leaving a cloud of her cloying perfume behind.

But somewhere in the midst of the perfume, Ella caught another whiff of pepperoni rolls. If only it meant Chaz were here. She shook her head. On second thought, maybe she wasn't ready to face him again.

She reopened her sketch pad and studied the rough outline of the turkey she'd been working on. Too bad she didn't have time to go back to that meadow and study the birds once more. How she wished she hadn't lost her best drawing from that day! But it had disappeared when she rushed to escape Chaz, back when she was trying to avoid him.

"Special delivery." Someone rapped on the doorway.

Ella glanced up, hoping to see the person she'd been thinking about. Instead, Jake stood there with a container in his hands. He lifted it up, and she realized it held what she'd been smelling.

"How long have you been lurking?"

"I don't lurk." Jake straightened and tried to look dignified. "Although apparently, I can be coerced into errands for friends willing to go hunting with me in the wee hours of the morning."

"You must have already snagged your deer if you're back in time for lunch." Ella grinned at her friend's brother.

"I did. An eight-point buck. My best yet."

"Very nice. I'm sure Kari will love that head being added to the fireplace at the hotel." Ella smirked.

"She decorates all the rooms and other areas. I get the fireplace." Jake shrugged and handed her the take-out container. "It's a fair trade."

"Are these from ..."

"Chaz. He wanted to come himself." Jake glanced over his shoulder then back at her. "But he figured you weren't ready."

"How much of our conversation did you hear?" Ella poked her thumb in the direction Bellamy had stalked off.

"Enough."

"We did get along for a while. When she first moved in." Ella leaned back and closed her eyes. "But it didn't last into our teen years. Something changed between us, despite only being a few months apart in age. And then Dad died, seemingly sealing our fate."

"You going to be okay? Living in the same house as her?" Jake shrugged. "We always have extra rooms. You're welcome to come crash for a while." He glanced over his shoulder again. "Other people do."

Was Chaz out there? Better not to know. Ella traced the edge of the warm container in her lap and shook her head. "Thanks, but I'm okay for now."

"You'll let me know if that changes?"

"I will, Jake. Seriously, thanks."

"See ya later, then." He saluted and spun around, walking away.

Ella opened the container and inhaled the spicy aroma. Could she fall in love with someone because he fed her? Whoa. There was a thought that had no right to be in her head. Must be her hunger talking.

* * *

"Would you like to go ahead and just tell her I was standing there?" Chaz hissed as Jake wandered over, hands in his pockets and looking quite pleased with himself.

"Didn't think I needed to." Jake passed him without waiting for him to catch up. "Ella's a smart girl."

"Especially when you make it obvious that you're not there by yourself."

"I wasn't there *for* myself." Jake glanced over his shoulder, brows raised. "I've never seen Ella in the light you seem to see her. To me, she's just Kari's weird friend."

"Weird?" Chaz fell into step beside him as they walked out into the cold Saturday afternoon.

Jake shrugged. "She's always been sort of quiet and secretive. When she stood up to Bellamy this morning, that was probably the fiercest I've ever seen her. Her jeans always have holes, and she never has a coat that looks warm enough. But if you offer to help her, she always turns you down. I'm sort of surprised she accepted the food."

"She really likes pepperoni rolls." Chaz contemplated Jake's words. He figured she wore the holey jeans because it was a style. But was that the only reason? And that night he'd loaned her his sweatshirt ...

"Who doesn't?" Jake rubbed his hands together. "And now that I've finished delivering hers, we can eat ours."

"Do you ever think of anything besides hunting and eating?" Chaz shook his head and climbed into the Jeep.

"Only when I have to." Jake opened his container and took a huge bite. "Mmm. Killing animals always works up an appetite."

"And you wonder why you're single."

"Says the other single guy." Jake wiped his mouth on his jacket sleeve.

"I'm working on changing that."

"By sending me to do your dirty work?"

"Delivering food is not dirty work."

"I mean, it could be." Jake finished off his meal.

"Did you get dirty?" Chaz fixed him with a stare.

"Not that time." Jake licked his fingers. "It did make me feel a bit like a spy, though. The movies make spies look much cooler."

"If you were a spy, what intelligence were you gathering? I heard everything you did."

"But you didn't see everything I did." Jake lifted one of his brows.

Chaz leaned back and waited. "Okay. What did you see that will help me?"

"What Ella was working on."

Chaz's curiosity stood at attention, but he wasn't about to give Jake the pleasure of letting him know. After all, he could be pulling his leg. Jake loved to pull pranks.

"You're not even going to ask?" Jake waggled his brows.

"Are you being serious right now?"

"Very serious." Jake huffed. "Fine. If you won't ask, I'll tell you. It doesn't matter to me. She was sketching what looked like a turkey."

"A turkey." Chaz searched his memory. Would she want to have her drawing back from the meadow? Would that win him brownie points, or make it look like he was favoring her over the other contestant? Not that he didn't favor her. "Man. I just thought of something."

"What's that?"

"I need to line up some other judges. I can't judge this contest. Neither can Dad. We know too much about the backstory. It wouldn't be fair."

Jake scratched his chin. "I guess that makes sense. But it doesn't seem right. I mean, we all know Bellamy is going to lose no matter what. Because if she can learn how to be an artist by watching YouTube, I'm going to start watching videos about how to be a billionaire."

"Oh boy." Chaz started the Jeep. "Why do I put up with you?"

"Because deep down inside, you enjoy it." Jake drummed his fingers on his legs. "So, tell me again why you're still going along with this crazy contest idea? It's obvious Ella is the real artist. Why allow Bellamy to embarrass herself further?"

"Ella needs to do this for herself." Chaz drove them back to where they'd left Jake's truck at the fast-food place. "She needs to prove she really is as good as we know she is, because I think she still doesn't see it herself."

"So crazy. How can she not see how good she is?"

Chaz shook his head. "How could my dad not see that there were so many great artists living in the same state as him just waiting for an opportunity? Sometimes we can't see what's right in front of our eyes until something big happens."

"Well, last night was big." Jake chuckled. "Whew. Bellamy sure can put on a show."

"Is it bad I'm dreading the next few weeks?"

"But you get to spend time with Ella." Jake punched his shoulder.

"And less time with you." Chaz punched him back. "You're right. This is going to be great."

"After I do all your dirty work." Jake put on a fake pout. "Some friend you are."

"I went hunting with you, didn't I? I took your picture with that big old deer. Even helped you load him into your truck to take to the processor. And bought you lunch."

"Okay, okay. So maybe you're not so bad." Jake pulled up the photo on his phone. "Man, that's a beaut."

Chaz chuckled. "Maybe you should suggest it for Bellamy to draw. She was looking for ideas."

Jake full-out belly laughed. "Yeah. I'll call it a landscape." Jake gathered his trash and moved to his own vehicle.

Long after Jake had gone his way, back at the gallery, Chaz contemplated the conversation they'd overheard. Why did women think he was some prize to win? Ella was actually the first one besides Kari who didn't look at him that way. Was that why he was so drawn to her?

No. She was much more than someone to win over. But more and more, that's what he wanted to do. His own personal contest.

22

When Ella arrived at the gallery on Monday, Bellamy's voice came from Chaz's office. Ella had seen him at church the day before, but besides exchanging a glance and a smile, they had no other interaction. Today, she didn't have a choice. She needed to turn in her list of supplies for the contest.

But there was no way she was facing Bellamy and Chaz at the same time. Not if she could avoid it. She waited in the hallway, where they couldn't see her through the door.

"Thanks so much for getting these supplies for me, Chaz. I'm sure you'll only buy the best of the best. And that will make my drawing even better."

"I thought you said you did a painting last time." Chaz's voice held no humor, but Ella couldn't stop her own grin.

Bellamy didn't even hesitate. "I use different mediums every time. I'm mixing it up, so to speak."

Ella rolled her eyes.

"Well, I'll be sure to get these purchased so you can start working. Any idea when you'll want to start? I'll set the room up for you."

"Can I see it today? I need to get a feel for the vibe. Is there lots of light?"

Ella sighed. This could take a while.

"Not today. We're still cleaning them out. But it does have a lot of sunlight. There's a big window in each room." Chaz's voice drew closer. "Just give Gertie a call when you're ready to get started on your drawing, and we'll make sure the space is ready."

"Perfect." Bellamy simpered. "You're so great, Chaz. Thanks again."

"You're welcome, Bellamy. I'll see you soon." He practically pushed her through the door. Ella ducked farther down the hallway and into an alcove, where Bellamy wouldn't see her. Chaz's door shut with a firm click. Bellamy huffed but left the gallery.

Ella drew a deep breath, waited a few more minutes, then approached Chaz's closed door. Would he take her list and push her out as quickly as he did her stepsister? If he did, he did. She needed to give him the list, no matter his welcome. She knocked and sent up a quick prayer for peace.

"Look, Bellamy—" Chaz swung the door open and froze. "Ella."

"Hi. I have my list." She held up her paper.

He glanced both ways up and down the hall, then grabbed her hand and pulled her into his office, closing the door behind them.

"Chaz, I—" Ella wasn't sure what was going on. He'd left the door open with Bellamy. Was he about to scold her and didn't want anyone to hear?

When he wrapped his arms around her and pulled her in close, her breath caught in her chest, and her throat tightened. She squeezed her eyes closed and let herself relax for a minute, inhaling his spicy scent and his warmth. Then propriety kicked back in, and she squirmed free.

"Sorry, Ella." He traced her cheek with a finger. "I couldn't resist. I've been so worried about you the last few days but didn't know how to help."

"Technically, I don't think you're allowed to help." Ella ducked her head and took another step back. "That wouldn't be fair to Bellamy."

Chaz shook his head. "I'm not actually a judge anymore. Or, at least, I'm working on that. I've been trying all morning to line up other judges from various galleries around the state. It hit me the other day that it wouldn't be fair for my father and me to judge this time. Because I know who I would choose."

Ella shook her head. "Still ..."

"I have something for you." He tugged her hand until she followed him to a shelf. He lifted a piece of paper and held it out.

"My turkey." She ran a finger lightly over the pencil marks. The tom had shown off that morning in the meadow, fluffing his feathers for full effect. This was the very thing she'd been wishing for the other day. "Where did you find it?"

"You left it behind on the rock when you ran away from me that day." His hand touched her arm. "I had no idea it was yours when I discovered it, though I should've made the connection. There were so many signs—like your colorful fingers." His own fingers trailed along her arm until they entwined with hers.

"I can never seem to keep them clean." She tried to pull free, but he tugged.

"I love it, honestly. It shows your passion and love for art."

A laugh burst from her. "Try telling that to Bellamy. She makes fun of me all the time. Says it's embarrassing."

"Well, we'll see how she likes it when her fingers look the same." He pointed to a pink piece of paper on his desk. "She asked for charcoal."

"Did she?" Ella moved over to study the curlicue letters. "Interesting. I always use charcoal on an element of my drawings. It makes me feel close to my dad—silly, I know. But he worked with coal. She doesn't have that connection. I guess she just wrote down what I mentioned using in the ..."

"In the train drawing?"

She pressed her lips tight. After months of hiding the truth, had he figured it out? Was she supposed to continue acting like it was Bellamy's since it was a finalist in the contest?

"You don't have to hide it anymore." Chaz shrugged. "I figured it out."

"Then why the contest?" Ella motioned toward the room where everything had blown up a few nights before.

"I didn't connect all the pieces until we were in the middle of that craziness, sadly. I should've, but I guess I was blind or something." Chaz ran his fingers through his hair. "Anyway, I still think this contest is a good idea. After all, what better way to prove once and for all that Bellamy isn't as talented as she keeps claiming she is?"

"Do you think it will really work?" Ella warmed at the idea of Bellamy getting her comeuppance, but she also wondered if it would backfire.

"I'm praying it will."

Ella nodded then remembered why she'd come in the first place. "Speaking of lists, here's mine."

He accepted the list and laid on his desk with Bellamy's, not even glancing at it.

"You don't want to see what's on it? It might be more than you bargained for when your dad offered to buy supplies for us."

"You painted the last piece with homemade watercolors, right?" Chaz lifted a brow. "Isn't that what you meant when you said 'natural' ingredients?"

Ella's cheeks heated. "My ... supplies ... weren't accessible at the time. I was making do."

"What happened to them?"

Ella looked away. No way would she let him know that Bellamy had destroyed so much in one day. Not only was it demeaning, but Bellamy already looked bad enough. No need to make it worse, even if it was. Even though they didn't get along, Angela and Bellamy were the only family she had left. And sisters in Christ.

"It doesn't matter. It all worked out." She tapped her list. "Please make sure this is okay and not too much."

He covered her hand with his. "It's fine. No matter what's on it."

"Chaz, please. I don't understand. Why are you treating me like this?"

"Like what? Like you're special? Like I care about you? Like I'm so glad to see you that I'm probably going to look for a way to spend as much time with you as possible before you insist on leaving?"

Her heart twinged as his words penetrated the broken places. Was he serious? Why? How?

For so long, Bellamy's taunts about Rendersella's dirty fingers had her believing no one could ever find her attractive. But Chaz liked her colorful fingers. He liked ... her?

Half of her brain fought to believe it, while the other half clung to what she'd always held as true.

* * *

She still didn't believe him. He could see it in her face. Had her life been so bad that she couldn't accept that someone loved her? How could he fix it? Because he wanted to fix this more than he'd ever wanted to fix anything in his whole life.

And she probably wouldn't let him. He might be a fixer, but she consistently turned down any help offered her. She wasn't the kind of girl waiting on a knight in shining armor. Not if her truck wasn't broken down, at least. Time to change the subject.

"So, you think that turkey sketch will help?" Chaz leaned against his desk as if he didn't care what her answer was. "Jake said you were sketching one at the flea market the other day."

"Were you spying on me?" She raised a brow, one side of her mouth tipping up. Everything in him yearned to close the gap between them.

He gripped the edge of the desk to help him resist the temptation. "I wouldn't say ... *spying*, per se. That word comes with such evil connotations, after all. Let's just say Jake happened to notice what you were doing while he was delivering the food."

"You don't have to keep plying me with food, you know." She ran her finger down the edge of his calendar. "I'm not starving or anything."

"I never said you were. I just know you like pepperoni rolls, and we happened to grab some, so I figured I'd send some your way too. And considering what happened the night before, I sent Jake instead of coming myself."

"I wasn't upset with you." She hugged herself. "I actually figured it was the opposite. That you assumed I had schemed with Bellamy to get more attention or something."

The idea was so preposterous, he couldn't resist teasing her. "Did you?"

Her head jerked his way. "No!"

Reaching out, he clasped her hands and tugged her closer.

"I never assumed it. Ella, I know you well enough by now to know you'd never even think of such a thing. Remember? I didn't even realize you'd entered. You signed your painting as 'E. Renders.' How was I supposed to know that was you?"

"You weren't." She looked away.

"Ella." He let go of one hand to reach up and turn her chin back his way. "Talk to me. Why did you hide your art from me? Didn't you think I'd be interested?"

"I didn't really think my art was good enough. Sure, it's been a dream for most of my life to have a painting displayed here, but when I entered the contest, I was only hoping to win one of the runner-up prizes. I wanted the lessons. And I figured if you knew about my drawing, you'd think I was spending time with you to try to get my artwork into the gallery."

He chuckled.

"What's so funny?"

"The only reason you spent time with me the last few weeks was because I basically forced you to. I invited you to lunch and showed up at the flea market and volunteered to come help with your truck. You weren't trying to spend time with me."

Her cheeks turned the most beautiful shade of pink he'd ever seen.

"So, do you think you can believe that I never would've assumed you were only spending time with me to display your artwork here?" He tugged her a tiny bit closer.

"Okay, so I concede that point. But can you see how it might've looked that way if I had tried to spend time with you instead of ... not?"

"Yes." He grinned. "I can see that. But you don't need more lessons. Your artwork is stunning already."

"There's always room for improvement." She shook her

head. "My pictures don't show any movement. And I'm horrible at faces."

He cut her off before she could protest any more. "Okay. I'll concede the point that you have some areas you can be stronger in. But you're already strong. Can you believe that?"

"I'll try. But it's hard."

"Ella, you were one of the winners. Two, if you think about it. Because Bellamy's drawing was yours too." Chaz shook his head. "If you win a third time, will you finally admit that you're a great artist?"

She giggled but repeated, "I'll try."

"I guess I'll accept that for now." He placed his hands on her waist. "Now, can I talk you into having dinner with me tonight?"

She blinked. Opened her mouth and closed it again. Shook her head, though she didn't look like she wanted to.

"Is there something about me you don't like?" It had never happened to him before, but there was a first time for everything.

"No, Chaz. No." Ella squirmed, but he refused to let her go. "I just don't want people to get the wrong idea. How would it look to others? To see someone fighting for a spot in your gallery who is also seen around town with you? To see us spending extra time together could make ... people ... think I'm trying to win by gaining your affections first. Rigging the contest."

"Well, you're not rigging the contest, because I'm not a judge. And you're not gaining my affections, because you already have them." He pulled her flush to his chest and pressed his forehead to hers. "But I can see what you're saying."

She closed her eyes and took a deep breath.

"These next few weeks are going to be really long." How

could he not try to spend as much time as possible with her when she was going to be so close?

She nodded, causing his head to nod along with hers.

"But you promise it's not that you're not interested?" he whispered.

Her eyes fluttered opened, the blue of her irises sending a jolt through his middle. "I promise."

Before he could stop himself, he pressed a quick kiss to her lips. When she drew in a sharp breath, he only wanted more. Instead of giving in, he leaned back and loosened his grip, letting her step back as well. She stayed in front of him, but not as close as he wished.

She touched a finger to her lips. "You're serious about this."

"Very."

"We have to get through the contest first." She lifted her chin, stubbornness and determination shining through.

"I know." Once again, he gripped the edge of the desk.

She nodded and stepped away, grabbing her turkey drawing and her purse. "When will you have the supplies and room ready?"

"Tomorrow." Shopping would give him a distraction, at least. Except for the fact that he'd still be thinking of her as he purchased the items on her list.

"I'll be back then." She pinched her lips together, and he wished he could kiss her one more time. "You should probably let Bellamy know everything will be ready then too. To be fair."

His heated middle cooled slightly at the reminder that he'd also have to see Bellamy a lot over the next few weeks. "Right."

He reached out and squeezed her fingers until she moved away and out his door. A lungful of air whooshed from him. So close. But still several weeks too far away.

23

She could do this. Fae believed in her. Kari believed in her. Chaz believed in her.

Chaz not only believed in her—he liked her. How did that happen? And why at such a bad time? She couldn't let their relationship—if that's what it was—progress until after this contest was over. Bad enough she and Bellamy had to compete.

Ella parked her truck in the gallery parking lot late Tuesday morning and sat for a moment. *Okay, God. You brought me this far. What now? Are turkeys really the way to go?*

She couldn't shake the image from her head. The meadow, the early morning light, the birds all fluffed up in their gray-and-black glory. She would paint a turkey whether it was right or not.

"Okay. Here goes nothing." She left the mostly warm interior of her truck and headed inside.

Bellamy's car was parked outside, too, so she had to be here somewhere. Would this be completely awkward? Would they have to see each other while they painted, or was there a wall between their rooms? Had Bellamy watched enough videos to have an idea of what to do?

Angela was making Bellamy live up to her claims, saying she was done bailing her daughter out of trouble. To say the tension was thick in their house the last few days was an understatement. It was almost enough to make Ella sell one of her mom's paintings just to have rent to live elsewhere.

"Good morning." Gertie met her in the office lobby. "Chaz has your supplies waiting in his office."

"Thanks." Ella pressed a hand to her belly as she approached the room where a dream had been born the day before. She didn't even realize she desired affection from a guy like Chaz until she had it.

No time to analyze any of that now. Time to focus and get serious about winning this contest. Her bag bumped her hip as she stepped up and knocked on his open door.

"Ella." He hopped up so fast his office chair rolled back and banged against the wall.

"Hey. Gertie said you have my supplies." She tucked a strand of hair behind her ear.

"Right. Yes. Come on in." He grinned so big both of his dimples made an appearance.

"Were you able to get everything?" She glanced around the room but didn't see a stack of art supplies.

"I was." He stepped in front of her and took her hands in his.

"Chaz"—she glanced over her shoulder, through the open door—"Bellamy is here somewhere."

"I know. I set her up in her own studio space a little while ago." He pulled her into an embrace and pressed a kiss to her temple. "I couldn't resist a real greeting."

When she shook her head, his chin bumped the bridge of her nose. "This is risky. What if Bellamy sees?"

"Maybe she'll quit thinking she has a chance with me?" He

pulled back enough that she could see the ornery expression on his face.

"All fine and well for you, but what about me?" Ella tugged free of his arms.

"What are you talking about?" Chaz frowned. "What aren't you saying?"

"Never mind." Ella scanned the office again. "Where are my supplies?"

"Ella." Chaz caught her as she moved past him to explore the bookshelf against the wall. "Is Bellamy threatening you? Blackmailing you?"

Ella pinched her lips together. Even though he guessed right, she couldn't admit it—in part because it was humiliating, in part because the threats still hung over her head, making her wonder what might happen if Bellamy realized exactly how close Ella was growing to Chaz. And that Bellamy wouldn't get what she thought she wanted.

"Are you safe?" His voice was just above a whisper, right next to her ear.

"I'm okay, Chaz." Ella glanced at him then at a painting behind his desk.

"Promise?" He caught the tips of her fingers.

"Promise." She squeezed, hoping to reassure him. "I'm okay. Now, my supplies?"

"May I have a kiss first?" He lifted one of his eyebrows.

Ella crossed her arms over her chest. "Is this how you made Bellamy ask for her supplies too?"

Chaz jerked back. "Of course not!"

"She probably would've willingly blessed you with as many kisses as you wanted and more." Ella grumbled the words under her breath, but he heard.

"I don't want kisses from anyone but you." Chaz fixed her

with a stare that sent a tidal wave through her belly. "Even if I have to wait three more weeks before I can ask for one again."

She groaned, wishing she didn't have to push him away. "You're not being fair. I don't like this any more than you do, but we both agreed that while the contest is going, we need to cool it. Please, please, just—"

Chaz held up a hand. "I know. I'm sorry. You're completely right."

She took a deep breath, trying to calm her trembling insides.

"Will you forgive me?" Chaz ran a hand through his hair. "I got so excited to see you more than one day in a row, I couldn't help myself."

Ella squeezed her eyes closed. "Of course I'll forgive you. If you'll give me my supplies. The sooner I get this piece painted, the sooner this contest will be over, right?"

He stared at her for a few more moments before moving to a drawer next to his desk. He lifted out a sack bulging with paints and brushes. "If I picked anything wrong, please let me know. A few of the brushes, I guessed on. Your canvas is already in the studio waiting for you."

She blinked moisture from her eyes. "It's too much. I only needed small tubes of paint. And you bought top-of-the-line brushes. I've never had anything this nice."

"It's not too much." He traced her cheek with a finger before he yanked his hand back. "You're worth this and much more."

"You got the same quality for Bellamy, right?"

"Of course."

She nodded, her heart overflowing. "Thank you." Rising on her tiptoes, she pecked his cheek before she could stop herself.

She left his office before the temptation to give in to his earlier request overcame her. To let him fold her into his warm embrace, breathe in his spicy scent, and allow him to shower her with the affection she longed for. It couldn't happen today. The stakes were too high.

"This way." His voice startled her before she made it very far down the hallway.

She followed him through the room still full of all the contest entries and then through another room, full of dark and intense pieces. Past that, through another room displaying vibrant landscapes, were two doors. Through one, Bellamy stood at an easel, her phone in hand, looking first at the screen and then at the paper before her. Pencils were scattered all around her, as well as some high-quality charcoal sticks. Light streamed through the window behind her like a spotlight.

Chaz opened the second door to show a similar setup. Another large window looked out onto a field of stubble, with woods on the far side. Sunlight poured through, perfect for catching nuances in shades and color. Her easel faced the wall, and a table stood nearby, ready to hold the supplies in her hand.

"Everything look okay?" Chaz leaned against the doorjamb as she moved past him to survey the space. "Can you think of anything else you might need?"

Ella noted the blank white walls. Not exactly inspiring. "Would it be okay if I pinned my sketches up here? Or taped them?"

"What if I find a bulletin board?"

She nodded without looking his way. "Perfect."

"Anything else?"

"This is all so amazing." She spun in a circle, almost hitting a stool that stood to the side. "You have no idea. I normally just paint on my bedroom floor. Or outside."

"The floor is yours too." One of his dimples winked at her.

"Let me know if you think of anything else. You know where my office is."

She glanced at the wall between her space and Bellamy's, then at Chaz. "Thank you again."

How she yearned to rush to him and let him wrap her in his arms for one more minute. But a sound of frustration filtered through the wall, reminding them they weren't alone. He stared at her for a second, then nodded and eased out of her space.

* * *

"Chaz?"

Chaz glanced up from his desk, where he'd been checking messages once more, hopeful that at least a few of the other gallery owners were willing to judge this confounded contest. His mom stood in the doorway with a large package under her arm. He jumped up and relieved her of the burden.

"Thanks so much for doing this for me." He set the board down and hugged her tight.

"My pleasure." His mom leaned closer. "Besides, I was curious and wanted to meet this Ella I keep hearing about."

He grinned. "I should've known you didn't do this only to help me."

"Let's just call it killing two birds with one stone."

"Right." He motioned her back out the door. "Right this way."

Music played from the other side of the gallery, piercing the normally quiet atmosphere. It wasn't anything he expected Ella to play, but he hadn't known her that long. He had all sorts of things to discover about her.

The hard rock filtered from Bellamy's side of the work area. He thought she'd left for the day. A peek in her room showed her staring at her phone for a moment before doing something on the paper. A frown wrinkled her forehead.

Chaz quickly led his mom to Ella's area. The music was so loud that the thumps of the bass practically shook the wall. Ella glanced up as he knocked on her door.

"Special delivery." He held up the bulletin board.

"Wow. That was fast. Thank you so much." Ella hopped up and moved out of the way.

"My mom just happened to be at the store earlier. She agreed to grab it for me." He motioned behind him, and Mom stepped into the room.

Ella froze, eyes wide. "Oh."

"Ella, it's so wonderful to meet you." Mom stepped forward, both hands outstretched. "I loved your painting. And your mom was one of my dearest friends when we were younger."

"You knew my mom?" Ella's voice came out soft.

"I did. I'm honored that her dishes are now sitting in my kitchen. So many memories wrapped up in them and her painting on my wall." Mom let go of Ella only to pull her into a hug. "Dear girl, you look so much like her."

Ella shook her head but blinked away moisture. Mom was so good at knowing exactly the right thing to say. He'd forgotten to mention to Ella that their moms had known each other.

"Where would you like this?" Chaz broke into the emotion fest before it got out of hand.

Ella glanced around then pointed to the wall between her and Bellamy. "Maybe it will help muffle the noise."

"If it gets to be too much, let me know. We can ask her to turn it down. After all, this is a gallery where people come to enjoy artwork. They probably aren't expecting to hear … that."

"Unfortunately, I'm used to it." Ella shrugged and moved her painting out of the way.

The quick glance he snuck at her art showed only several streaks of color across the top. What would she paint? Would she include her turkey? What else? He wanted to know everything but didn't feel he had the right to ask.

After prepping the board, determining the right height, and penciling everything in, he hammered the nail into the anchor. A few more bangs, and he was able to get the board in place. It looked straight. Nice. Maybe hanging all those paintings over the last few weeks had helped him find the perfect method.

"What is going on?" Bellamy strode into the room, her face full of fury, and froze. "Oh. Sorry, Chaz. I didn't realize you were in here."

"Just hanging a bulletin board. Sorry. Didn't think about how it would sound on the other side of the wall." Sort of like how she didn't think about how her music sounded to others. Or did she?

"Not a problem. Just wanted to make sure it wasn't going to continue. Throws me off my vibe, you know?" She gave him a grin that was probably supposed to be sultry but turned him off.

"You must be Bellamy." Mom stuck out her hand.

"I am." Bellamy shook his mom's hand. "And you are?"

"Lydia Prince." Mom smiled. "Chaz's mom."

"Oh! Mrs. Prince." Bellamy clasped his mom's hand in both of hers, looking like she might never let go. "What an honor to meet you. You've raised such an amazing man in Chaz. He's absolutely the best."

"Thank you." Mom slid her hand out of Bellamy's grip. "How's your work going so far? I know you both started today, but every artist works at their own speed."

"It's … coming." Bellamy fluffed her hair. "Guess I better get back to it. I'm sure Ella will want to as well."

Ella nodded with a small grin. "Yes."

"Of course." Chaz grabbed his hammer and the trash. "If either of you need anything else, let me know."

Ella moved back to her spot, straightening her easel. "This is great. Thanks."

"You bet." Chaz started to walk away but stopped and dug in his pocket. "Oh. Here are the thumbtacks."

He held them out, enjoying the moment his fingers grazed her palm. She already had some pink paint on her fingertips, and it made him smile. Would he get to see all the colors she used through this process, or would he have to stay away? The idea of staying away knotted his stomach.

Bellamy raised a brow as he turned back toward the door and escorted her and Mom back to Bellamy's space.

"Do you need anything else in your area?" he asked.

"Not at this time." Bellamy glanced back into Ella's room and narrowed her eyes. "But I'll let you know if I think of anything."

"Sounds good. See you later." Chaz gently touched Mom's arm and steered her away before Bellamy could compliment him more. Why did she fixate on him? Especially after he'd given her absolutely no sign of mutual interest?

"I like her." Mom's voice threw him for a loop.

"What?" Chaz stared at her.

"Ella." Mom squeezed his bicep. "I know we didn't chat very long, but hugging her was like hugging Sara again, with a bit of her dad mixed in for good measure. She seems very sweet. I'd love to get to know her better."

"You and me both," Chaz sighed.

"What's that sigh for? She'll be here quite a bit until she

gets her painting finished, right? What's stopping you from spending time with her? Besides work."

"She suggested it wouldn't look right if we spent time together during the contest." Chaz dragged his hand through his hair as they reentered his office. "Said it might appear like I was biased toward her over Bellamy."

"I see her point. Have you considered trying to find other judges so you don't have to be one? That would take the pressure off."

"I'm trying. So far, I've heard back from one gallery owner up near Parkersburg. He's agreed to come down and judge. But I need a couple more."

"Why not get your father to help? He has a lot of contacts. Maybe they'll respond faster to him."

Chaz slumped into his chair and buried his head in his hands. "I was hoping to not have to utilize his help anymore. I was supposed to be proving myself with this contest. Showing him I could step up and do more around the gallery."

"What's your motivation?" Mom perched on the sofa in front of his desk. "Why do you need more responsibility?"

He lifted his head and met her concerned gaze. "For one, because I felt like I wasn't doing anything worthwhile. Like I was a paper pusher and there was no meaning to being here at all except that it's the family business. I wanted a purpose."

"And?"

"And I'm starting to think I'd like a place of my own. But I need a bit of a raise to do that. To get something big enough to … well, to maybe get married down the road."

Mom gave a little bounce and squeal before calming again, though her smile still beamed. "You could probably move out anyway, even if it's not something as big as you'd like. Start smaller. Something tells me Ella wouldn't care."

Chaz opened his mouth to protest but stopped himself. He

couldn't deny Ella was the one he had in mind when the future ran through his head. And his mom was right, though he hated to think of asking Ella to live somewhere less.

"She deserves more."

"Agreed. But here's some advice. When you start out, live within your means. Work your way up to where your dad and I are now. We didn't start out in a four-bedroom house. We lived in a tiny, one-bedroom apartment. For three years. And those were some of the sweetest years of our marriage." She reached across the desk and squeezed his hand. "If you have love, it doesn't matter where you live."

"I don't know if there's love yet, but ... I definitely feel like I'm headed that way."

"I'll pray for you." She gave one more squeeze before standing. "But I do recommend asking your father for help on the judging situation. Sometimes the way to prove you're capable is to admit when you need help."

She was dishing out all sorts of advice this afternoon. But he couldn't deny he needed it.

"Thanks, Mom."

"Anytime." She kissed his cheek. "Anything to speed up the process of gaining a daughter-in-law."

He chuckled as she left but quickly sobered. Time to swallow his pride and ask for help. And pray his dad had better luck finding more judges than he had.

24

Did that tree look right? What about that feather? Ella tilted her head as she worked on details of her painting. The background was done, the sky streaked with morning colors. The meadow was ringed with trees casting their shadows over everything except the middle of the scene, where a cluster of turkeys showed off among grasses and flowers.

She'd worked both Tuesday and Wednesday last week, then Sunday afternoon, and the last two days as well. It was coming along nicely. A good thing, considering she had to work the flea market again for the next three days.

She had no idea how Bellamy was doing. She'd thrown a huge fit last week, claiming Chaz's supplies weren't what she needed and demanding different materials. Apparently, most of the videos on YouTube she'd been watching were for paint instead of pencil. Needless to say, she'd gotten what she wanted, but not without several strange looks from Chaz.

A rap at her door caused Ella to jerk her head up. She didn't get many visitors, although occasionally, a guest would peek their head in to see her progress. Of course, with her canvas facing away from them, they couldn't tell what she was painting. She wanted it to be a surprise for the big reveal.

"How's it going?" Chaz smiled from the doorway. He'd done a great job of maintaining distance over the last week—mostly. She couldn't blame him. She chafed at the self-set boundaries too. But they were there for a reason.

"I think it's going okay." She rinsed out her brush.

"Have you eaten today?" He leaned against the doorjamb as if he hadn't a care in the world, but concern came off him in waves, evident in the wrinkle between his forehead and the way his stare never left her.

"I had some breakfast this morning." She worked on screwing the lids onto her paint tubes to keep from having to look his way.

"And since then?"

"I'll eat when I leave."

He tutted. "You're going to waste away, the way you skip meals. How do you do it?"

"I'm used to it."

He let out a groan. "That's not a good thing, you know."

"It is what it is." She wiped her hands on a cloth, though color still showed under her fingernails.

"Ella ..."

"Chaz, we talked about this. I can't eat with you." She fixed him with a stare. "Thank you for caring, but I'm okay."

He sighed. "You're sure?"

"I'm sure." She softened her voice. "Thank you. It's nice that someone cares."

"More than you know." His glance practically smoldered her.

She was figuring out how much he cared. Whew.

"I'll see you later."

She nodded, and he was gone as quickly as he'd shown up.

Letting out a long breath, she glanced around to make sure everything was put away. It all looked good.

"What did Chaz want?" Bellamy glared from the doorway Chaz had just vacated. "He didn't talk to me."

"He was making sure I had everything I needed." Ella shrugged. "Maybe he didn't come by because he talked to you earlier."

Bellamy didn't appear convinced. "He was inviting you to eat with him, wasn't he?"

"He wasn't." Not technically, anyway. He'd never said the actual words. "He just asked if I'd eaten today since he never saw me leave the gallery."

"Maybe you should leave the gallery and get some lunch during the day like I do. Then he won't have to check on you." Bellamy sniffed. "And he's never expressed such concern for my well-being."

"Probably because he sees you come back with a cup from wherever you ate lunch and figures you're doing okay." Ella dropped one last paintbrush into an old metal can and brushed her hands off, removing her apron.

"I guess you need to start doing the same, then." Bellamy didn't move out of the way when Ella attempted to go through the doorway.

"I can't eat out every day. I don't have that kind of money."

"Figure out a way. I'm tired of you stealing Chaz's attention."

"Look." Ella got as close to Bellamy as she dared. "I can't help who Chaz gives attention to. I'm just here painting like I'm supposed to. Nothing else."

"Nothing else?" Bellamy narrowed her eyes. "I don't believe you."

Ella waited. When Bellamy got this way, there was no reasoning with her. Better to wait it out.

"I don't think you're keeping up your end of our bargain."

"Bargain" was a word that had nothing to do with what was actually taking place. Ella shifted her weight and remained silent. Bellamy would get to the point soon enough.

"Remember what I said—Chaz is mine. If you're making moves on him, that means I get to destroy even more of the things you love."

Ella's breath caught. There wasn't much left at the house, but there was enough. Not to mention her own health. If Chaz thought she wasn't taking care of herself now, what would he think if she remained in such a situation? Enough. She wasn't going to sit back and let Bellamy destroy more of her life.

"Well, I'm not making any moves on Chaz." She didn't have to. He'd made moves on her. "So no need for any of that."

Ella pushed past Bellamy and motioned for Gertie to lock the room behind her. She didn't want to tempt Bellamy with the opportunity to sabotage her painting. With the door secured, Ella shouldered her bag and headed out into the cool night.

Time to take matters into her own hands.

She parked in Fae's drive instead of her own. This was a task that needed an army, and Fae would know how to round up enough troops. Her neighbor welcomed her in, set a plate full of stroganoff in front of her, then started making phone calls. With a nod, she sat down and cut into a fresh pan of brownies.

"Kari has an extra room. It's all yours until you find something better. And she's sending Jake to help heft the heavy stuff."

"I don't have much, but it will be nice to have an extra truck and some muscles." Ella took a deep breath. "I probably should've done this weeks ago, but I couldn't bring myself to leave my home."

Fae glanced through the window at the two-story lemon-yellow house Ella had lived in all twenty-three years of her life. "It's a lovely place, but it's only a house. The people who made it a home for you aren't there anymore. It's time to make a new home."

Ella nodded, though moisture waited right behind her eyelids, itching for an excuse to let loose. Would Angela care? Would she celebrate? What would Bellamy think? She hadn't made it home yet, and Ella hoped it stayed that way for a little longer. At least long enough to get this process started.

* * *

"Guys, it's time." Kari appeared in the doorway.

Chaz looked over from where he'd been venting to Jake about how hard it was to stay away from Ella.

"Time?" Jake glanced at his watch. "Did I miss a memo? I don't remember scheduling anything with you tonight."

"It's not for me." Kari waved her phone. "Fae called. Ella is moving out. I need you to go load up her stuff and bring it over to the spare apartment next to mine."

Chaz blinked, and Jake didn't move, either. What did she say? Moving Ella?

"Now," Kari snapped.

"Right. On it." Jake pulled on his boots.

Chaz jumped up and grabbed his jacket.

"Is everything okay? Why does Ella need to move out?"

"Guess." Kari spun on her heel and headed back down the hallway.

"Does your sister ever give you all the information?" Chaz scratched his head as he followed Jake.

"Never." Jake spun his truck keys in his hand. "But this

situation doesn't surprise me. I'm amazed Bellamy hasn't chased her out before now."

"Bellamy? She's the reason Ella has to leave her house?" Chaz slid into Jake's passenger seat. "But isn't it Ella's house? The one her parents owned?"

"Her dad left everything to Angela." Jake revved the engine. "Everything."

Chaz blinked. That explained why Angela was selling all Ella's parents' possessions. Technically, they were Angela's. An idea niggled in the back of Chaz's head, but he couldn't focus on it right now. Ella needed him.

Jake pulled into the drive of a pretty two-story house. It was slightly older than his parents' but in good shape, as far as Chaz could tell. Jake pointed to the house next door as Fae and Ella exited and slipped through the hedge.

"I take it you're my cavalry?" Ella wrapped her arms around her thin coat. Why did she never wear a thicker one? Now that it was mid-December, the cold had set in to stay for a while.

"At your service, ma'am." Jake tipped his hat. "Point the way."

"Nothing is really packed, so we're going to have to wing it." Ella stepped up onto her porch and paused, as if bracing herself for battle. "And I want to grab a few things from the garage too. The good news is, if we can get the door open, the boxes and chest are in the front, so we should be able to get them out fairly easily. The bad news is, no one else knows about them except me, so ... we may get some pushback."

"Let's start with those." Chaz caught her arm before she could open the door. Something told him the garage items were more important than anything else.

Ella nodded and entered the warm house. The air was the only warm thing about it, though. The decorations might belong on the cover of a magazine, but not in a home where someone actually lived. More of a showcase. Except the walls. They were strangely bare, though some spaces appeared a slightly different shade, as if frames had hung there for a long time.

"That you, Belle?" Angela's voice filtered through from another room.

"It's me, Angela." Ella pointed to her left. She walked through the kitchen where Angela was cooking something at the stove.

Her stepmother spun around, her mouth gaping, as the guys and Fae followed Ella through. "What is going on here?"

"Just grabbing a few of my things. I won't be in your way long." Ella opened a door and entered the chilly garage.

She hit the door button, and it slowly rose, creaking in protest. Between them and it stood a veritable maze of boxes and furniture and other items. All Ella's parents' things? Or discards from Angela?

"What do you think you're doing?" Angela hit the door button again, causing it to stop.

"Grabbing a few things."

"Nothing out here is yours. Remember, this house and everything in it is mine." Angela set her chin. "Your father left me little enough, so it's only fair he provide in other ways. He's supplying the products for our flea market booth."

"Not everything is yours." Ella hit the button once more. "That chest in the front is one my grandmother had. Dad gave it to me when I turned ten. It's mine, and it's going with me. The rest of this, you can keep."

Angela narrowed her eyes. "Can you prove it's yours?"

"You're really going to keep her from taking a chest her grandmother owned?" Chaz stepped into Angela's space.

"Oh. Mr. Prince." Angela backed up. "I didn't recognize you at first. You're not helping with this craziness, are you?"

"I'm helping my friend move, if that's what you're asking." Chaz folded his arms as Jake stepped closer.

"Move? Where exactly are you going, Ella?" Angela donned an expression that was probably supposed to look like maternal worry.

"I'm staying at the hotel for a while. Not sure after that. I'll find something."

"A hotel?" Angela clutched at her neckline. "How will you afford it?"

"Now you're worried about me?" Ella pinched her lips together. "I'll be okay. And this won't take long. As you reminded me, I don't own much."

Angela stayed another minute, her mouth moving as if trying to figure out how to respond. Then, she turned on her heel and marched back to the stove where an acidic scent of scorched noodles wafted up.

Ella pointed to the trunk and the two boxes next to it. "That's all that needs to come from here, boys. Fae and I will gather the things in my room while you load that."

"On it, ma'am." Jake tipped his hat and started sidestepping through the mess.

Chaz smirked and followed.

"What do you think is in this?" Jake bent his knees and lifted the old cedar chest. A heart was carved on the front. "Hopefully not books."

The furniture was heavy, but not so heavy they couldn't carry it between the two of them. "No idea, but it's not our concern. All that matters is Ella wants it."

"Agreed. Just seems like she cares a lot about this old piece of wood."

Chaz shifted so they could raise it into the back of Jake's

truck. "We probably need to wrap it so it doesn't get scratched."

As he pushed on his end, something shifted on Jake's, and the chest tilted enough for the lid to flop open and bang against the back. They quickly set it down in the back of the truck, and Chaz scrambled up to get it situated. Inside, he glimpsed records, an old afghan, photos, a few books—though he wasn't telling Jake that part—a kettle, and a conglomeration of other bits and pieces. Probably things that had belonged to her family that she hid away from Angela instead of selling.

Good girl.

Back in the house, they went upstairs and found Ella and Fae stuffing a few more things from drawers into another chest. The room was small and still held a few pieces of Ella's childhood. An old quilt sat folded on the end of the bed. A rag rug covered a circle of the floor.

"What all goes, Ella?" Jake stepped in, flexing his muscles. "I'm here for you."

"The dresser." Ella pointed. "We may have to remove drawers and carry them down individually. And this chest." She glanced around, as if at a loss. "My quilt."

"Mind if we wrap the quilt around the top of the other chest?" Chaz picked it up and ran a hand over the soft, hand-stitched fabric. "Don't want it to get scratched."

With moisture in her eyes, Ella met his gaze and nodded. "Sure."

His own throat clogged with emotion. He set the quilt down and pulled her into a hug, not caring a bit if anyone else saw. She needed this more than anything.

After a minute, he pulled back and they got to work. Within short order, her room was empty of everything but the bed and rug. Ella stared at her bare room, breathing deeply.

"What is going on here?" Bellamy's voice cut through the silence, and Ella stiffened.

"Don't worry. We're leaving." Jake pushed past Bellamy where she stood farther down the hallway.

Fae and Chaz walked on either side of Ella all the way down and out into the cold. Ella slid into her own truck and started the engine.

"You okay to drive?" Chaz caught her door before she closed it.

"I'll be okay."

After another moment, he let her close the door and pull out into the night. He jumped into Jake's truck before Bellamy could catch him, though she was headed his way. They followed Ella to the hotel and helped unload all her things into the tiny studio-style apartment next to Kari's. Even though the space was small, Ella's things barely filled it.

She pulled the afghan from the chest and wrapped it around her shoulders as she surveyed her new domain. "I won't outstay my welcome."

"Stay as long as you need." Kari squeezed her friend's shoulders.

Ella nodded.

Jake tugged on Chaz's arm, but he didn't want to leave. He yearned to hold Ella, to let her cry, to give her any comfort he could. But now wasn't the time. She needed to mourn. Needed to adjust.

And he needed to finalize some plans.

25

Ella parked in front of the gallery on Monday morning. It would be her first time facing Chaz since he helped her move. What would he think of her bumming a room from their friends?

She climbed out of Humphrey and squared her shoulders. It didn't matter right now. She had a painting to finish in just over a week, which really meant only a few more days for her. So far, Angela hadn't stopped her from working the flea market booth, so Ella would continue to do so until told otherwise.

"I suppose you think you're some kind of smart, huh?" Bellamy waited for her outside her workroom. "You think I can't touch your things now?"

Ella didn't even deign to answer. What was the point?

"Mom said you better not come back. Nothing else belongs to you. A few of the things you took probably don't, either, but she's willing to overlook your selfish attitude so she doesn't have to feed you anymore."

As if Angela had fed her all that much to begin with. She shifted her bag on her shoulder. Most of the time Ella ate with Fae, or not at all. Or scrounged something from the pantry she didn't think Angela would notice missing.

"Oh, good. You're both here." Chaz approached, jangling the keys. "I'll unlock your doors so you can get started."

Bellamy smirked as she straightened and moved out of the way. No telling what that meant. It didn't matter. Ella stepped into her space and flipped the light switch. The sky outside was gloomy, and she wanted as much light as possible.

"You good?" Chaz caught her fingertips for a second, hardly long enough for anyone but her to notice. But she noticed. Oh, how she noticed.

"I should be." She set her bag on the stool and surveyed her area while Chaz left to unlock Bellamy's door. It was a shame they couldn't trust each other enough to leave the rooms open.

She reached for a brush and froze. Every bristle had been hacked off. Same for the next one. And the next. All those costly brushes, shorn down to the metal. She ran her finger over the stubble, her heart breaking. How did someone get in and do this? Why?

The why was obvious, though Ella still couldn't understand the how. The door had been locked. Chaz had opened it with a key. Right?

She glanced up at the knob, but everything appeared right. Quickly, she skimmed the rest of her workstation. Something was missing. But what?

Her hand hovered over each section until she realized most of her paint was gone. All that was left was white and black.

"Okay, God. I know Bellamy is a soul who You love, too, but I don't understand how You can expect me to love her. She's evil, God. What am I supposed to do now? What lesson are you trying to teach me this time?"

"Did you say something?" Chaz poked his head back through her door.

"No." When he started to leave again, she rethought her answer. "Hey, Chaz?"

"Yeah?" The expectation on his face almost shattered her. How could she admit what Bellamy had done? That all that money he'd spent was wasted?

"Ella? You okay?" He stepped farther into her room, a wrinkle marring his perfect forehead.

"Just curious about something." Ella scooted the cup full of brushes over an inch. "The door this morning. It was locked, right?"

He stiffened. Great. Now she'd offended him.

"I didn't try to open it without sticking the key in first. Why?"

"Just curious."

"There's more to it than that." He folded his arms over his chest, widening his stance. "If someone was able to get in here, I need to know about it so I can fix the problem. Is your painting okay?"

Ella let her gaze caress the canvas next to her. All looked to be in order, thank goodness. Missing paint she could deal with, but more sabotaged work—that would have broken her.

"It's good. But you might need to have the locked checked just in case. A few things were ... out of place this morning." Ella pushed the brushes further back where he couldn't see them.

"Noted." He studied her for a few more seconds, then spun on his heel and strode away with purpose.

Okay, time for a new plan. The good news was that the biggest part of the painting was almost complete. She still needed white and black paint for the turkey to finish out the details. For the other colors she'd hoped to use more of, she still had a bit of yellow, some red, and a tiny smidge of brown in her bag—tubes Bellamy hadn't destroyed in her earlier attempt to eliminate Ella.

It's You and me, God. And a few little dabs of paint. Please let it be enough.

She uncovered a few old brushes from the bottom of her bag, the paint, and even a few charcoal nubs. Perfect. Everything she needed. At least, it would have to be.

Halfway through the day, when Bellamy's music had stopped long enough that Ella assumed she'd gone to lunch, a rap sounded on her door. Chaz stood in the doorway with someone else beside him. A locksmith, according to the logo on his shirt.

"How about we nip this door problem in the bud?" Chaz lifted a brow. "Is it going to disturb you if he works on this while you're painting?"

"As long as he doesn't get dust or anything in here, it should be fine." Ella grinned. "Thanks."

"Sure." Chaz nodded to the locksmith and left him to it.

Okay. This should help things. If Bellamy had somehow found a way to get in with the old lock, surely the new one would stop her. The paint and brushes were working okay. She could do this. She *would* do this. If only to show Bellamy.

Not the best reason. Not even a good one. But Bellamy had declared war, so Ella would take up her colors. Literally.

At the end of the day, Ella rinsed everything out, stuck her supplies in her bag just in case, then hunted down Chaz. She studied him a moment while he sat behind his desk, frowning at a computer screen. Looked serious, but so was her request. "Hey. Can you lock my door?"

He jumped up and moved toward her quickly. "Of course. How did today go?"

Ella tucked a strand of hair behind her ear. "It went okay. But I'm beat."

"Sure." Chaz peeked out the door of his office, then ducked

back inside and pressed a quick kiss to her lips. "I've been wanting to do that for days."

"Chaz!" Ella gasped.

"I know, I know. I won't do it again. But you can't blame a guy when you come in looking like that."

She glanced down at her ratty overalls, plaid shirt, and paint-stained fingers. "You're kidding, right?"

"Nope. Prettiest girl I've ever seen." He pointed out the door. "Let's get your room locked up so you can leave. I probably won't stay much longer. Just waiting for Bellamy to finish so I can lock hers too."

"Does she usually stay late?" Ella's gut clenched at the idea of Bellamy here alone with Chaz.

"She's usually gone before you are. Not sure what's going on today, unless she's working extra to try and finish." He rested his hand lightly on the small of her back, and she had to fight the urge to turn and let him wrap her in his arms.

Her door remained open, but they discovered something inside they weren't expecting. Or some*one*. Bellamy looked up from where she stood on the other side of the easel.

"What are you doing in here?" Chaz's voice was steel.

"Just curious about how much more Ella has to do before her painting is finished." Bellamy pouted. "But I can't figure out how she's done anything at all."

"What are you talking about?" Chaz frowned.

"How did she paint with these?" Bellamy held up a fistful of the mutilated paint brushes.

"What in the world?" Chaz lunged for them, but Ella jerked him back.

"It's fine. I made do with a couple old ones I had." She marched around and shoved Bellamy out of her space—after making sure nothing had been added to or changed on her painting. "This is almost over. Can we please just finish?"

"Ella, those brushes ..."

"I should've thrown them away. You weren't supposed to know about them." She pointed to the doorknob. "Please just lock my space, and let's leave everything for tonight. I have a headache and want to go ho—"

She stopped herself before uttering the word that held no meaning anymore. She had no home. And she definitely wasn't about to admit to Bellamy that she'd moved into a hotel.

Chaz squeezed her shoulder. "Okay. We'll leave it for now."

She nodded.

He jerked his head toward Bellamy. "But I better not find anything else like that again, or you're disqualified."

"Me? What did I do?" Bellamy pressed her overly manicured hands to her bosom. How had she kept her nails so free of paint? "I would never!"

"I'll see you tomorrow." Ella slipped out before she could witness anything else. It was all too much. She wanted the contest over already.

* * *

Chaz paced his parents' living room, hands in fists. He had to do something. What happened today was the final straw. He could not let Ella continue to put up with abuse from that ... that ... ugh!

He couldn't even bring himself to say a word nasty enough to describe how he felt about her.

"Chaz, sit down." His mother pointed to the sofa.

"I can't. I'm too antsy. Too riled up."

"I can see that. You need to calm down and think rationally." She grabbed him by the biceps and pushed him onto the couch.

He thought about hopping right back up but thought

better of it when he saw her expression. Instead, he shoved his hands under his thighs and jiggled his legs. How would sitting here solve any of the problems going on in Ella's life? He needed to do something.

"Now, I understand you're upset, but you can't just rush in and fix things. For one, most women don't want a man to do that. For another, you don't know the whole story. What you try to fix might actually make things worse."

He stilled, his mother's words sinking in. "But I can't leave things the way they are, either."

"You're not. You're giving Ella a chance to get out from under her stepsister, the hope of a spot in your gallery, and from there, who knows? Her artwork is good. She has potential to go far, but she needed this opportunity to be discovered. And you did that. I thought that was one of the reasons you hosted this contest in the first place."

"It was." Chaz shoved his hands through his hair. "It is. But it doesn't feel like enough."

"Well, when Bellamy is finally proved a fraud, maybe she'll learn she can't go around claiming to have talents that belong to other people. I pray she learns many lessons from this. Because that child desperately needs to be taught a few things —and I'm not talking art."

Chaz chuckled. "Agreed. I think she's using YouTube videos as tutorials for her painting. Do you think it will look anything like the original?"

"Even if it does, that means you can sic her with copyright infringement. Her work is supposed to be original, right?" Mom lifted her brows.

"Brilliant."

Mom nodded. "But you can't rush in like a bull after a red painting. You need to stay calm and think things through from every angle. Did you talk to your father today?"

"I didn't get a chance. I was coordinating things with the judges he lined up."

"I told you he would help."

Chaz shot his mother a look that told her exactly how he felt about her rubbing it in. "Yes, well, thanks. I also had to deal with calling a locksmith."

"Calling a locksmith?" His dad stuck his head around the front doorway. "What are you talking about?"

"Somehow, *someone* got into Ella's room before she arrived, and ... well, she killed the paintbrushes, for lack of a better term."

"What?"

"Fortunately, she seems to have left the painting itself alone. But I changed the locks, just in case."

Mom shook her head before leaving and returning with cups of coffee and fresh cookies. Apparently they were going to be here awhile.

"Ridiculous. I say let's end this charade of a contest and declare Ella the winner. I don't want that Bethany girl to be in my gallery any longer."

"Bellamy." Chaz rubbed his forehead. "And I agree, but we had so many witnesses to her fit about Ella stealing the painting. If we don't follow through, how is that going to look?"

Dad groaned but conceded. "So what now?"

"Mom thinks we should ride it out. Let Bellamy make a fool of herself and let Ella shine on her own."

Dad nodded.

"Kingston." Mom touched Dad's shoulder. "Did you talk to Chaz about your plan?"

Dad shook his head.

Another plan? What now?

Hands steepled in front of him, Dad leaned forward. "What

do you think of a yearly artist in residence? Using one of those rooms to have a local artist come in a few times a month to work where people can see the creative process in action, maybe even ask questions. And display her pieces."

"It's a great idea." Chaz leaned back. "Why didn't I think of that?"

"Well, it was your local artist idea that spurred this one on, so in a way, you helped think of it." Dad pointed at him and winked. "I'm going to put you in charge. That will give you the local artist contest each year, the artist in residence bit, and the few things you were already doing. Which means you need a raise, doesn't it?"

Chaz's heart skipped a beat. "It does?"

"Only seems fair." Dad stroked his beard. "Mom said you're wanting a place of your own. Why don't you shop around and see what's out there? Then we can talk about what kind of raise you might need."

Chaz had some money stashed away already. Definitely enough for a few months' rent, including a deposit. But he needed something else more right now.

"If I'm going to move out, I probably need some things to furnish the place with." Chaz traced one of the swirls on the couch. "I have an idea about that, but it's a little ... different. Will you hear me out?"

Mom and Dad exchanged a look, but then settled in, their attention all his. Chaz laid out his idea piece by piece. And amazingly enough, his parents didn't flinch or frown. Instead, they were nodding by the end.

This might actually work.

26

The locks must have worked, since nothing else appeared to have been tampered with the last two days. And Ella had left a bit of charcoal dust near the door as a booby trap so she could see if anyone entered. There were no signs of extra footprints.

She had finished her painting yesterday, adding the final touches of charcoal to the dark parts of the turkey feathers and the shadows of the rocks at the edge of the meadow. It was as good as she could do in the time frame allotted. Next week, various judges from other parts of the state would stop by and examine the pieces, marking which one they thought should win.

Ella pressed a hand to her tummy. Worrying over it wouldn't help anything, but a niggle in her middle didn't seem to believe that. What if Bellamy had actually pulled off a miracle?

No. She straightened her bag as she walked through the maze of the flea market. In spite of tampered supplies, loud music, and threats, she had finished her painting in the allotted time frame. And it was good. Probably the best she'd ever done. No more worrying. She had used her God-given talents, and the rest was up to Him.

"Good morning, Ella!" Marjorie waved as Ella walked by her booth at the flea market. "I'm surprised you're here today. What else can you possibly sell?"

That was an odd greeting. Marjorie was normally more optimistic.

"There's always something." Ella moved down the pathway and to their booth.

Jiggling the lock, she finally undid it and pushed back the trellis that made up their door. She froze. Their spot was nearly empty.

Dad's wingback chair.

The records.

Books.

Even the old ottoman that desperately needed a new upholstery job was missing.

With shaking hands, Ella pulled out her phone to call Angela.

"Ella. I thought I might hear from you this morning." Her stepmother's voice was as smooth as always, as if she didn't care one whit about what Ella might think of this situation.

"What did you do with all of it?" Ella swallowed the lump trying to choke her.

"*It?* That's a terribly vague term. Please be more specific." Ella could practically see Angela examining her perfect nails while she talked, as if she didn't have a care in the world.

"The items in our flea market booth. Everything is gone."

"Not everything."

Ella glanced around again. A few little pieces of pottery, some old toys Angela insisted were vintage and could bring in money, and an ugly lamp remained. Not much else.

"Do you want me to work here today? There's not much to bring people in."

"Totally up to you." Angela's voice hardened. "You wanted to be free of me. Well, you're free. Everything is gone, and you no longer have to worry about trying to keep it from selling. I got a very nice offer and grasped it immediately. He even came and hauled it all away yesterday. I didn't have to lift a finger."

Ella choked back a sob. She should be past this by now—crying over possessions. Grieving again and again.

"If you want something to do today, clean whatever is left out of there and take it to the local charity. Then I can quit paying rent on that awful space."

Click.

Ella slid her phone back into her bag and nodded, though no one was there to see her. Angela had never treated her like a daughter. Not really. She'd been a bit nicer when Dad was alive, but only if he was in the room. Instead, Angela had acted like Ella was an unwanted parasite that came with her marriage to Dad.

And she'd finally found a way to get rid of the parasite. Ella rubbed her hands up and down her arms, trying to decide her next steps. Angela said she didn't have to work today, but what else did she have to do? She'd declared her painting done. And she had no other real job. Not even a prospect.

Angela is a soul too. One God loves as much as He loves you. What would God want you to do? Fae's voice ran through her head, making her wrinkle her nose with a sigh. Right. Treat others as you would have them treat you and all that stuff.

Setting her bag on the stool that had been hers the last few years, Ella found a couple empty boxes and a broom and started emptying the last few items from the booth. It took less than an hour to finish. She loaded it all in the back of her truck, grabbed her stool, locked up, and left for the last time, waving at everyone as she went.

Free.

Funny how such a wonderful word didn't sound so great right now.

After dropping the items at the charity thrift store, she drove to Fae's. The older lady welcomed her with open arms and a cup of spice tea. Nestled on Fae's sofa, she filled her in on the last week.

"You need to be doing something." Fae nodded.

"Like what?" Ella traced the sweater pattern on her mug. "I can't exactly go get a job when I don't know what's going to happen next week. What if I'm chosen to be the artist in residence?"

"Atta girl." Fae patted her thigh.

"Although, there are two other artists who were finalists in the original contest. They'll probably choose one of them instead of me. Someone with more experience."

"And there she goes again, stewing in her own stupidity." Fae slumped back against the couch.

"Thanks a lot."

"Listen to you!" Fae flopped her hands around. "One moment you're certain you're as good as we all say you are, and the next you're wondering why you're even in this contest in the first place. Let me tell you why. It's because you're good enough." Fae poked her.

"Ow!"

"You need to wake up and see the truth. And the truth is you're a great artist, your stepsister is a nincompoop, and that boy who runs the contest is head over heels for you."

"Fae!"

"You know I'm right."

Ella's cheeks heated.

"Ha. See? This old biddy can still spot a thing or two. And the way he hovered the other night told me he cares more than a bit. I say as soon as this competition is over and judged, you snatch him up before he realizes you can't see a good thing when it's practically smacking you in the face."

Or literally smacking her, as the case may be. Ella stifled a groan. Now her inner thoughts were just as sarcastic as Fae. Though Fae's kind of smacking didn't mean kissing, that's immediately where Ella's mind went. His kiss had been so sweet. And much too short.

"What are you thinking about to make your face look that way?" Fae cackled. "Ooh, boy! Maybe you can see a few things, after all."

"Fae. Enough."

"Fine, fine. I've got a few projects you can help me with over the next week." Fae rubbed her hands together. "After all, we have a dress to find."

"A dress to … find?" Ella's gut clenched.

"I have the perfect outfit for that ball they're throwing to announce the final winner. I just can't quite remember where I stored it away."

"F-a-e …"

"Trust me." Fae wiggled her way up from the sofa. "Have I ever let you down before?"

No, she had not. But that didn't mean she made it easy on the journey. Ella sighed. One more adventure.

* * *

"It looks good." Mom placed a hand on Chaz's shoulder.

"Yeah?" Chaz looked around at everything again.

"Yeah, but I think the table needs one more thing." She crooked a finger at him and motioned for him to follow her. He shivered as he walked out his new condo's door and down to her car. What was she up to?

"I know it's not Christmas yet, but it's close enough. So this is a Christmas and housewarming gift all wrapped up in one." Mom popped the trunk and pointed to a box.

Chaz moved to lift it, but she stayed him with a hand. "It's fragile."

More carefully, he grasped the edges of the box and heaved it out of the trunk. It was heavy. And it clanked. What in the world?

Inside the condo, he set the box on the small dining table his mom had helped him find at a thrift store and then pulled back the flaps. Dishes. He traced the familiar, delicate roses. Not just any dishes. The ones he gave Mom for her birthday.

"Mom!" Chaz jerked his head up. "No take backs."

"Chaz." She pressed both hands to his cheeks. "I'm only giving you six place settings. I still have all the others. You can't have those until I die." She lifted a brow. "And don't hold your breath."

A chuckle burst from his lips. "You're something else."

"So are you." She lifted some plates from the box and unwrapped the paper from around them—the very same newspaper he'd thought had discolored Ella's fingers. He'd learned much since then.

Silently, they both worked to fill the small cabinet against the wall. Six dinner plates, six dessert plates, six bowls, and six teacups and saucers. And if he had his way, he knew exactly who he wanted to use them with first. One more day until this eternal contest was finally over.

One judge wouldn't be able to come until tomorrow night. Chaz straightened a dining chair. The other four had given surprising results. Two for Ella and two for Bellamy. He picked at the spot on the table where the price tag had been. Was this going to backfire?

"Why are you worrying?" Mom poked his shoulder.

"What?"

"You get that wrinkle in the middle of your forehead whenever you're worried about something. What is it?"

"This contest." Chaz shook his head. "What if Ella doesn't win?"

"Ridiculous. I've seen her work. How could Bellamy teach herself to do something that well in such a short amount of time?"

How indeed? It was a question he and Dad had talked about at great length. But neither of them could figure out the answer.

"You still have proof that she tried to sabotage Ella's painting. Those beautiful brushes, all destroyed." Mom tutted. "Someone needs to sit that girl down and give her a spanking."

Chaz turned so his mother wouldn't see him smirk. His condo was ready for its tenant. Filled with items that already had so many memories attached to them, plus a few extras. And a new bed.

If his plan worked, he'd officially ask Ella to be his girl at the ball tomorrow night. After a bit longer, he could ask her to be a more permanent girlfriend. He even knew what kind of ring he wanted to buy. He just had to make sure tomorrow night went well first.

"I think she's going to appreciate what you did." Mom straightened a throw pillow she'd insisted on adding to the chair. "But she might not at first. Not until she understands."

Chaz nodded. "I guess it could come across as really weird, huh?"

"It could. You just need to explain it to her. Tell her why you did it. That you have a plan that includes her."

"Right. So easy when she's as skittish as a rabbit and hard to pin down for a conversation." He rubbed the back of his neck.

"But she promised you that you could pursue a real relationship after the contest was over, right?"

Chaz tilted his head. "I think that's what she meant. I don't know. It just makes me want to confirm that she wins even more. I mean, why would she date me if she loses?"

"No." Mom slashed her hand through the air. "You are not basing your relationship on whether or not Ella wins tomorrow. That's part of why she didn't want to pursue anything until it was over. The two need to stay separate. Because your love can't be based on anything beyond your mutual attraction and admiration. It needs to be solely between you two and God."

"But if she loses, she won't want to be around me." Chaz hated how whiny his voice sounded, but he couldn't help it.

"Then that's on her. If she can't see a good thing right in front of her, you deserve better."

"But—"

Mom held up a hand. "I know you think I'm biased and that I think no one is good enough for you, but that's not what this is about. I do want the best for you. But more than that, I want you to have someone who loves you as much as you love her. Not for what you can give her. Not for what she can give you. But for what you can bring to each other to make your lives as good as they can be and to help each other get to Heaven."

Chaz sighed. His mom was right, but that didn't make it any easier.

"Whether or not she wins tomorrow, you have to trust God. He's the One who knows best." Mom kissed his cheek.

"Now, get some rest. Tomorrow is a big day, and we wouldn't want you looking haggard."

Chaz grinned as his mom slipped out the door. He looked around his new domain one more time, and his grin widened. Almost perfect.

Okay, God. Help me trust You with this. But please, God. Please let everything work out the way it's supposed to.

27

"You have got to be kidding me." Ella crossed her arms. "It's thirty-two degrees outside. I'm not wearing that."

Fae held up the hanger, pride coming off her in waves. "Of course you are. What else would you wear?"

The dress in question was light blue, which wasn't the part that disturbed Ella. The fact that it had thin straps and was made of a filmy, lightweight fabric was what concerned her. This was more of a summer dress, and Fae wanted her to wear it in the middle of winter.

"I'll freeze to death."

"You won't freeze to death. Remember how warm it was in the gallery at the last shindig?" Fae pressed the garment to Ella's chest and started digging in the closet again. "I'll loan you a coat to wear until you get there."

"Fae, this is ridiculous."

"Agreed. I can't imagine why you wouldn't want to wear your own mother's dress to a ball being held in your honor. Ridiculous."

Ella blinked and almost dropped the gown. "My mother's?"

Fae tossed out a few shoes, barely missing Ella's ankles. Rufus, who had been batting at the hem of the gown, hissed and rushed out of the room. Poor cat. "That's what I said, isn't it?"

"But why on earth would you have something that belonged to my mother hanging in your closet?"

"Because after your dad decided to marry that ... Angela, he needed to make room for all her things. So, he brought everything of your mom's over here and told me to go through it and save out the pieces I thought you might want one day. I stashed them away and forgot about them until recently. I honestly didn't save much. Only a few things. Like this dress."

Suddenly, the gown didn't seem as impractical. Her mother's dress. Ella fingered the silky material, wishing it still held a bit of the spirit of the woman who had originally worn it.

"I'm mad at you for not remembering this sooner," Ella said over her shoulder as she carried the gown into the small bathroom to change.

"Noted." Fae surfaced from the closet with a triumphant "ha!" right before Ella closed the door.

Ella didn't even want to know what her dear friend had uncovered. She was too busy trying to zip the gown all the way up. Maybe this dress wouldn't work after all.

"Are you decent?" Fae asked through the door.

"Mostly." Ella yanked again, but to no avail. "The zipper is stuck."

"Let me in. I'll help."

Reluctantly, Ella pushed the door open and turned her back to Fae. Fae's fingers were chilly, but she got the job done. The dress settled into place as if it were made for Ella. It even had pockets!

"Perfect." Fae's hands rested on Ella's bare shoulders,

reminding her why this dress wasn't the best idea. She shivered. "You look just like your mama. She'd be so proud, Ella-girl."

Ella blinked back tears. No time for sentimentality. She had to fix her hair. And find shoes. And maybe even put on a bit of makeup.

Fae set a pair of silvery heels on the bathroom counter as Ella blinked against the mascara wand. She stared at the shoes for a full minute and then shook her head.

"Never gonna happen. They're the wrong size."

"We'll have to make them work." Fae moved about, slipping into her own fancy dress covered in green sequins. "I don't have any shoes as small as your feet."

"I'll just wear my Converse." Ella picked up a strand of her hair then dropped it again, unsure what to do. She didn't have Kari's hair skills, and Fae had insisted she get ready here this time.

"You'll do no such thing. You're wearing a fancy dress, which calls for fancy shoes." Fae pointed to the torture devices known as stilettos with a long finger. "Those have buckles, and we'll do them up as tight as we can. It's not like you're going to do much more than stand around. You can handle wearing something pretty for a few hours."

Ella glared at Fae but huffed, "Fine. But I'm taking my Converse with me, just in case."

"Stubborn child." Fae pushed her down onto a bench in front of a little vanity table. "Sit and let me do your hair."

"I'm going to be late."

"No. You're going to make a fashionable entrance."

"Fae."

"Sit still or I'll pull." Fae gave a little yank to prove her point.

Ella squeaked but sat still. Fae's fingers moved adeptly

through Ella's tangles, weaving bits and pieces on the sides until they formed small braids that wound back to where the rest cascaded down her back in golden waves. Fae tucked in a few little white flowers and clapped her hands.

"Gorgeous. He won't be able to keep his eyes off you."

"Who?" Ella slid her feet into the shoes and buckled them as tightly as she could, though they still slid around more than she liked as she walked.

"Who? As if she doesn't know who she's been falling in love with for the past few weeks." Fae slid into her own flats—how was that fair?—then draped a fur coat around Ella's shoulders. "Let's go knock them dead, sweetheart."

Ella wrapped the older lady in a big hug, overwhelmed by all she'd done for her—not only this night, but always. "Thank you."

"Pishposh. What's all this about?" Fae fluttered her hands between them. "I'm only loving you like I always have."

"I appreciate it. More than you'll ever know."

Fae rested a hand against Ella's cheek for a moment, her own eyes misty with emotion. But she quickly snapped out of it. "If we don't get a move on, we're going to go from fashionably late to actually late."

Ella shoved her sneakers into her bag and followed Fae down the stairs and out into the cold. The wind bit into every single one of her bare toes and found its way up her skirt. She practically threw herself in the front seat of her daddy's truck and turned the key. Nothing happened. Of all nights ...

Fae tapped on the window and held up her own keys. "Let's go. Into the pumpkin."

"The pumpkin," Ella groaned. Fae's car was bright orange and slightly rounded on top, which had earned it the nickname early on. With Ella always getting teased about being

Cinderella, she'd sworn she would never ride in it. No choice now. The irony was not lost on her.

Ella slid into the gourd-shaped vehicle, holding the coat closed around her as she shivered. The coldest night of the year, and she was wearing open-toed shoes and a dress made for spring. Because of Fae.

And now she was going to be late. It normally wouldn't matter, though she hated being late. But to be late to a party where she was one of the main guests seemed rude.

Fae peeled out of the driveway. Was she feeling the time crunch as much as Ella? Ella had never seen her drive so fast. Maybe they wouldn't be as late as she'd thought.

"No parking spots, of course." Fae stopped at the gallery doors. "Go on in, and I'll be in after I park. They really should've saved spots near the front for the guests of honor, though. Tell that guy of yours, will you?"

Fae's words floated behind Ella as she exited the pumpkin and steeled herself to face what waited inside. She hadn't been back since finishing her painting but knew most of the judging was already done, with only one left for tonight. How would she face it?

"There you are." Kari rushed out and tugged Ella's hands until Ella moved her feet. "We were beginning to worry."

"Humphrey wouldn't start."

"You and that truck." Kari shook her head. "Come on." She helped Ella out of the coat, handing it and Ella's bag off to an attendant near the door.

Ella wanted to protest leaving her bag behind, but Kari had already pulled her into the main room of the gallery, and she was suddenly surrounded. News cameras hovered nearby, people asked questions all at the same time, and Ella wished to escape and hide somewhere. Anywhere but here.

* * *

"Have you seen Ella?" Chaz stood on tiptoes, searching the crowd for her glorious blonde hair, but every time he spotted someone with the right shade, it wasn't her. Even Bellamy's light tresses threw him off for a minute—until she laughed.

"Not yet." Jake leaned an elbow on Chaz's shoulder, pushing him back down to his heels. "Aren't you supposed to be in charge of this thing?"

"Technically?"

"Yes, technically, and in all the other ways too." Jake smirked.

"Yes." Chaz rubbed a hand over the back of his neck. "It just doesn't feel right to start the final judging until both Ella and Bellamy are here. Has Kari heard from her?"

"I actually lost Kari a few minutes ago." Jake glanced around. "One minute, she was next to me, chiding me for eating too many appetizers, the next, she was gone."

"Some help you are." Chaz moved to the left to see if the view afforded anything better. It didn't.

"What's the delay?" Dad appeared out of the thick of the crowd and motioned around them. "We've all been here half an hour."

"I haven't seen Ella yet tonight." Chaz frowned. "Have you seen her?"

"Oh, dear." Mom looked around too. "Let me see what I can find out. Surely someone has seen her. Maybe you missed her in the crowd."

Mom moved away, mingling with each person for a second before making her way to another section. Working a room was her talent and one of the ways she'd first met Dad.

From another direction, Fae rushed up. "Sorry we're late." The older woman patted her chest. "You really do need more parking if you're going to keep hosting these fancy shindigs."

"Good to see you, Fae." Chaz squeezed her shoulder. "Have you seen Ella?"

Fae straightened and frowned. "I brought her in the pumpkin. Sent her in before I parked. You don't think she ran instead of coming inside, do you?"

"Ran? Why would she run?" Dad shook his head.

"The pumpkin?" Chaz blinked.

"My car, darling." Fae patted his cheek. "And she'd run because she is not a fan of these big crowds. She never wants to be the center of attention."

"Kari found her." Jake held up his phone. "But they're trapped somewhere over that way." He pointed to the right. "A bunch of news and media people pounced on her."

Chaz exchanged a glance with Dad. This had all grown out of control. They'd had no idea so many news sources would cover the event. Or that it would attract so many extra guests. Next year, he would sell tickets. But that didn't solve tonight's problem.

Dad jumped up on the dais they'd set up in the middle of the room—where each canvas sat covered by a sheet to make sure no one peeked—and gave a loud whistle. The crowd stilled and everyone faced them. Chaz shook his head. One of these days, Chaz was going to have to learn how to do that.

"May I have your attention, please?" Dad smiled at the crowd. "We're trying to get started, but we need both contestants to make their way up here now."

Bellamy and Angela sauntered over from a short distance away. A smug grin played on Bellamy's face. Her dress was light gold and barely covered her. Chaz looked away quickly.

Mom appeared on his right, Ella and Kari linked in each of her arms. Ella's eyes were wide, her face pale. But her light-blue dress and her cascading hair created an aura around her that took his breath away. Wow. He pinched himself to make sure she wasn't a dream.

"And now, let me tell you how the rest of this is going to work," Dad continued, addressing the crowd.

"I thought you were in charge," Jake whispered in Chaz's ear.

Chaz swatted at him, barely keeping himself from easing over to stand next to Ella. As if he could find room, considering the way Mom, Fae, and Kari surrounded her. If ever he were jealous, it would be now.

"We have lined up five judges. Four of them have already viewed the paintings and made their decisions. The final judge is here tonight. He will see the paintings for the first time the moment you do, so I'll request you all stay quiet so he can make his decision."

Murmurs ran through the crowd, but everyone seemed to be in agreement.

"Once he has made his ruling, he will let my son, Chaz Prince, know which one he's voting for. Chaz will tally the votes." Chaz almost laughed out loud. There was no need to tally. The paintings were tied, and tonight's vote would settle things.

"And then Chaz will announce our winner. Are you ready to see the final paintings?" Dad looked around, keeping everyone on the edge of their seats as he liked to do. "To keep things fair, I won't tell you which piece belongs to which artist. Not until the final judging is complete. Which will begin ... now."

Two employees gently yanked the sheets from the easels, and the crowd gasped. On the right sat a painting displaying a beautiful forest scene with a stream running through sun-dappled trees. On the left sat what looked to be a meadow with some sort of animal, but the canvas was covered with white streaks, as if the artist had tried to make it look like sunlight was streaming from above but overdid it. The streaks blotted out all the little details and made it appear more like an alien invasion.

A cry of anguish sounded to his right, and Chaz spun to see Ella buckling at the knees. Her mouth was open, brows furrowed, and anguish was clear in every inch of her expression. Tears ran down her cheeks. Her whole body trembled as she shook her head.

Chaz searched the space around her, trying to figure out what had upset her so much, but then realized her focus was on the paintings. On one painting. The one on the left. The one with the streaks.

His eyes darted to Bellamy, who gave him a smug smile and wiggled her fingers as if she already knew she had won. What had she done? How? How had she pulled this off?

After a closer examination of the painting on the left, he could barely make out what the animals were. Turkeys. It was definitely Ella's work, but he knew she hadn't added those streaks.

He had to fix this. But how?

Every news camera was focused on the disaster unfolding around him. Dad was going to rescind his offer of a raise and additional responsibility. All because of Bellamy.

Chaz blinked. It didn't matter. He'd give up everything he had gained if it would fix Ella's painting. She meant more to him than working at this gallery, even if it was the only job he wanted. He wanted her more.

If Bellamy thought he had any interest in her before, she better believe he couldn't stand the thought of her now. But that didn't do any good. What he needed was to reverse time and protect Ella's painting. With no way to do that, what was his next best option?

28

Ella's pulse pounded in her ears as she stared at her painting. Ruined. Mutilated. All those hours of work, dealing with the brushes being destroyed, the missing paints, the pounding music from next door. This was how she was rewarded for avoiding Chaz the last few months? For denying one of the few pleasures in her life?

She'd lost her other artwork and supplies, her house, and now this? It was too much. *Do you hear me, God? It's too much!*

Fae's hand under her arm was all that held her up. She drew in a shuddery breath. How could this happen? She swallowed the shriek wanting to escape. They'd changed the locks. Chaz had promised everything would stay locked up, that no one except the judges could get in. Surely a judge wouldn't have slashed white paint over her meadow scene. Blinking rapidly didn't keep the tears from escaping.

The little bit of lunch she'd eaten earlier that day roiled in her belly. She couldn't do this. Couldn't stay here. She needed out. Now.

"Ella?" Kari's voice seemed to come from far away as she spun and started forcing her way through the crowd, back toward the door.

"Ella!" Chaz's shout didn't stop her. She couldn't let him convince her to stay.

She'd been humiliated enough. No more. She wiggled between two cameramen, not bothering to apologize. Maybe she'd go where no one else in the world knew who she was. She could start over anywhere—assuming she could get Daddy's truck started. Pushing past a lady in a hat, she narrowly avoided someone else's elbow. Maybe Jake would fix Humphrey one more time for her. Then she'd load up as much as she could and leave. Drive until she ran out of gas, find a job, and just be one more person in another town.

Was the crowd getting tighter? "Excuse me." She maneuvered through two more people.

She didn't need artwork. Didn't need to have a painting in some fancy gallery. Not if it meant things like this would happen—where everything was claimed by someone else or taken or destroyed. Her sandal slipped and she barely kept from falling. It wasn't worth it.

"Ella," another voice called after her.

Why wouldn't these people leave her alone? Nothing happening was all that interesting. Nothing except her horrible, ugly, sabotaged painting being displayed as if she meant for it to be that way.

She nudged her way past three more people before the heel of her left shoe twisted and she fell. Stupid shoes. She should've stood her ground with Fae. Her Converse were much more sensible.

She slipped the straps of the heel from her foot and started on the other, but the voices were getting closer. No time to linger here, where they could stop her from leaving. She moved to her hands and knees and crawled as modestly as she could in the beautiful, impractical dress.

"Sorry, Mama. But sometimes a girl has to do what a girl has to do."

Surprisingly, it was easier to crawl through the crowd than walk. The people still stood close together, shifting randomly and blocking her path. But, she made it.

The cool air of the foyer caressed her shoulders and legs as she stood and wobbled on one heel. She plucked the second shoe off and strode down the hallway to find her coat and bag. Aha. A rack had been set up beside Gertie's desk, fur and wool and leather all crammed onto it. A quick search turned up Fae's fur coat and Ella's bag.

Sliding into her tennis shoes, she grabbed the coat and turned to leave, not even bothering to tie her laces.

But Chaz stood between her and the door, watching her with an unreadable expression. Not good. Could she make it past him? She wiggled her toes inside her shoes. Without those stupid heels on, maybe she could sprint fast enough. She gauged the distance between him and the wall. Probably wouldn't work.

"Ella, I think you dropped something." Her first heel dangled from his finger.

"Could you give that back to Fae?" She willed her words to come out strong. They mostly did. "They're actually hers. Here's the other." She set it on the desk.

"Going somewhere?" He lifted a brow and took a step closer.

Her heart leaped in response, and he wasn't even within six feet from her yet. Bad. This was very bad.

She swallowed. "Didn't think I needed to stay. It's obvious who won."

"Is it?" Another step. Another leap of her betraying heart. "I didn't think so."

"Don't be ridiculous. Who on earth would vote for my

painting over hers? She somehow found a way to destroy it." Ella's voice broke on the last word.

Chaz closed the distance and pulled her into his arms, crushing her to his chest. "We're going to fix this."

She shook her head, some of her hair catching in his stubble. "She's finally won. I can't keep fighting her."

He pulled back a bit and lifted her chin, swiped at the tears on her cheeks, and looked her straight in the eyes. "No. One more fight."

She pinched her lips together. She was so tired. No matter what Ella did, Bellamy found a way to retaliate. And yet, did she really want to let Bellamy win?

"Not for me." Chaz shook his head, squeezed his eyes closed. "Don't fight for me. Fight for you. For your talent and your artistry. You cannot let her win."

It was like their minds were synced. "But how do I fight her? This was it. Those paintings were supposed to be sabotage-proof, without any way to cheat."

"Cheat." Chaz snapped his fingers, then grabbed her hand and pulled her after him. "Come on."

"What? Where are we going?" At least this time she could move more easily, because her shoes actually fit. And Chaz had a much easier time parting the crowd than Ella had. He moved like a putty knife through a new smear of paint.

Chaz tugged Jake's sleeve and pointed to the painting on the right. The one that wasn't ruined. How had Bellamy been able to do such a good job when a few weeks ago she hadn't even been able to paint a wall? Something was off.

Jake nodded, a grin spreading across his face. He pulled his phone out and tapped a few times before snapping a picture of the artwork. After a few seconds, his smile grew even more, and he showed the screen to Chaz. Chaz's grin grew so wide, his dimples deepened enough to plant a seed in. What were they up to?

Chaz jumped up on the dais, startling the man who had been looking back and forth between the paintings with a score sheet in hand. "Thanks so much for coming to judge tonight, but I don't think we need to continue this charade any longer."

The man stepped back, his eyebrows nearing his hairline. "Excuse me?"

"Chaz." Kingston Prince moved to the edge of the stage and leaned close to his son. "What are you doing?"

Chaz bent his head and met Ella's gaze before focusing on his dad again. "Do you trust me?"

After a quick second, Kingston nodded. Fae, Kari, and Lydia Prince surrounded Ella once more. What would she do without them? She'd be long gone, that was for sure.

"What's going on?" Kari whispered on her left.

"I don't know."

"Ladies and gentlemen." Chaz held his hands in the air, and everyone quieted again. "When we set the rules of this contest, I thought they were foolproof."

Murmurs skittered through the crowd.

"I was wrong."

Ella's heart stuttered again. What was he doing? Surely he wasn't going to take the blame for what happened to her painting?

"I didn't take into account the fact that locks can be picked and tampered with," Chaz continued. "That some people are cruel enough to want to ruin someone else's chances by destroying their supplies. That cheating was a possibility. Or that pure sabotage would take place. If we ever have a contest again, I will be making sure things go more smoothly."

Bellamy's glare met Ella's from across the space. Ella

straightened and stared directly back. She had nothing to do with this, but in her head all she could hear was Chaz's soft admonition to *fight*. One more fight.

* * *

"This painting"—Chaz pointed to Ella's work—"doesn't look like it should. Someone has destroyed it by painting these white streaks over the top. I never got to see the finished product because it was supposed to be a surprise to everyone, but I've seen other pieces this artist has made, and I know it was absolutely lovely before the white paint was added."

The judge in front of him folded his arms but gave a sharp nod, as if he'd deduced the same conclusion. Dad also nodded. Okay. So far so good.

"This painting looks great." He pointed to Bellamy's finished piece. "But we cannot accept it."

Bellamy's sharp shriek pierced the otherwise quiet room.

"While the saying goes that copying an artist's work is the highest form of flattery, in this case, it's almost an insult."

Angela gaped at her daughter. Interesting. Apparently, she had no idea what Bellamy had done.

Jake handed Chaz his phone, which he held out for anyone with good eyesight to see. "The picture here is exactly the same as the one beside me. It's a paint-by-number kit and also comes with step-by-step tutorials online. While she did a great job, I cannot accept this as a piece to hang in my gallery."

"You never said I couldn't paint something someone else already painted." Bellamy pursed her lips and straightened her shoulders. "I don't think that should be terms for disqualification."

"How about you ruining the other painting? Should that be

terms?" Chaz spoke lower, trying to save her some embarrassment, but Bellamy didn't seem to care.

"You cannot prove I did any of those bad things to Ella. Bad luck seems to follow her wherever she goes." Bellamy shot a cocky look at her stepsister.

"Actually, I can prove it." Dad stepped forward. "I had the video cameras repaired a few weeks ago, after a ... paintbrush incident. And one just happens to be in that room outside the work spaces. It'll show me anyone who went in and out, and when."

Bellamy pinched her lips and lifted her chin. "I don't think Ella should get to have a painting hung here, either. You have no idea what hers looked like. She painted some dumb birds, for crying out loud!"

Several gasps ricocheted through the room, and Bellamy's eyes widened as she realized she'd just admitted she was the saboteur. Angela clenched Bellamy's arm and yanked.

"Thank you for this chance. My daughter will not be bothering you again." Angela whisked Bellamy out of the room.

When things quieted down once again, all eyes turned to Chaz. Now what? He'd ousted Bellamy, but how would he wrap this up?

"She's right in one way, son." Dad hopped up on the dais with him. "As much as I hate to say it, this painting doesn't prove Ella deserves to be in this gallery."

Chaz's heart gave an extra thump. The battle wasn't over yet. He still had to fight for Ella's right to be here.

"You've already seen her other paintings. From the first contest." Chaz leveled his dad with a stare, daring him to disagree that those had both been Ella's. "Do you want more proof?"

"Does she have more?"

Chaz glanced down at Ella. Her skin was so pale he was afraid she might pass out any minute. He took in her whole image—her wavy hair, her blue dress, and her ... sneakers. Perfect.

He stepped down and stood in front of her. "Do you trust me?" He searched her eyes.

It was the same question he'd asked his father. It had been a weighty question then, but somehow it was even heavier now. After an eternal few seconds, she gave the slightest nod, but it was enough.

He tugged her fingers and pulled her up onto the stage with him. Then he looked around until he spotted a chair a few feet away. He had Jake grab it and bring it up on stage. Gently, he sat Ella in the chair and knelt before her.

More gasps.

"May I remove your shoe?" Chaz asked, ignoring the crowd.

Ella blinked, glanced around, then blinked again. "Okay?"

With a few tugs, he freed her sneaker and lifted it to Dad's eye level. "Do you see this?"

The high-top canvas shoe wasn't plain white. It wasn't plain anything. Paint covered every inch—a floral bouquet with ornate details. His dad cradled the shoe in his hand, his bushy eyebrows lifting into his hair.

"Do you need the other one too?" Chaz barely contained his grin. He knew he'd won. "Ella painted them both."

"Is all your work this intricate?" Dad glanced at her before studying her shoe once more.

"Yes." Her whisper was just loud enough to be heard.

"I'd say we have a winner." Dad handed the shoe back. "Now please put this back on her foot before she freezes."

Fae's laughter burst from nearby. "And to think I told her not to wear those things tonight!"

Ella's giggle soon joined in, and before long, the whole gallery was laughing, the tension fleeing in the midst of joy. Chaz gently clasped Ella's ankle. He slipped the shoe onto her foot, tying it back in place. The perfect slipper for his Cinderella.

Dad whistled once more as Chaz tugged Ella up to stand beside him.

"Not only did Ella win the contest to be one of our new artists here at the gallery, but she has also been chosen for a new honor." Chaz waited for everyone's attention, though he kept his fingers firmly wrapped around Ella's in case she decided to bolt again. "She's going to be our new artist in residence, starting in January."

Ella's gasp was barely audible over the applause, but he heard it. There was much to explain and discuss, but not now. Now was the time to celebrate.

29

"Oh, my darling girl." As soon as Ella stepped off the dais, Fae pulled her into a hug so fierce she almost couldn't breathe. "I knew you could do it. All those weeks of you saying it wasn't going to happen were for nothing, weren't they?"

"You can't let a girl win without rubbing her face in past mistakes, can you?" Ella mumbled into Fae's shoulder.

Fae pushed her back but held onto her arms. "I want you to remember. Because you are perfect just how God made you. And He saw you through, like I told you He would."

"I can't decide if this is a sermon or an 'I told you so.'" Ella smirked.

"Does it matter?" Fae pinched her cheek.

Ella shook her head.

"Good." Fae smiled, moisture in her eyes. "Oh, dear girl. Your parents would be so proud. I hope you know that."

Ella's lower lip wobbled as she nodded. "I wish they were still here."

"As do I."

"Okay, enough tears." Kari shoved in for her turn at a hug. "This is a happy occasion. No more sadness tonight."

"I'm not sad." Ella laughed. "It's bittersweet."

"More sweet than bitter, though." Kari poked her arm. "And don't forget it."

"Fae." Ella turned back and caught her neighbor before she was lost in the crowd. "What about Bellamy?"

"Something tells me you don't have to worry about her anymore." Fae *tsked*. "But that girl definitely needs a heart change. I'm not sure what will bring it about. Only God can fix those kinds of problems. And I don't think she's ready to let Him."

Ella swallowed. As much as she'd hated having to put up with Bellamy, she never wanted anything bad to happen to her. How awkward would church services be from now on? To see them but have no ties or connections?

As her friends fawned over her and the reporters asked to take photos of her shoes, Ella was still very aware of Chaz and his father answering other reporters' questions on the opposite side of the dais. Her heart twinged as her line of sight slipped over to her painting. Could she fix it after all this was over? It would never be the same, but maybe ...

Chaz met her gaze, and he winked before turning his attention back to those next to him.

"Sweet girl." Lydia Prince appeared and wrapped her in a lilac-scented hug. "Oh, I'm so happy. I know your painting isn't what you wanted it to be, but now you have so many chances to wow people even more." Lydia blinked. "No pressure, of course."

Ella grinned. "I'm trying not to think about any of that tonight."

"Smart girl." Lydia held her at arm's length and looked her up and down, shaking her head. "You are so like your mother. I remember the first time she wore this dress. It was when she met your father, actually."

Ella's breath caught. "You knew them back then?"

"Sara and I were friends in school. I have one of her paintings in my dining room." Lydia snapped. "Oh! You must come to Christmas dinner. You can see the painting then. And I can show you pictures of your parents from when they were younger."

"That sounds lovely, but ..." Ella glanced in Fae's direction.

"Bring anyone you want, honey. I always cook too much. Besides, I have all these place settings now, and I need to find people to use them." Lydia winked.

Ella laughed again. "If you're sure."

"Absolutely. Won't take no for an answer." Lydia gave her another squeeze.

"What are you forcing Ella into, Mom?" Chaz slid his arm around Ella's waist.

"Just inviting her to Christmas dinner." Lydia pressed a kiss to his cheek. "I'm sure you can help convince her."

"I'll do my best." Chaz's answer was barely out before his mom started talking to someone else.

Ella followed Lydia with her gaze as she flitted through the room. "She's amazing."

"I agree." Chaz turned to face her. "Everyone has received a hug from Ella except me."

"That's not true." She held up a finger before he could get closer. "I didn't hug any of the reporters. Or Jake. Or most of the people here."

"I'd rather you didn't hug Jake, if it's all the same to you." Chaz's dimple flashed a message she longed to interpret.

"Oh? Why's that?" Was she flirting? Ella didn't flirt. And yet, here she was.

Chaz leaned closer, his breath tickling her neck as he whispered, "Because it would make me jealous."

"Oh."

"Is that a good enough reason?" Chaz tucked a piece of her hair behind her ear.

Ella pretended to think about it, ignoring the waves of emotion rolling through her tummy. "I suppose."

Chaz tugged her into his arms, nestling her head beneath his chin. "Congratulations."

Who cared about anything else she'd won tonight? This, right here, was a big enough prize. To know this man was interested in her, willing to chase her through a crowd of people, and even willing to remove her shoe. How was she so blessed?

"I thought you said this was a ball." Jake shoved Chaz's shoulder, breaking up their lingering hug. "There's no dancing. You can't call it a ball if there's no dancing."

Chaz smirked. "Says who?"

"Anyone who's anyone." Jake rolled his eyes. "We need to work on your marketing skills. I mean, where's the DJ?"

"Over there." Chaz pointed to a far corner of the room. "Go tell him to get things started."

Jake lifted a brow. "Okay. I did not see that coming."

As Jake strolled away to direct the DJ to start some music, Chaz twined his fingers through Ella's. "I'm hoping you'll let me have at least one dance tonight."

"As many as you want." She had no desire to dance with anyone else. Not when she had Chaz Prince.

Her chest fizzed with tiny bubbles of happiness. It didn't matter if any of them burst, because there were plenty more. She might not come down off this high for weeks.

* * *

The DJ played up-tempo beats for about forty-five minutes before putting on a slower song. The little hitch in Ella's breath told Chaz this song had a special meaning to her. He gently spun her out and back into his arms, enjoying the way she fit there so well.

"Do you like this song?" He nestled his cheek close to hers.

"It's one my parents used to dance to in the living room. I have the record in my chest at the hotel. It's one of the things that wasn't sold at the flea market because I hid it away." Ella closed her eyes.

Chaz's heart pinched. This was his opening. He should tell her he'd bought most of those items. Had her dad's record player set up in his own living room, waiting to create a moment like this for them.

"I remember sneaking out of bed late at night when I heard the music. The lights were low. Mom was barefoot, twirling on her tiptoes. And Dad had eyes only for her." Ella's own blue eyes blinked open. "That was when I decided I wanted a relationship like theirs. It was more romantic than the fairy tales Daddy used to read me."

"Who says it wasn't exactly like the fairy tales your dad used to read?" Chaz kept his voice low. "Who says those princes and princesses didn't get to dance barefoot in their living rooms to old records? They did live happily ever after, you know."

"Mm." Ella grinned. "True. I just wish my parents' happy ending lasted longer."

"I wish it did too. I would've loved to meet them." Chaz moved one of his hands up to rest against her soft cheek. "They raised an amazing daughter."

"You barely even know me." She ducked her head.

"I'd love to change that. To get to know you better."

Ella searched his gaze for a few seconds. "What are you saying, exactly? What does that mean?"

"I'd love to take you on dates." He dipped her back as the

song ended, then slowly lifted her up and walked her toward the refreshments, where Jake filled a plate for what had to be the fourth time that evening. "I'd love to spend time with you here. Sit by you during church services. Let you get to know my family. Even hang out with this bozo every now and then if you can stand it." Chaz bumped Jake playfully.

"Hey!" Jake mumbled around a meatball.

"What do you say?" Chaz pulled her into a more secluded corner. "Does that sound like a plan you could get behind?"

"I've never ... Well, I've never really dated anyone before." Ella tucked a strand of hair behind her ear. "This is all very new to me."

"I promise you"—Chaz wove his fingers through hers—"that when I say I want to date you, I'm serious. I don't want to casually go out. I want to date you with the end goal of us never dating anyone else."

Ella's breath caught, and her eyes widened. "That's ... serious."

"When you think about your future, do you think you could picture me in it?" He pressed his forehead to hers.

Her eyelids fluttered shut, her breathing coming in shallow puffs, but ever so slightly, she nodded. "I think I'd like that very much."

He couldn't resist any longer. He leaned forward the last inch and pressed his lips to hers. Snaking his arms around her back, he pulled her as close as he dared. The ends of her hair tickled his fingertips, urging him to let one of his hands wander up into the depths of her glorious tresses. But he couldn't let himself kiss her too long. Not here. Not now.

He gently broke away, pressing his lips to her forehead once more. Slowly, her eyes fluttered open again, shimmery and full of emotion. But this time, the emotion wasn't sadness or anger. Her eyes held hope instead.

"Darling, I'm bushed." Fae appeared at their side out of nowhere.

Chaz leaped backward a few more inches, glad he'd already ended their kiss. Ella grinned, her cheeks a pretty pink. She must be used to Fae's sudden appearances.

"I can go now, Fae. I just need to grab my coat." Ella freed herself from his arms, though he was tempted to pull her back.

"No, no, hon. I don't want to break up all your ... fun." Fae's eyes twinkled. "Besides, your truck isn't working, and my house is the opposite direction from where you're staying. Surely someone here can give you a ride back to the hotel?" She winked at Chaz.

"I'll gladly see her home this evening, Fae. Are you okay to drive? You said you were tired." Chaz couldn't resist grinning at the conniving woman.

"I'm quite all right, thank you. I sent young Jake to get my car for me so I don't have to walk all the way across three parking lots again. He's probably waiting for me at the door now." Fae pointed at Chaz. "There's another idea for next time. Valets, darling."

"Noted." Chaz chuckled. "Thanks for coming tonight."

"I couldn't miss this." Fae squeezed Ella's arm. "I knew my girl would win."

Ella started to protest, but Fae was already gone. She shook her head. "I love that woman with all my heart, but she is something else."

Chaz let out a belly laugh. Yes, she was. And he also looked forward to getting to know the woman he secretly referred to as Ella's fairy godmother better. This was a package deal, after all.

"So, you're seeing me home, *hmm?*" Ella lifted a brow.

"Seems that way. Unless you want to ride with Jake and Kari."

"No." Ella rested her hand on his sleeve as they wandered back into the crowd. "You already volunteered. I'd hate to keep you from fulfilling your word to Fae."

"Is that the only reason?"

Ella tapped a finger on her lips. "Isn't it a good one?"

Chaz leaned close, whispering in her ear. "I'm also hoping for a good night kiss."

Ella's lips spread into a smile, something he hadn't seen her do nearly enough. "That could be arranged. But you know, I'm in a borrowed dress and I arrived in a pumpkin. You might want to get me home before midnight, lest this dream disappear with a swirl of fairy magic."

"Something tells me this isn't only magic tonight. Though it does feel magical."

Chaz glanced around at the dwindling crowd. As the host, he should probably stay and see out the last few guests. But he had absolutely zero desire to talk to anyone but Ella tonight.

Dad caught his eye from across the room and waved, giving him permission to leave. Chaz wouldn't wait for Dad to change his mind.

With Ella bundled in the fur coat he'd taken from her earlier, he bustled her out to his Jeep—parked in the back where they didn't have to walk as far as Fae had. Inside, he leaned across the console and pressed a quick kiss to her lips. She blinked, her mouth open.

"I've been wanting to kiss you for weeks now, and you haven't let me." He waggled his brows. "I have some making up to do."

Her laughter pealed through the vehicle. Perfection. He wanted to make her smile and laugh as much as possible from here on out.

The ride back to the hotel was quiet, as each of them became lost in their own thoughts. They wove their fingers together between them, and he couldn't complain. Ella was the one he hadn't known he was waiting for. Could he even make it to Valentine's Day before proposing?

But her words from earlier reminded him to slow down. Until she was as sure as he was, he didn't want to do anything that might scare her off. So instead of getting down on one knee, he pressed another kiss ... or several ... to her lips as they stood outside her door.

And then he whispered, "Good night."

"Good night"—Ella opened her door but looked back at him—"Prince Charming."

30

Valentine's Day

Ella stood beside Kari, Jake, and Chaz at the back of the church building. Chaz was itching to leave, but their friends needed them. Kari's hand shook as she held the letter she was reading.

"So, our uncles need us to go help for a bit. Now that we've helped our aunt get her hotel under control, they think we can do the same for them." She twisted her lips to the side. "I have no idea why. I mean, I don't think we did anything special."

"The Starbright Hotel is an amazing place." Ella touched Kari's arm. "And I'm not saying that just because you've let me live there for a couple months. It's stunning. If you can help your uncles pull the same thing off at their inn, maybe you'll believe in yourself more. Because I think they're seeing what the rest of us see."

"Says the girl who couldn't even see that she was an amazing artist." Jake smirked. "But Ella makes a good point. When we got to the Starbright, it was nothing to write home about. One by one, we redid each room and the foyer, and now it's a five-star hotel. We can do it again, sis."

"But we've put down roots here. There's nothing in Georgia for us." Kari flapped the letter in the air.

"Except our uncles. Who need us." Jake lifted a brow. "And it's not like it's forever. We could come back here when we're done."

"But we'll definitely miss you." Ella pulled Kari into a hug.

"What about you, Ella?" Kari's words were muffled against her shoulder. "Where will you live if we go? We're the ones who made the deal with you. I'm not sure Aunt Millie will agree to keep the arrangement."

"We'll figure it out." Chaz wrapped an arm around Ella's shoulder.

We will? Ella tucked his words away to ponder later. Over the last few months, she and Chaz had grown closer than she ever thought possible, but were they to a point in their relationship where they could make decisions together about living arrangements?

Bellamy's perfume wafted over Ella before her stepsister moved past with her head held high. "Rendersella."

Angela touched Chaz's arm and exchanged a look with him Ella didn't understand. "Our agreement stands," Angela murmured before following Bellamy out into the cold February day.

"Agreement?" Ella and Kari asked at the same time.

"I'll tell you later." Chaz squeezed Ella's arm and gave her a genuine smile. Whatever he was hiding, it must not be too bad. Though Ella had trouble imagining anything to do with Angela could be good.

"How are all my darlings today?" Fae breezed over, a vision in red with a large, heart-shaped pink brooch on her shoulder.

"We're great, Fae." Chaz turned her way.

"Wonderful, wonderful."

"Speak for yourself," Kari tucked the letter back into her purse.

"It'll be okay, Kari." Ella didn't know how, but she knew it would be. Kari was her dearest friend. She deserved an ending as happy as Ella's.

"What's wrong now?" Fae looked back and forth between them.

Ella offered a quick recap, and Fae pulled Kari and Jake into a floral-scented embrace. "My dears. Let me know if I can help in any way. Any way at all."

"And on that note, I think we're going to head out." Chaz lifted his brows and tugged on Ella's arm. "Our lunch is waiting."

"You're actually crazy enough to go out to eat on Valentine's Day? Don't you know the crowds are going to be insane? And that the restaurants have jacked up the prices to double?" Jake shook his head.

"Good thing I planned for us to eat at my place." Chaz winked. "I'm cooking spaghetti."

"You're going over to his apartment?" Fae spun around from where she'd been talking to Kari.

"Just for lunch." Ella clasped the older lady's fingers. "I haven't actually seen his condo, and he's itching to show it off."

Fae shot him a look Ella couldn't interpret. What was going on today? Why did everyone keep giving Chaz confusing expressions?

"I even cleaned it up. Bought a brand-new vacuum." Chaz grinned.

"Fancy." Jake laughed. "Remind me never to take dating advice from you."

"Says the man not dating someone." Chaz playfully punched Jake's arm before they headed out into the cold.

Ella tugged the fur coat Fae had insisted she keep more tightly around her to ward off the wind. Spring might be just over a month away, but winter hadn't given up yet. The chill contradicted the bright sunshine.

Chaz drummed his fingers against the steering wheel on the way, betraying his nervous energy. She wasn't sure what its source was. They were going to eat lunch. They'd had lunch together pretty much every Sunday since Christmas. Was he afraid she wouldn't like his place?

He parked in front of a light-blue condo with brick trim. The bushes out front were neatly trimmed. A wreath hung on his front door, and Ella assumed it was his mother's work.

"It's nice, Chaz." Ella looked over in time to see him rub his hands on his pants legs. "You okay?"

"Yep." He exited and quickly moved around to open her door. "Ready to see the inside?"

"Sure." Ella shot him a funny look as he fumbled the key twice before unlocking the door.

He gave her a nervous grin then motioned her inside. She stepped into a small area and noticed what looked to be a dining room to the left. A hallway led past some stairs into what she assumed was a living space and kitchen. Chaz flicked on the light switch, pulling all the details into focus.

Her eyes caught on the painting over the dining table. One of her mom's paintings. The table itself was set with dishes that looked exactly like her mom's. She ran her finger over one and looked around some more. Down the hallway and into the living room.

Dad's chair sat in the corner. The record player was on top of a familiar cabinet. Books she'd know anywhere lined the top shelf next to the fireplace. She spun to face Chaz, her heart pounding in her chest.

"You?"

"Me?" He looked more uncertain than she'd ever seen him. Was this what had him so nervous?

"You're the one who bought out the flea market booth?" She whispered the words as a question but didn't need him to confess. The truth was evident all around her.

"I couldn't let you lose any more of your memories, your heritage."

In two steps, she was in his arms, her head burrowed into his shoulder. He'd paid money for what should probably have been hers to begin with. To make sure she didn't lose it. Even before he knew they were going to date or get serious. Where on earth did such an amazing man come from? And how did she end up with him?

"Please tell me these are happy tears." Chaz ran his thumb under her eyes, wiping away moisture. "I meant to tell you forever ago, but every time I thought I'd do it, something else interrupted. I decided this was the best way to let you know, but then I started second-guessing myself after Fae gave me that look."

"Fae knew?" Ella shook her head. "Of course she knew. Fae knows everything."

"She asked me to work on a secret project for you, actually. Figured I had the connections." He tugged her hand, leading her to the other side of the room, and pointed to the wall.

Her gaze rose to the painting, the one he'd had restored. A tiny smear was still visible where it had rubbed against something in the trash can, but it was mostly back to its original state. Mom's painting of the bird. Beside it hung the one of Ella as a child, in all her sweet, innocent perfection. Before she'd had to live out the harsh part of her fairy tale.

"Chaz." The way she breathed his name made him feel ten feet tall. He'd done something right.

"When Fae approached me about this one, she told me about the other things she'd stashed away for you too. That's why she knew I had all this. She insisted those come to live here as well. Said something about how you'd be living here soon enough, anyway."

Ella spun to face him. "Why would she say something like that? I can't live here. We're not married."

Chaz held up a finger. He hadn't planned for this conversation to come up so quickly, but the timing seemed to be right. He walked over to the record player and flipped it on, setting the needle on the record he'd already prepped. It wasn't the song they danced to back at the ball, but another one of her dad's old tunes filled the room. Ella covered her mouth with her hand.

Instead of pulling her into a dance, Chaz knelt down before her and took her hands in his. "Ella Marie Renders, my very own Rendersella, how would you feel about becoming a Prince?"

"When I was a little girl, I always wanted to grow up to be a prin*cess*." Her lips tilted into a grin. "I never realized I could be a Prince instead."

He chuckled. "I mean, the girl does have to marry the prince to become the princess, right?" His heart beat so hard there was no way she couldn't feel it through his fingertips. He took a deep breath. "Ella, will you marry me?"

Instead of nodding or answering or even throwing herself in his arms like the girls did in the movies, she dropped to the floor in front of him until they were both on their knees. She took his face in her hands and looked straight into his eyes, her own rather misty.

"When I dreamed of growing up to be Cinderella, I never

realized what it might mean. The hard times. The struggles. The evil stepsister." She made a face. "But I also didn't realize how wonderful it would be when I reached the happily ever after."

Chaz waited, but she remained silent. "So, does that mean you'll marry me?"

Her laughter filled his small home. "Yes, Chaz. I want my happy ending to be with you."

"Well, in that case"—he pulled a ring from his pocket, the princess-cut diamond sparkling in the sunlight streaming through the window—"I guess you can have this now."

Her smile rivaled the sun as he slipped the jewelry over her finger. He leaned close and sealed the promise with a kiss. The best part was that he would get to do that for the rest of his life. Because she'd agreed to be his wife.

"Is this what you meant by working out my housing situation earlier?" Ella leaned back with a frown. "Because I don't think we can get married that quickly."

"Actually, I have one more surprise." He stood and helped her to her feet before heading to the kitchen. "But let's start lunch. I'm starving."

As they boiled the noodles and he heated the sauce and meatballs he'd made the day before, he explained the conversation from earlier. "Angela is selling the house."

Ella dropped the knife she'd been using to butter the bread.

He caught her hands before she could get hurt. Maybe this wasn't a great conversation for a cooking session.

"Dad is helping me finance it. It's going to be ours, if you want it to be. Dad talked her down from her ridiculously high price."

Ella blinked. "You're buying my house too?"

"Is that okay?" Suddenly, he wasn't sure he'd made the right choice.

"Oh, Chaz." She launched into his arms again, and he took that as a good sign. "My house. With all my memories. Really?"

"Really and truly. If you want to move in before the wedding and start fixing things up, I can keep renting this place for a while."

"How does this happy ending keep getting happier?"

"I don't know." Chaz grinned at her beaming smile. "But I expect it to continue in this trend, okay?"

"Sounds good to me." Ella spun out of his arms and started buttering the bread again. "Now, let's get this lunch ready. I just had an idea for a new painting, and I want to start this afternoon."

"What color am I going to find under your fingernails this week?" He pressed a kiss to her cheek before fixing their drinks.

"Yellow." Ella hummed a happy sigh. "The color of my house. And happy endings."

AUTHOR'S NOTE

Dear Reader,

I have always loved fairy tales. Especially Cinderella. But I never thought I could write a retelling until we took a trip to West Virginia. For some reason, all the artwork and the beautiful surroundings and the history wove together in my soul. I could picture a girl with the coal under her nails. And then I realized it was charcoal because she was an artist. And the story grew from there.

What did you think of my modern take on a classic tale? I have to admit, I had a lot of fun having "evil" characters to blame things on. Don't worry. There's plenty more to come. Fairest Inn All, my Snow White retelling, will release March 2026, and Beauty School and the Beast will release March 2027. This is one of those cases where I set out to write one book and my muse let me know there were actually three stories needing to be told.

I hope you'll continue to join me as I write books. I love having you along for the ride.

Feel free to reach out through social media, sign up for my newsletter so you never miss an announcement, and be sure to leave a short review to let other readers know if you enjoyed the story.

Love and Happily Ever Afters to you!

Amy

DISCUSSION QUESTIONS

1. Ella sees God as the first and best artist, and she often stops to thank Him for sharing His beauty with her. Are you ever struck by the beauty of a sunset or the majesty of an animal or the awesome sight of a mountain? Do you find your soul whispering a thank you like Ella's does?

2. Chaz is restless as he wishes for more responsibility in the gallery. Do you think he goes about gaining his father's respect in the best way? If you were his dad, would you have given him a raise after the way everything ended?

3. Ella has to watch many of her household items leave via the flea market booth. Have you ever had to let go of an item wrapped up in memories or with family connections? How did you deal with that loss?

4. Fae reminds Ella that God made her exactly how he wanted her to be. Do you ever struggle with self-doubt and need a similar reminder that if you're not where you're supposed to be yet, maybe God is still teaching you lessons you need to learn?

5. Chaz often spends the night at Jake's hotel when he's not seeing eye to eye with his dad. Is this the best way for him to handle things? If not, what could have been a better way to deal with the situation?

6. Bellamy wants Ella to stop painting and drawing in the hopes that Chaz will notice Bellamy instead. Obviously the plan backfires. Why do you think Bellamy is so desperate to gain Chaz's attention?

7. Ella is determined to do things on her own instead of accepting help. Chaz often has the same problem. Often, when we don't let others assist us, we're denying them the opportunity to serve and show their love. Do you ever struggle with this? Or have you been on the other side, being like Fae, who wants to help and is denied over and over by Ella's stubborn pride?

8. Ella reminds herself several times through the story that Angela and Bellamy are souls loved by God. While this doesn't always help her to love them as she should, it is a good reminder. Even when we're hurt by or furious with someone, knowing God loves them anyway can change our view enough to calm down and think more clearly. Have you tried this tactic with people before, reminding yourself to love them as God does?

9. Cinderella originally wore fancy glass slippers to the ball, but I couldn't imagine Fae pulling those from her closet. Do you think the shoe solution I came up with was close enough to the original story to keep the fairy tale vibe? What's another item from the original story that was changed that

might have been done differently? The pumpkin?
Deer and turkeys instead of mice?

ABOUT AMY R. ANGUISH

Amy R Anguish grew up a preacher's kid, and in spite of having lived in seven different states that are all south of the Mason-Dixon line, she is not a football fan. Currently, she resides in Tennessee with her husband, daughter, and son, and usually a bossy cat or two. Amy has an English degree from Freed-Hardeman University that she intends to use to glorify God, and she wants her stories to show that while Christians face real struggles, it can still work out for good.

Follow her at https://amyranguish.com or http://www.facebook.com/amyanguishauthor

Or https://x.com/amy_r_anguish and https://www.instagram.com/amyranguish

ALSO BY AMY R. ANGUISH

Window of the Heart—Stained Glass Legacy Book 3

Lennox Malone may not believe in love, but she's determined to do the best job she can as her friend Sara Beth's maid of honor. Problem is, the man in charge of fixing up the chapel doesn't match her determination. Fighting against preconceived notions, a past that catches up to her, and an attraction she wants nothing to do with, this wedding is turning into more than she can handle.

Ty Dunne might be laid back and easy-going, but he's determined to make sure the chapel is ready for his cousin's wedding. Not only is it his duty as best man, but he wants to preserve the family's history in the building. If only he could live up to his family's other expectations —or those of Lennox Malone, the fiery redhead he can't stop thinking about. Before he can go any further with her, though, he has to convince her that love is real and worth the risk.

Lennox has built her walls high and sturdy, but Ty is determined to find a way in—even if it's a window. Maybe the history of the chapel itself along with the romance of a wedding will help.

https://scrivenings.link/windowoftheheart

Destination: ~~***Fun***~~ ***Romance***

Roadtrip Romance—Book One

It's not every day you bring a boyfriend back as a souvenir.

Katie Wilhite is ready to settle into her new job as a librarian now that college is through, but friends Bree and Skye want one more girls' trip, and when Bree insists this is her bachelorette fling, Katie agrees. What she didn't agree to was allowing fun and flighty Skye to dictate the itinerary or for her anxiety to kick in harder than ever ... right in front of a cute guy.

Camden Malone had no idea when he agreed to be the voice of reason on his cousin Ryan's vacation that the trip wouldn't stay in New Orleans as planned. But when Ryan plots with Skye so that the guys can tag along with the girls all week, he isn't nearly as upset as he should be. Not with Katie's fiery temper and flashing eyes intriguing him more by the minute.

Can Katie relax enough to trust Camden and a possible future, or will she continue to push him away as only a vacation fling? And can Camden move past a rocky history of his own to be able to jump into a better future? For a trip that was supposed to be all about fun, there's a lot of romance going around.

https://scrivenings.link/destinationromance

Roadtrip for ~~One~~ Two

Roadtrip Romance—Book Two

Recovering from heartbreak is hard when

the ex-fiancé tags along ...

Dallas wasn't in the plans when Bree Henley set out to use the nonrefundable honeymoon tickets from her canceled wedding. Nor was running into ex-fiancé Nathan Hart. But their mutual friends and the weather have other ideas. A hurricane cancels their cruise and Bree decides to turn the disaster into a roadtrip for one, never imagining Nathan would object.

Nathan is furious when he uncovers the plot to get him back with Bree. But he can't just let her go roaming around the big city of Dallas alone. Though he knows calling off their wedding was the right thing to do, he still cares for Bree. And before he knows what hits him, he's volunteered to tag along. Suddenly, it's a trip for two.

Spending the week together might remind them of why they fell in love. But is it enough to overcome the obstacles standing in the way of "til death do us part"?

https://scrivenings.link/roadtripfortwo

Operation Find a Job Guy

Roadtrip Romance—Book Three

by Amy R. Anguish

She's set on saving her car ... and her heart.

Skye Jones has one goal for the summer—keep her father from taking away her convertible. That's the *only* reason she agrees to work at her sister's bridal shop in Boulder, Colorado, while she searches for a non-boring job. Why else would she have anything to do with weddings when she has no interest in marriage?

Benjamin Smith somehow ended up as a groomsman in two weddings over the summer, so he's spending a lot of time at Happily Ever After events. Falling for a blonde with no dreams of settling down wasn't in his five-year plan, yet the more he sees Skye, the more he wants to figure her out.

But all she sees him as is a boring attorney–her complete opposite.

Besides, romance is supposed to be for Skye's friends, not her. And she's in Colorado to get a job, not a guy. Right?

https://scrivenings.link/operationfindaguy

No Place Like Home

Can love secure Adrian's wandering heart?

Roots are overrated, at least to someone like Adrian Stewart, preacher's kid, who has never lived anywhere longer than six years. That's why her job with MidUSLogIn Inc., is so perfect for her—lots of travel, and staying nowhere long enough to have it feel like home. But when work takes her to Memphis, closer to her family for the first time in years and in the same small office as Grayson Roberts, she starts to question her job, her lack of home, and even her memories of her rocky past with the church.

Gray is intrigued by Adrian from the moment he sees her, and he's determined to get to the bottom of why this girl, who loves old movies and hums when she works, won't go to church with him. As they grow closer, he wants more too, but how can he convince her to stay in Memphis when she doesn't believe in home—or God? Can he use his own broken past to break through hers?

https://scrivenings.link/noplacelikehome

Saving Grace

Michelle Wilson's one goal in life was to become a top journalist at the local paper back in her hometown of Cedar Springs, AR. But on the way to bringing that dream to reality, a life-changing wreck interrupts Michelle's plans and adds an orphaned baby into the mix. Now, she has tough decisions ahead—did God put her in that accident to save baby Grace? And if so, why is it so hard to convince everyone else she should be the baby's new mommy?

Greg Marshall has been Michelle's best friend his whole life. He's thrilled she's moving back home, but not so sure about her sudden desire to be a single mom. His feelings for her have grown through the years, but she's never seemed to notice. Can he help Michelle with the adoption and grow their relationship at the same time?

https://scrivenings.link/savinggrace

Faith and Hope

https://scrivenings.link/faithandhope

An Unexpected Legacy

https://scrivenings.link/anunexpectedlegacy

Novella Collections:

Pets Amore

A novella collection, including "Out-of-the-box Valentines"

https://scrivenings.link/petsamore

A Match Made at Christmas

A novella collection, including "A-parently Christmas"

https://scrivenings.link/amatchmadeatchristmas

Love in Any Season

A novella collection, including "The Missing Piece"

https://scrivenings.link/loveinanyseason

Love Delivered

A novella collection, including "Romance at Register Five"

https://scrivenings.link/lovedelivered

Candy Cane Wishes and Saltwater Dreams

A novella collection, including "Mistletoe Make-believe"

https://scrivenings.link/candycanewishes

* * *

Stay up-to-date on your favorite books and authors with our free e-newsletters.

ScriveningsPress.com

www.ingramcontent.com/pod-product-compliance
Lightning Source LLC
Chambersburg PA
CBHW060625100726
47907CB00006B/1772